The

Karina Cory was born _____
French and Italian at Ox_____ lived in Italy for
four years. Since then she has worked in marketing and is now Marketing Director for a business
consultancy. She lives with her husband, son and
cat in London.

Karina Cory

The
Pinprick

Mandarin

Lines from 'I'll never fall in love again' (Bacharach/David)
© 1968 Blue Seas Music Inc/JAC Music Co. Inc. Reproduced
by kind permission, MCA Music Ltd. (50% controlled in
the UK & Eire by Windswept Pacific Music Limited.)

A Mandarin Paperback
THE PINPRICK

First published in Great Britain 1996
by Mandarin Paperbacks
an imprint of Reed International Books Ltd
Michelin House, 81 Fulham Road, London SW3 6RB
and Auckland, Melbourne, Singapore and Toronto

Copyright © Karina Mellinger 1996
The author has asserted her moral rights

All individuals, companies and events represented in
The Pinprick *are fictitious, and no resemblance to*
actual persons, living or dead, is intentional

A CIP catalogue record for this title
is available from the British Library
ISBN 0 7493 2287 X

Printed and bound in Great Britain
by Cox & Wyman Ltd, Reading, Berks

Phototypeset by Intype, London

With love to all my family and friends, and with thanks to Araminta Whitley at Peters Fraser & Dunlop, to Louise Moore at William Heinemann, to Greg Bradford at CACI Information Services, and to my superlative brother, Simon.

FOR DERIC

One

Hey, it's just a new Monday dawning in London's sunny West End.

Like the updated set for yet another dreary Dickensian BBC series, London is coming to life. The coffee bars are dusting down yesterday's croissants and shoving them into microwaves for a spot of reincarnation. The newsagent outside the Palladium is readjusting his mags so the girl with the nice big titties takes pride of place over Boris Yeltsin staring out gloomily from *The Economist*. The vendors of tittiless issues of the *Big Issue* get strategically positioned on the pavement.

Up and down W1, the whole world prepares itself for the arrival of the worker ants.

It's 8.30 a.m. If you put your ear to the ground, you'll hear the shudder of the tube trains lurching into the station and then the pitter-patter of executive feet announcing their arrival. And, all of a sudden, here they come, here they come, marching up from Oxford Circus underground, little anty eyes hitting the morning light as they dart forth, up from the underworld.

Here they come, spilling off the buses and out of taxis, the armies and leggies of the little worker ants, their little antennae twitching as they march off decisively this way and that towards the place that will give them the means to pay their mortgage and buy that nice jacket in Debenhams this month. All the worker ants, twitch, twitch, up and down the street they go, here, there and everywhere, left right, left right, crossing the road at the zebra crossing, not crossing the road at the zebra crossing, not looking when they cross, I defy you to run me over, I'm a worker ant, zip, zip.

The boy worker ants are tired and already dreaming of their beds that night. Their suits are crumpled, their heads still ache from the pub. They're mad about that girl in accounts but she's doing it with that bloke in IT. Stop to look quickly in the window of Liberty's to see if that pimple's still there. Yes, it is, of course it is. Zip, zip, get along, get along.

The girlie ants, hello Noreen! Hello Rita! What time did you stay till last night? Oh, he never did! Oh, what a bloody cheek! That's it, today I'm telling him he can shove his job, I mean shove it, I'm going back to Office Angels in my lunch hour, I'll tell 'em. Gabble, gabble, scamper. Up Great Marlborough Street they go, down into Soho, what you doing lunchtime Angie, d'you fancy a drink? Remind me to go to Boots when we're out later to see if they've got that new shampoo. You never read that article in *Options* about orgasms, did you? Omigod, let me tell you!

Yes, it's another day of bustle and hustle in the metropolis, there's letters to be typed, people to be sacked, deals to be done and excuses to be invented. But hang on a sec! What's this?! Emerging (and Botticelli, I'm treading on your copyright here) from the scrum, from the masses, from the twitching froth of anonymous worker ants, is, well, I think it's Venus. It certainly looks like Venus. It's a vision, a vision of loveliness, the woman that you and I always hoped we might wake up one day and find ourselves to be.

There she goes – can you see her? No twitch, no zip for her. She's late, she's in a hurry, a woman like her always is you know, but she doesn't twitch. She glides, she flows, she sails forth. Honey brown hair streaming in her wake, dissolving into the honey brown silk of her this-did-not-come-from-Marks & Spencer's shirt, a gliding streak of female apex – just use your imagination if you can't keep up. Serene, supreme.

Some boy worker ants stop and stare for a moment but they know she's out of their little league. Well may you dream, young chaps. A thing of beauty is a joy for ever. Make way, make way. For this is Sarah, queen amongst ants, and Sarah is late for work.

Two

So – who is this Sarah? I hear you ask, and well you might, ladies, as Sarah and her foibles are soon to become icons for your very own. Sarah works for a very smart company in some very smart offices in London. She's in advertising, but I don't want that to put you off her. She's in advertising with integrity, which means no cigarettes, no time-shares and no misrepresentation of women. So feel free to like her.

Sarah is an account director, if you please. She's just been promoted, just last week, so you're meeting her at an interesting time in her personal development. No glass ceiling for Sarah. She's done everything right, from eleven plus and up. Her CV is the sort they pin up in the primary school back in the home town of Little Crumbledene in deepest, darkest Yorkshire to inspire the seven-year-olds.

Sarah is the proverbial achiever. What's more, she didn't stick a knife in anyone's back to get there. What's even more, she looks gorgeous. Face, body, hair – you dream it, she has it. Her staple diet is milk chocolate bars, but her skin couldn't spell zit if it had z-i-t on the scrabble board. She eats pasta like a horse, but size twelve bags at her hips.

Are you with me so far – or has this already entered the twiglet zone of your imagination? Her thighs have had the meaning of cellulite explained to them a million times and they still don't know what it is. She

4

has tits that stand so proud that their Red Indian name is 'Stand So Proud'.

So, I hear you grizzle through clenched teeth, is this woman perfect? Doesn't she have any problems? Yes, of course she does. She has lots of them. And they've all got willies. And every night, before she goes to sleep, often against the snoring back of some lump of male flesh which has just expelled itself into her, Sarah says to God: 'God, I understand you had to do a trial run before you took the spare rib and did the job properly. But, God, the usual thing is to dump the faulty prototype, not to let it run amok!'

See what I mean: she even has a sense of humour.

The agency where Sarah works is very well known and is considered to be very successful. DFDDG is, like all other agencies, an acronym of all the surnames of the men (they're always men) who originally had something to do with setting it up. But D and F and D and D are now long gone, whitherto we know and care not a jot, and only G remains. G is James, the big man at the top of the heap. You can make your own suppositions as to why the other four founding fathers left him to get on with it on his own; suffice to say that some people just have that effect on their colleagues.

If you know anything at all about advertising, you'll know about James. Next time you find yourself singing a catchy little ditty in the bath, James probably wrote it. Next time you lean instinctively for brand A rather than brand B in your supermarket, it's probably because one of James's ads told you why you should.

Sarah works in James's agency. Up till now, she's heard him speak at conferences and a few client business meetings, she's seen his face in the trade magazines and read his books and articles (lots of stuff with titles like *Living Above The Line* and 'Creative FMCG Communications', which do supposedly mean something to the happy campers in adland), but she hasn't seen that much of him face to face. He's smiled at her once or twice in the corridor. He sits in on her annual promotion and pay review. He came in to congratulate her when her team won the washing-up liquid account from their arch-rivals across the road.

And now, because Sarah's been promoted to director (her Dad back up north made her send him a pack of her business cards so he could prove it to family and friends), she's been invited to her first weekly directors' meeting with the other ten directors in the agency, chief amongst whom, *primus inter non pares*, is, of course, James.

I have to make a confession here, which is that James is Sarah's Achilles' heel. Like, I know it's the oldest trick in the book to fall for your boss (actually the boss of her boss), but that's what she's done.

A lot of her getting to the top so quickly has been inspired by James. She thinks he's absolutely marvellous. He's her guru. It's not his looks – although James is still a bit of all right, notwithstanding his near half-century of wear and tear. It's the fact that he's so good, that he's so clever at what he does. Because Sarah really believes in advertising; she thinks we're all happier human beings for it. And to her, James is the poster site for which you drive three times round the roundabout just so you can see the ad again and again.

She may well be right. He has done some great ads in his time. On the other hand, I'm very keen on penne alla vodka, but I don't have to take a bowl of it to bed with me to prove the point. Whereas Sarah definitely wants to get very close to James. All that power, all that glory. They could sip Australian Chardonnay deep into the night and discuss the fragmentation of consumer markets, they could debate priorities on brand strategies and, before they knew it, they'd be in each other's arms, putting product penetration to the ultimate test. So it's essential for Sarah that she puts on a good show today, her first full and formal exposure to the big man.

6

Unfortunately, the hours leading up to this presentation have not been the best for Sarah. She is still recovering from a particularly seedy session the night before with a bloke called Adam, and here's a good example of why you shouldn't feel jealous of her, notwithstanding her total adorableness.

Adam – shoulder-length blond hair slicked back à la mode – six-foot-two – perfect features – cheekbones like tomahawks – grey Armani suits – Armani shades worn outdoors and in – Armani socks – Armani underpants – did everything except wear a badge that said 'Hi, I'm Adam. Why not let me screw up your life?' but she still went for him.

Basically, what Sarah is no good at is men. Men she just can't do. Give her a piece of business to win, an account to handle, and you've got the best. Give her a man and it's a mess. Give Sarah a roomful of earnest, altruistic, interested men (you've found enough of them to fill a room? – I'm impressed!) and she'll part them, Moses-like, to make a beeline for the one right at the back who's on his mobile to the wife telling her he'll be working late that evening, sweetheart, better not wait up.

That's the one she wants, yes sir! The one that'll blow her out at dates wherever, whenever? Yes, sir! The one that'll treat her just as mean as can be? Yes, sir!

It's quite endearing really. Endearing like a cute puppy that gets a kick in the face every so often from its owner, that cowers and howls, and then goes slobbering back to lick the foot that kicked it. Sarah sniffs out bastards like pigs snout around for truffles, and when she's found one, no treatment they mete out is too contemptible, no behaviour too bad. The fouler they play, the more she wants the ball. She likes it when it hurts.

Were, however, by hapless chance, a good guy to wander innocently into her life and make the absurd mistake of trying to be pleasant to her, he would soon get the exit sign chucked at his goolies. When men are

7

nice, she can be just as mean as the mean ones are to her. Sitting duck becomes bird of prey. With Sarah you certainly get two for the price of one. It's just that, somewhere along the line, she's got her pleasure/pain wires crossed. She's developed her own private S&M club in her head, where all the nice blokes get barred at the door and the jerks are made life members.

It's odd isn't it, because I was telling you how smart she is, how good she is at her job, how attractive she is and all that. How can she be so smart at work and so daft everywhere else? Did only one side of her brain develop in the womb? Is she putting herself through this, like one of those masochistic Japanese game shows where they have to swim underwater through a bath of live worms, because someone's offered her a special prize at the end of it? Is it nature? Is it nurture? Is she nuts?

Oh, who knows, who knows, why us gels love shits. Why the safe and reliable types appear so bloody dull that we break up good marriages to leave them and get our noses bloodied by bastards; why we grind ourselves into the ground grovelling after the ones who make us feel like dirt.

I'll tell you about Sarah when she was a kid, but who's to say if the clues are there. Everything she's had or done, many others have had or done as well, without turning themselves into a self-inflicting Ms Whiplash.

Let's start with study and work, God knows Sarah always does. Even at nursery school, Sarah made her classmates feel inadequate. While the others in the class were grappling with p for panda, she was reading her dad sections from his copy of *The Times* over breakfast and beating him at chess. She was a triple-A-rated student all the way through school, got a place at Cambridge to read French and Russian, and then won the big prize on the milk round: a traineeship to become Assistant Brand Manager for Cherish Fresh.

Talk about the jackpot. That's only Cherish Fresh as

in the largest advertising spend on any sanitary product in the UK if you don't mind! Plus – as if any plus were needed – it was around the time when Cherish Fresh first launched wings on its towels, so a pretty seminal moment in the development of the sanpro industry, as I'm sure you'll appreciate. Nothing to do with French and Russian, but who's to care.

Sarah grasped the Cherish Fresh product opportunity with both hands, so to speak. She got wings on the agenda of every magazine with 'woman' in the title, she promoted it as the biggest breakthrough for the female sex since the pill. Through advertising and PR, she showed her sisters how life before wings was not really any kind of life at all, and before long Sarah was made brand manager and then marketing manager.

Well, a star like that soon gets noticed. She was headhunted by every manufacturer of personal care products in town, but somehow sensing the need for a new challenge after four years of promoting the benefits of women's nappies, Sarah took the offer to join Unilever to champion their fishfingers and then, two years later, to help Pepsi spend some of their considerable advertising budget on life-enhancing sponsorships for racing drivers and rock stars.

Diversity is the name of the game in advertising. By the time you've got the best part of a decade's worth of sanitary towels, fishfingers and Pepsi cola under your belt, you have what is officially called 'significant experience in fast moving consumer goods' and the world is your oyster. The recruitment consultants actually return your calls, they actually read your CVs.

By now, Sarah had decided that the time had come to try the other side of the fence and move to an agency. She more or less had her pick of offers, but DFDDG had to be the one, because, you guessed it, James ran DFDDG and James was where it's at in ads. And of course, as soon as she got there, it was foot on the old mental accelerator, endless long hours and smart moves which have culminated now in this precocious promotion to a board directorship at the age of thirty-two.

So that's the good news, all the job stuff. Now for the not so good news: her life. Anything that didn't have to go into a CV was the agenda that Sarah never quite got round to. She was so busy getting A grades when she grew up, to make her dad proud, that she kind of forgot to make friends, forgot to fancy men, forgot to question why she was pushing herself as hard as she did and why she was doing it in the first place. She was very clever, everyone had always told her she was very clever, much cleverer than her little sister Caroline who was not so clever.

You hear that ten times a week when you're growing up and it's hard not to take it all a bit too seriously. You get your dad showing your school reports to people when they come to the house ('the headmaster says he's never known a brain like it') and you begin to feel the pressure is on. You get your dad saying that his eldest is going to achieve all the things he never did, and failure is no longer an option. So you start to think of life as a series of goals – end of year exams, O' levels, A' levels, S' levels, Oxbridge, finals.

By then, you're so sucked into the system of life as an endless sequence of personal achievements, of endless personal ambitions, that you start to treat everything you do as part of the ladder of self-improvement. You buy a flat – the next one has to be bigger and better. You get a job – you immediately start pushing for promotion. If you go out with a man, he has to be smarter, better-looking, better-off than the last one. You don't ask yourself why you're doing it. You're not even particularly happy doing it. You just have to do it, because you've always done it.

Meanwhile, your younger sister, of whom nothing is expected, has lots of friends, doesn't do much at all really and seems quite happy. Meanwhile, although you do eventually make friends, you've never really got the time or energy to see them. Meanwhile, you are always tired, always a little bit sad, always going out with prats, always working and never stopping. Late nights, take work home, in the office at weekends. Spending money on things just to show yourself you can. Never stopping. Always more, always relentlessly more. The successful career woman.

Men were optional accessories for Sarah for a long time. Her sexual metabolism was far more geared up to the adrenalin of a good exam grade than a bit of a snog with a pubescent face of acne in her local cinema.

In fact, it has to be said that sexual relations of any kind were never Sarah's forte. She wore her regulation grey grammar school knickers up to the age of fifteen, long after they stopped being compulsory. Her idea of teenage provocation was to douse herself in Johnson's baby powder before the fifth form disco. At Cambridge she moused away in libraries, behind sandbags of vast volumes of *Le Petit Larousse*. More than a late developer, Sarah showed no interest in physical progress of any kind. Beyond a few fumbles with a couple of sincere types at parties, her toilet parts were reserved for just that, and Sarah felt at no particular loss because of this.

As the years passed, however, Sarah began to discover more about herself and her needs as a woman. Specifically, she found out that these needs were to surround herself with men who were unkind to her. The nastier the tactic, the more she was drawn to them.

It all started when she was twenty-three and she was getting dolled up to go to a party with Kevin. Serves her right for wanting to go out with a bloke called Kevin in the first place, I say. At that age she should have known better. Just as the third layer of eyeshadow went on, Kevin rang to say that he had slipped on a bar of soap in the shower, that he had fallen and banged his chin on the handbasin and that as he was now semi-concussed he wouldn't be going to the party at all. Well, at least he'd made the effort to think up something original. Total crap, but original. As the hosts were really Kevin's friends, people that Sarah hardly knew, Sarah, not disbelieving him for a moment, said she wouldn't go either. She put the phone down and suddenly realised that she would die if she had yet another Saturday night with no one but Cilla Black and a spring roll to keep her company.

So she went to the party and guess what. Kevin was there. Guess even more what. Kevin was there with another woman. So did Sarah feel angry? Did she want to go straight over and wallop him one? No. Sarah felt admiration. She felt desire. She was impressed that he should treat her so bad. It meant he must be a man worth fighting for.

Then they say women are illogical! Goodness me, we've got so much logic, it's spilling out of our ears! And ever since then she's been hooked. The secret to Sarah's heart: forget the chocolates, the love letter, the bouquet of flowers. Put the boot in – she'll love you for it.

Anyway, enough of all this analysis, I think you get the picture by now. We were talking about Adam, the man she'd been dating for a couple of months. It's important to stress the dating bit, because putting the date in the diary was about the most congenial thing that ever happened with him. From then on it was all downhill.

Adam is a thrusting thirty-something who's a PR. PR people use that abbreviation because to add 'ick' all the time would make the word a bit too long for them. He's a very attractive man, but his own appreciation of his looks spills down over him like egg on a baby's bib.

Adam, the man with the voice which swoons at its own sound. The kind of guy who, when he's chatting you up, is already looking over your shoulder to see what else he might be missing out there. The type whose eyes mist over with a dull opaque if you're talking about anyone but him. (Sounds like someone you know?)

Sarah first met Adam at a business conference. At the end of the conference he asked Sarah back to his place for a drink. Sniffling the opportunity for a bit of shitty treatment, she readily accepted and back they went. Adam was very taken with Sarah. She had that detached, virginal look about her. And as Adam does not care, as the expression goes, to stir other people's porridge, this aura of purity appealed to him.

Adam has very distinct preferences. Amongst other things, he likes tall, elegant women who carry themselves proudly with straight, graceful spines. Yes, he likes 'em tall and straight. The straighter they are, the more they snap when he breaks them. Adam is very good at breaking women.

They went back to his place and Adam poured her a glass of wine. He talked to her for a while about the merits of PR as an imperative force in today's multi-media environment. All of a sudden he turned and said to her: 'You're very beautiful. I have to fuck you.' Adam's romantic rhetoric was never his most impressive feature but he couldn't be arsed – he knew that the rest of him made up for it.

Sarah was entranced by this flourish of male will. Like when you go to Regent's Park Zoo and you see an ape snorting and belching and swinging its way from branch to branch and you think – gosh, I find that ape very exciting and I must let it abuse me. Adam smiled and waited for his charm to take effect, like a nerve gas that needs a few minutes to permeate the victim's lungs fully. Five-four-three-two-one, they were in the bedroom and he was stuffing himself up her this way and that. Sarah told herself it must be love.

For three months, life followed this charmingly atavistic pattern. Sometimes he rang, very often he didn't. She rang, sometimes he rang back, usually he didn't.

When he did, they met at his place and he put his germy foreskin inside her. Until one morning, this morning, straight after a night of this passionless, primeval poking, he told her that it wasn't going anywhere. That it was all over, he respected her, would always want her as a friend, etc, etc. You know the jargon. She started crying.

Oh, Sarah. Praise the Lord and leave, don't cry!

She cried and cried. She cried herself back to sleep. When she woke up, he'd gone to work. There was a set of keys and a note. The note said: 'Please double-lock the door then post the keys through the letter box when you leave. Adam.' God! It never happened like this in 'A Reader's True Experience'. So she lurched out of his house, semen seeping through her tights (Adam doesn't like condoms because he can't feel anything when they're on, you see) and forged her way through the London traffic into work, to this big directors' meeting where she's got to impress everyone.

When she got to work, the secretaries looked at her with disdain. Everyone in the office knows that Sarah always has man trouble. One disaster after another. But she brings in the business so no one says anything. To her face. This morning it was obvious that her latest bit of chest hair had booted her out. Dishevelled, I think, is the word normally used to describe a woman in this state. Her hair was all over the place, her mascara looked like a squid had peed in her eyes, and she definitely had that post-shagged morning after, just been fucked and chucked look.

The *University Challenge* panel of secretaries watched her run into the loo with her make-up bag. 'Bet she's got his juices still running down her leg,' said Anita, the directors' head secretary, sagely, as one who understands these things.

After a swift but effective repair job with the old *maquillage* kitbag in the ladies' loo, Sarah was ready to go into the meeting – a good twenty minutes late. A final check in the mirror. Suck in the cheeks, stick out the chest. Yes, we're looking good. Deep breath, count to three, make your entrance girl. This is big-time now and, late or not late, you're going to make it happen.

One of the older guys, Tony, who'd been at the agency for ever, was in mid-sentence as she walked in. 'Glad you could join us,' said Peter, her boss, loudly and sarcastically, feeling embarrassed that he had pushed so hard to get her promoted to director if this was how she was going to repay him.

OK, so not the best start to your first directors' meeting. You're twenty minutes late and your boss gets his loud-hailer out to make the point. So what's she going to do? Get lost in another mascara mudbath of tears? Mumble a dismal apology and sink down into her seat as low as it will let her go?

Not on your nelly: this is work. This is different. This is where Sarah suddenly self-transforms from domestic doormat into corporate hobnailed boot; where the business hairs sprout on the backs of her slender fingers and her corner teeth mutate into fangs of assertiveness; where she metamorphoses from victim fatale into businessperson extraordinaire, as Little Bo Peep strips off her blue shepherdesses frock to reveal – dan der dan – the Queen of Sheba, Boadicea, Cleopatra, Madonna, Joan of Arc and sundry other positive female role models all rolled into one.

No more Ms Nice Girl. This is work, this is ambition, this is what Sarah allows herself to be good at. Her internal connections meet, spark, and some light that reads 'self-respect' flashes into her mind.

'Pete, you're right to be pissed off,' Sarah replied. Calmly. Charmingly.

She sat down, smiling her most serene smile, looking like the photo on the cover of the training video, 'The Successful Woman At Work: Winning Through Confidence': tough while radiant. Never would you have guessed, unless I'd told you, that only a couple of hours beforehand this face was caked with the snot and tears of rejection and despair.

'Pete, you're right to be pissed off,' she replied. Calmly. Charmingly. 'I had something very pressing to attend to which demanded my full attention. But I'm here now' – at this point she looked across the table and assaulted James's eyes with her own – 'and I'm raring to go.' More big smile, this time laced with just a snifter of flirtation, in James's direction.

Round the table, reactions were mixed. Sarah's fellow female director was impressed by her nerve. Her fellow male directors made a subconscious mental note to attend these meetings more regularly from now on. They scratched their balls nervously under the table – they can't tell whether they're in awe of her or whether they want to give her one. Sarah makes them feel confused. I know that's easily done, but Sarah always seems to do it.

Watching her performance, James's nostrils had started to twitch like the pink snout of a cat when someone takes the smoked salmon out of the fridge. 'No problem,' he mumbled. 'Let's just get on, shall we?'

'Thanks,' Sarah mouthed silently across at him, using muscles her lips didn't even know they had to give maximum impact to the red of her so-moist-you-could-drown-in-it freshly applied lipstick. By now James had more than his nostrils twitching.

So the meeting carried on. Sarah's late arrival was forgotten. Tony continued with what turned out to be a rather sad, butt-covering explanation as to why one of his key clients, a cereals manufacturer, had told him they were thinking of putting the entire account up for review.

Tony was a nice man, and you know what it means in business when you're described as nice. It means you ain't got no future. It means that you either go off and teach marketing to twenty-year-olds or you set up a small business in Essex doing direct mailshots for medical publishers. It means you do not stay in London, at the top, where nice people don't make it beyond the rush to get out of the tube first thing in the morning, much less as far as the office.

However, today Tony was a driven man. With this bad news to relate, he was particularly desperate for his fix of Brownie points, which he retrieved on a regular basis from somewhere up James's rear passage.

James had a soft spot for Tony. By coincidence, they had been to the same dull little country public school together, and James was sure that Tony was aware of an unpleasant adolescent incident that James had been involved in there. Although neither of them had ever mentioned it, James had felt more comfortable knowing that Tony ate out of his hand. Also, Tony had at one time been very useful during James's various *coups* in liberating him from the company of the other four men with whom he had first set up the agency. Tony was handy for spreading rumours, telling tales and gleaning gossip: a nifty fag who could do a lot of the dirty work required in putting about stories to undermine a good man's reputation.

But that was then and this was now. James had got rid of the others and built the agency up into one of the biggest and best. Tony's sleazy loyalty was no longer necessary, his arse-licking was getting irritating and his business acumen increasingly in doubt. And who cared if he knew that James had been caught with his face in another boy's trousers thirty years before? No one would believe him, and anyway, all that kind of stuff was considered par for the course nowadays. Even desirable for a real life-player.

'Well, my feeling is it's pretty obvious we're on the inside track here,' Tony yabbered on. 'Looking at the financials, I'd say we're over and above the limit. We could take it to two ten but I only want to deal in year ends here. I mean, all bets are off if we don't have his buy-in. I reckon it'll be all over bar the shouting at this rate. They're going to need a decision in place by Q2. We got stitched last time, but this time we can re-jig the figs and get back on track.'

A handy tip here, folks: lots of media people like to talk in rhyme. It helps them get into the swing of things, and even (or especially) if what they're saying is nonsense, it means they can ignore the words and get off on the beat alone. Think of Baloo Bear adorned with coconuts: you've got the picture.

Tony was coming to his incomprehensible crescendo. With each point he made, he waved one hand in the air like he was conducting a symphony orchestra. 'I say we go out there, market aggressively, and lobby at strike position. Right now, we're up a gum tree. We need to ride herd, hit the head of the pack and keep running. Let's gatecrash this one and just do it.'

Having made no sense to anyone for quite a while, he came to what obviously represented a conclusion in his own head. There was a pause. Everyone waited nervously for James to speak.

'Well,' said James.

'Well,' interrupted Sarah, who had heard on the grapevine about Tony's predicament. 'I don't know whether I missed something before I arrived, but that sounded like crap to me.'

Roger, the FD (that's finance director, although other interpretations have been known), choked coffee all down his jacket. 'I see the new girl wants to make a good impression,' he said loudly into his chest as he wiped himself down.

Sarah turned on him like a glamorous pit bull terrier. 'Well, Roger. Old boy. I've heard that these meetings are often full of toss, and if I'm going to be part of this set-up, I'd like to make my input real.'

You have to imagine this all coming out of the mouth of a very beautiful woman. Notwithstanding the damage just done by Adam, Sarah is visually extremely pleasing. I do stress this, to make it more credible for you. If a plain, flat-chested female tried this little number, she'd be out on her ear. So, as they say after an episode of *Batman*, don't try this stunt yourself, viewers.

Roger's jaw gaped with a gravity attack. When it was clear she would not have to suffer further comment from him, Sarah eloquently turned her back on him and continued to savage her previous prey.

'Tony,' our heroine strode on, 'that account has been withering on the vine for months now, and you know it. You had a long time to do something about it, but you just hung on in there, hoping that your regular golfing sessions with their marketing director would see you through. It didn't, and now it looks like they're pulling out. We've got what we deserved.'

Tony went very pale. He opened his mouth to answer back, but no words came, leaving just a few sticky lines of spit running like a couple of greasy stalactites from his top teeth to his bottom dentures.

'That's rather harsh, Sarah,' said Peter. 'Although I'm afraid that she's probably right,' he added more quietly.

While all this was going on, James, sitting on his bigger-than-everyone-else's chair at the top of the solid teak table, was electrified. He had an erection so huge he was worried that it was going to tilt the table, and no amount of surreptitious fondling would dampen it down. Who is this woman?

He was trying hard to think why he hadn't noticed her before. That is, he had noticed her before, but he hadn't noticed her so that he wanted to lock himself in a room with her for a week before. James was elated, inflated. Finally – a bird with tits, guts, and lips that looked like a bloody suction pad. And he knew a sink that needed unblocking. Fast.

Unaware that she was causing the man of her desire a nether-region hurricane, Sarah carried on defiantly. There was no stopping her now. She does have this tendency to show off a bit when the going gets good, but when she's talking so much sense, it's hard to complain.

'Tony, we're talking cereals here. In my view, the issue is the identity: the name and the packaging. Consumers have no real relationship with the product because the name's so bloody boring. Brekky Chunks. Who the hell's going to want to be seen with Brekky Chunks in their shopping basket? And that awful box, it looks so dull and dated. The product has no personality, no charisma. Right now, it's no more than a series of E numbers and flavourings, some weights and calories and kilojoules. You need to make it sing off the gondola at Safeways, dance out of the TV screen, get kids nagging their mums for it, make it a part of the essential identikit of today's fashionable family. Hi, I'm Andy, I jog, I read the *Guardian*, I care about my wife and my nose hair and I eat it.'

'Charisma?' snarled Tony grumpily. 'We're talking about a bloody breakfast cereal, not a dinner date.'

'Well, it's that kind of a comment which shows me how little you must understand about why people buy the brands they do buy. No wonder the last issue of *Marketing Week* showed that consumer awareness of Brekky Chunks was trailing behind almost every other advertised breakfast cereal. Even that new banana-flavoured crap which was launched only a few months ago, what is it, Banana Bonanza, has overtaken Brekky Chunks. I'm not surprised the clients are pissed off.'

'You don't want to believe those consumer surveys – the trade press make it up as they go along,' whimpered Tony defensively.

'Look Tony, it hardly matters whether you believe it, or I believe it, the fact is that everyone who reads *Marketing Week* sees it, and that includes our clients and our competitors and all the retailers and if they think Brekky Chunks are no longer top of the hit parade, they're going to start playing a different tune. Let me put that more simply for you, Tony, they're going to drop the product lower and lower on their shelves and stock fewer and fewer boxes on the gondolas until you're going to need trained sniffer dogs to be able to find any of them.'

'Now you're just being silly, Sarah – '

'I'm being silly? No, I tell you what, Tony. You want silly, I'll tell you what's silly. Silly is over two million pounds of the client's money on the last campaign you ran for the "Brekky Chunk Brigade", a bunch of girls, dressed up like majorettes, who were supposed to give you a voucher for £500 for every "lucky pack" of Brekky Chunks they find in your house when they came calling.'

'Look, I agree that – ' Tony stammered. But Sarah's on a roll, ain't no stopping her now.

'Silly is advertising the campaign in parts of the country where there were no participating retailers. Sillier still is dressing up a bunch of women not old enough to have left school in indecent costumes as the "Brekky Chunk Girls", sending them out after dark to knock on people's doors to see if they've got packs of Brekky Chunks at home, and then being surprised when you read front-page news that one of the girls was almost raped by some perve in his house when he lured her in to check his larder. And most silly of all is sending all thousand packs with the winning "lucky pack" token inside to that one Gateway store in Surbiton, where they thought Christmas had come early, but which left every other customer in the rest of the country vowing never to buy another pack of Chunks for the rest of their breakfast-consuming days.'

You can't blame Sarah for having an upper torso which is so richly endowed that, when she's animated like this, her bosoms bounce up and down like a mini chorus-line, robustly echoing her every sentiment.

By now Tony's head was in his lap.

Sarah paused for breath and then concluded: 'Anyway, as I said, I think it's all a question of identity.

So tell the clients you're going to change the name, tart up the packaging, and I know of a brilliant little design outfit that I've been working with recently who'll wave the magic wand for you.'

Forget her magic wand. Any minute now, James's own magic wand, leaping uncontrollably with her every word under his flies, would be spewing forth six white doves and a rabbit.

'OK, OK, Sarah,' he said, 'you've made your point.' (God knows, she'd certainly made his.) 'Look, Tony,' he went on, 'it's clear this has to be sorted out. Why don't you get together with Sarah sometime soon and discuss this in more detail. I know you've got an understanding of the ins and outs of this account that perhaps the others don't have, but a piece of fresh advice never did any harm.'

Tony assented with a surly nod in James's direction. Like hell he was going to discuss his account with a bloody woman. He'd sort things out his own way, he didn't need this pushy cow telling him what to do.

Peter gave himself a mental pat on the back — he'd picked a winner in Sarah. He'd have to make sure that James didn't forget that it was he who had hired her and nurtured her right from the start.

Roger wished he hadn't made that snide comment: this was obviously someone he needed to get on with and, now that he thought about it, she had tits you could rest a tea-tray on. He scribbled himself a reminder to ask her out for lunch next time his secretary could get a table at a decent restaurant.

James made a tacit agreement with his dick that if he settled down now, James would make it up to him later.

The pressure went out of the room and they continued with their agenda. Sarah realised that she had made enough impact for one meeting, and, apart from the occasional intelligent and salient remark, sat quietly like a good girl.

Three

At the end of the meeting James asked Sarah to stay behind. The others self-consciously filed out, jealous that they had not been chosen for a private interview with the chief, while Sarah demurely pretended to look through her notes, trying not to look too obviously delighted.

'Sarah, I just wanted to discuss a couple of things,' James began. He had no idea at this stage what these things were to be, but improvisation had never been his weak point.

'Sure,' she replied. Just then, James noticed that her brown eyes in fact had quite a lot of green in them, but it looked as if the left eye had a little bit more green than the other one, although maybe, no, they were the same it was just that the little flecks of green under the big dark lashes looked like they might be green or brown.

Then he saw her shoulders. The curve of Sarah's bare shoulders glinted through the thin silk of her shirt. He wanted to lick those shoulders. He was compelled utterly to lick those shoulders. If he did not lick those shoulders, he would surely die.

After what seemed like an eternity of being stared at, Sarah thought perhaps he expected her to start the conversation. 'Was it about Tony?' she asked.

Her words jumped him out of his trance. 'Yes, Tony. Yes, that's it. Look, go easy on the old chap.'

'Oh come on, James,' said Sarah irritably.

James may well be her hero, but she is still in work mode, and in work mode no one gets one over on Sarah. It's just out of work they get everything over her.

Her shoulders hunched in a sulk. He saw that this reprimand did not please them. They slumped into the folds of the shirt so the skin was no longer pressing against the silk. No, no. He could not offend those shoulders. That would not do.

'Well, I'm only saying that because, between you and me, his days are numbered here anyway.'

James saw the shoulders perk up again expectantly. His pulse quickened.

'My plan is to give him the old heave-ho on Thursday.'

Sarah leaned forward. The shoulders wiggled in anticipation. Their round, soft outline was pressed right up against the silk, bulging and straining at the fibre. He could almost taste them. His tongue sweltered in his mouth for them.

'Yes. Give him the elbow. And then give the account to you!' James heard himself say the words. The words had come before the thought. It made no sense at all to give the account to her when she was so well settled in with her washing-up liquid clients, but somehow his dick, not his brain, was now writing the script.

Sarah felt her stomach perform a triple-salco. She dug a nail very deep into her hand under the table so that the pain would stop her from leaping up and doing the okey-kokey with joy. 'Right,' was all she said.

Does it shock you that she's so thrilled about this proposition, that she cares so little about Tony? She's slagged him off in front of his colleagues, she's publicly humiliated him and made her own case. Now she's going to get his job and he's going to become another black plastic bag of personal desk contents in the rubbish dump of failed and past-it business executives. And her only instinct is delight?

Well, look see here now, it's like this. Sarah truly believes that Tony is doing a lousy job. She knows that she could make a better go of it, and probably save the account for the agency. She is genuinely frustrated by his total incompetence on the account, putting the jobs of everyone in his team at risk. Plus: this promotion fits in with her total work ethos about pushing back the frontiers of success every day, in every way.

And as if all this wasn't enough: James, her champion, master of her destiny, has not only noticed that she is alive but has given her one of the biggest accounts in the agency. He's looking at her now like he wants to eat her for breakfast.

So, yes. She is delighted.

'I like your style and I like your ideas,' continued James's penis, using James like a ventriloquist's dummy. 'I've been hearing a lot from Peter about your work. I think you could really do it for us.'

This was the royal we. We was James. This bint had gorgeous eyes, and truly fabulous knockers. Not only that (as if that weren't usually more than enough): she was also sharp, smart and highly original. She was brave enough to think laterally. Now James was thinking laterally. Horizontally.

'Look,' said his dick authoritatively, 'why don't we meet for dinner on Thursday evening. The dirty deed will have been done by then with Tony, and we can discuss strategy in greater detail.'

Bet you never knew that pricks could talk!

Sarah's reply was a weak and nonplussed smile. Was this the deal, then? Was she getting this account because he thought she was good at her job or because he wanted to bonk her? Was she good at her job because she wanted the account or because she wanted him to want to bonk her?

Is she in work mode, i.e. taking no shit from no one, or in romance mode, i.e. taking all shit from everyone?

25

Which one is it to be, Sarah dear? She's confused, bless her; we're all confused.

Either way, exultant as she was at James's obvious interest in her, she'd rather that a first meeting was lunch, not dinner. She knew what dinner meant: first date dinner is not ideal romantically and it's certainly not on professionally.

But right now, there was nothing she could say. There's nothing any woman can say when her male boss plays it this way. For if you say: actually, I'd rather we just kept business meetings to business hours – albeit with a smile – you are a ranting, dungareed harpie and you are foaming at your feminist mouth to turn a perfectly professional business arrangement into a sexual play because you've got so many cobwebs round your fanny you'd think the traffic light fancied you when it turned green.

But if you say, right, see you there, why, that means not only do you accept his divine right over your knicker elastic, you're gasping for a good rummage round you garden shed. Please don't tell me it's not like this. Lunch is lunch. Dinner is dinner. You don't need a Linguaphone language course in innuendo to know when an offer is an offer.

'OK,' she said.

James smiled his smile. They never said no.

When Sarah left the boardroom, Ralph was shuffling around outside, pretending to read the notice that had been up there since 1953 about what to do in the event of a fire.

Ralph was the director in charge of the agency's charity account. It didn't make much money, but it was good for the corporate image. Ralph was a regular guy. He was young, friendly and accessible, with those *Blue Peter* presenter kind of good looks, reliable and successful in a low-key kind of way, which meant no kind of way at all in Adsville. He chatted with the secretaries when most of the other directors treated them like skivvies, unless they were bonking them in which case they treated them like real dirt ('otherwise people will guess what we're up to, darling').

Ralph liked Sarah. Ralph liked Sarah a lot. He showed his affection for her in little things, most of which Sarah knew nothing about. He often watched her through the glass walls of her office. Nothing weirdo. Just friendly. He had often and anonymously passed on good PR opportunities when the press rang up, rather than taking the deals for himself. And he got very excited on Sunday evenings. Just about the time when the rest of us feel that dark cloud of dread settling on our shoulders at the prospect of another week at the coal face, Ralph would be quietly ecstatic at home in the knowledge that it was only a matter of hours before he saw Sarah again in the office the next morning.

Sarah had guessed that Ralph had some sort of above average interest in her when she'd casually mentioned that she preferred orange Smarties the last time he nervously sauntered into her office as he just happened to be passing by and offered her one. The next day, she'd found a tube full of orange Smarties on her desk with a note that said: 'Roses are red, violets are blue, but if you prefer orange then this tube's for you!'

OK, so it's a bit dire, but what the fuck. We can't all be miserable, cynical bastards and Ralph's not. Not any more. Ralph is a regular guy.

No wonder Sarah turns her nose up at him. He'd spent a fortune on packs of Smarties to get enough of them to fill up a whole tube with orange ones. Even worse, the orange ones were his favourites too, and it was agony to hand over a treasure like that and just be left with a whole stack of brown and red ones on his desk. He consoled himself that having the same taste in Smarties was surely a good omen for the future.

Sarah laughed when she saw the gift. She rang one of her friends and they both pissed themselves giggling at the idea of this guy up to his elbows in Smarties, fishing out the orange ones for her. Sarah thought Ralph was sweet. And now here he was, hovering outside the meeting room. He walked alongside her, trying to keep up as she steamed out of the room.

'Hello, Sarah.'

'Hello, Ralph.'

'Sarah, I thought you were great in there. I mean it. Just great.'

She stopped and looked at this ardent alsatian of a man. He had gorgeous eyes, like two pools of hot chocolate. 'Thanks, Ralph.'

'Sarah,' said Ralph, getting about as brave as Ralph gets, 'I wondered whether you'd like to come to the National Portrait Gallery with me this weekend. You know, they've got that BP competition thing and it looks pretty good.' He was all goofy Clark Kent, specs on the end of his nose, soppy smile. Except that underneath, there was no blue latex catsuit. Just a warm, hairy and slightly cuddly stomach.

'Sure,' said Sarah, to get rid of him as much as anything else. 'Sure.'

'Fine. That's great! I'll call you Friday and we'll fix a time for Saturday, maybe have a bite to eat at lunch as well?'

Sarah was still intoning 'sure' as she disappeared round the corner of the corridor, leaving Ralph in his tracks. Ralph was sweet. Really sweet. And therefore didn't stand a chance with her.

Four

Ever noticed how your life is governed by fate? Next day, which I believe was a Tuesday, Roger's secretary rings through at 11 a.m. to tell him there's a cancellation at the Ivy. (I know – unrealistic – but I can claim poetic licence, don't forget.) Just before he grabs the phone to dial Sarah's extension, let me fill you in on this delightful fellow. Roger has all the charm of tinned ravioli, i.e., looks bad, tastes worse, but notwithstanding this – oh, I'm sorry, I mean because of this – he seems to get more than his fair share of chicks ready to cut their fingers on his can.

The most interesting thing I can tell you about Roger is his hair, of which he now sadly has very little. So he and his barber have had to devise a complex coiffure for him which involves growing one very long lock of hair where he still has some of it, somewhere low down on the back of his neck, and then sweeping this lock forwards over his crown and then kind of flicking it sideways to simulate a head of hair.

It all requires an expensive mêlée of gels, cream and sundry other unctions to keep it in place. It also requires very skilful wrist action to whisk the thing into being each morning, but fortunately wrist action is something that Roger is particularly good at.

Still, I'm not going to have a go at a man because he hasn't got a lot of hair and because he's got a hairdo which looks like the thing you bought back from your nature trail at Brownies. I'm going to have a go at him because he's basically your archetypal shit, cheats on his wife, spends her money, confuses women generally with J-cloths, backstabs colleagues and practises a nasty line in deviant hobbies. His father got him a job in the city way back when, and somehow his dad's title, his old school tie and his wife's money have supported him through a very satisfactory lifestyle of mornings at jobs which pay well but demand little, afternoons at the golf club and nights playing poker with women. Yes, you guessed it: that's not poker as in the card game.

So, lucky old Sarah: this table has come up and now he's ringing his way through to her.

'Hello, Sarah, this is Roger. Look, I know it's rather short notice, but, given your recent promotion, I feel it's important that we meet.'

'You do?'

'Yes, you know, get together to discuss matters financial and all that. I'd like to give you a good grounding on the pounds, shillings and pence of the place. What do you say?'

'Fine. Well, I'll get my secretary to liaise with yours and we'll fix up for later this week – your office or mine?'

'Er, well, I was wondering, how are you fixed for lunch today?'

Sarah was taken aback. This man had never even acknowledged her presence. At the meeting the day before he'd tried to cut her down in front of everyone. Suddenly she was in demand.

'Well, I did have a lunch already planned, but I'm sure I can postpone it to another day.' After all, it's not every day that the finance director calls down to you from on high.

'Excellent. I'll book a car for twelve-thirty. I'll see you then.'

I don't know, it's tough at the top, isn't it, being whisked off for lunches and dinners, here, there and everywhere. I suppose that Sarah has now entered that stratosphere of corporate life where the number of hours of work you actually get done in the course of the average day has an inverse relationship to the number of numbers after the pound sign on your monthly pay slip.

But you go for it, Sarah. You're waving the flag for us all. All us mums who gave it all up to breed mobile nappies, all us women who didn't take promotion to keep our husbands happy, all us girls who turned down a place at university to stay in the same town as our fiancé who dumped us anyway, we're looking to you to live our lives for us, live out that corporate dream of glory which we sacrificed in the name of Persil.

Right, now I've got that little piece off my chest: here we are in the cab, and Roger, who's used to pretty much instantaneous capitulation (it's the thought of him handling all that money that makes the hooks and eyes on their bras go boss-eyed), ne waste pas un moment de temps.

'Well, Sarah,' he said, his hand swooping down like a hungry vulture on her thigh, 'it looks as if you're doing pretty well at the agency. The apple of everyone's eye, the jewel in our crown. Congratulations.'

'Thank you, Roger,' Sarah replied politely. 'And thank you also for taking your hand from my leg.'

Great. He loved it when they played games. He gave the firm skin a firm squeeze and then let go.

'Of course, you know what people are like, they love to gossip, to find excuses for success.'

'Is that so?'

'Well of course. A woman like you being promoted to director in such a short space of time . . . I suppose you know what people are saying.'

'No, Roger, I don't think I do; mind you, I don't think I care either.'

'Well, they're saying you've only got to where you are today because you took the right steps.'

Sarah detected that she was not going to like this man. 'Yes, that's right Roger, I did take steps.'

Aha! She's a one, this one. And he could drown in that cleavage. 'So, no denial!'

'No, no denial.'

'So tell me, Sarah, who is the lucky man?'

'The lucky man is Peter.'

'Peter? You shafted poor old Peter to get your promotion? Well, well, the dark horse. I wouldn't have thought Peter had it in him to put his cocktail stick in anyone's gherkin after that operation.'

'No, Roger, I did not shaft Peter. You asked me what steps I took. I worked very hard, and very long hours, for Peter, my boss, we won a lot of business together, including the Wondersuds account. These were the steps I took and this is why I was promoted. Do you understand? And shall we ask the cab to turn round and go back to the office?' She opened the little glass window. 'Would you mind turning back, please, driver.'

'Hang on, hang on,' said Roger. 'Ignore her, cabbie.' He slammed the window shut. 'Come on, I was only having a laugh, only teasing. Don't be so sensitive, you women always are so over-sensitive, so emotional about everything. Anyway, we're almost there now. We'll soon get a few glasses of vino inside you to calm you down.'

'OK, Roger, but get your act together, all right?'

Mmm, it gave him goose-pimples all over when they talked tough like that. 'Whatever you say,' he chuckled, then smiled and offered her his hand to help her out of the cab.

Sarah did not smile. 'I can get out of a cab on my own, thanks.'

In case you're wondering: Sarah does not fancy Roger. This hostile behaviour on her part is not, in fact,

32

a smokescreen for smouldering desire. She emphatically does not go for this one.

I know he's a complete bastard and therefore should be her cup of tea. I know he's a smooth-talking jerk in a position of power in business, and therefore has all the right ingredients for her menu. But, come on, I've told you about the hair. Give Sarah some credit: would you go out with hair like that?

Roger entered the restaurant with a flourish and greeted all the waiters by name as if they were old friends, although it seemed that they had difficulty in recognising him.

'My usual table, Henry, thank you.'

'I'm not sure what your usual table is, sir, but as you only took a cancellation last thing this morning, I'm afraid I can only give you that one over there. And by the way, sir, it's Dominic, not Henry.'

'Dominic, of course, of course,' said Roger, cursing the bugger under his breath for making him look like a fool in front of Sarah. 'Look, old man,' he muttered, hoisting him to one side by his elbow, 'that table won't do, it's right by the doors to the kitchen and the stairs to the bogs, for Christ's sake. The lady won't like it. Here's a little something to help you find us another table, something a bit more central, all righty?'

'I'm afraid not, sir,' said Dominic, pushing the money back into Roger's hand. 'We have this table available, and only this one. Do I understand you would rather leave it for today and go somewhere else?'

'Of course I won't leave it, you jumped-up tea boy,' blasted Roger. 'Where else are we going to get a decent table at this time? We'll have to take your rotten table and I'd like you to send the manager to see me at once.'

'I, sir, the jumped-up tea boy, I am the manager,' smiled Dominic.

Roger growled and stomped off towards the table. Sarah followed on behind him, incensed. 'I really think you ought to go back to him and apologise, Roger. You have no right to talk to people like that, your comments were really quite insulting.'

'Don't be so melodramatic, my dear, we're just having a laugh, Harry and I, we do it every time I come here, he's a bit of a joker, that one. Now what'll we have? A nice Pinot Grigio, how's that?'

'No thanks, I don't drink at lunchtimes unless a client particularly wants to. I'll just have some sparkling water.'

'Goodness, you're a cheap date, remind me to invite you out more often,' Roger complimented her. He went ahead and shouted for the bottle of wine anyway. They ordered food and Sarah tried to set a calmer tone for the lunch.

'I'm very grateful for your offer to meet. There are in fact a number of issues about which I'm curious, things I saw on the management accounts at yesterday's meeting which puzzled me, things like – '

'Oh you don't want to have to worry your pretty little head about nonsense like that. Here we are, having a lovely meal in one of London's best restaurants, just getting to know each other. Now, tell me about you, I suppose you're just beginning to feel your way around your new role?'

Sarah took a deep breath. What was she going to do with this prat of a man? 'Yes, I suppose you're right, I am just starting to feel my way around, especially the figures, and that's why . . .'

'Because people tell me I'm pretty good at feeling my way around, so if you would like someone to help you feel their way around you, make sure you let me know.'

'I beg your pardon?

'No need to beg, just give me the word. You know, a beautiful woman like you could go very far, if you know the right people, do the right things, talk the right talk. I could be very helpful for you.'

'Well, I'm not sure what my looks have to do with it, but thank you, I would be grateful for your help, given your very responsible role at the agency, Roger, so perhaps you can start by answering some of the questions I've drawn up on the management accounts.'

'For fuck's sake, Sarah, I didn't come here to talk about all that kind of tosh. You're in advertising for Christ's sake, is this how you are with your clients, all work and no play?'

'Please don't question my professionalism with my clients, Roger. I know perfectly well how to behave with them. You are not a client, you are a colleague, and I have to tell you that I find much of what you are saying not only completely unprofessional but also grossly offensive.'

Roger roared with laughter. Heads turned and he roared again. 'Offensive? Oh cripes, this is better than the theatre. What have you taken offence at, my sensitive flower? That a very senior colleague has invited you out for lunch, has tried to give you a helping hand with your career?'

'Yes, and it's that helping hand that I think I can do without, that hand fondling my thigh in the taxi, that hand you would like to feel your way around me with. You have no right to talk to female colleagues like that, and I shall make sure you don't get away with it from now on.'

'My feet are already trembling with fear in my shoes, my dear. If you want to go back to the office and make a complete idiot of yourself with stories that no one can verify, be my guest. But please be informed that I made sure that I mentioned to my secretary before we left that you'd been pestering me for weeks to take you out for lunch and that I was only giving in, busy as I was, to shut you up.

'Now try going back to the office and telling them whatever nonsense it is you want to tell them. It's your word as an ambitious little tart against mine as finance director of the company. Who do you think they're going to side with, eh? The fact is that you've got your

35

panties in a bit of a wad over me and you don't know how to deal with it. You know it, I know it. We've got the hots for each other. Why not just give in and enjoy?'

'Roger, I know this is going to distress you and come as a terrible shock to you, but the truth is that I don't find you in the least attractive. In fact, if you were to press me, I'd say I think you're one of the least attractive men I know, in every sense.'

'Is that what you'd like me to do, Sarah, to press you? Press you against me, eh? Where would you like me to press you?'

'The expression I'd rather stick needles in my eyes comes rapidly to mind.'

'Is it your little titties you'd like me to press, Sarah? Is that what you'd really like?' Roger whispered, with a Cheshire grin, his big, bulbous face close up against hers. 'Are your little boobies pleading and panting in their little cups to have me get a hold of them?'

Sarah looked at this creature, this bag of bones and fat and stupidity. She looked at him hard and saw the sweat glands of lechery throbbing in his eyes.

Slowly, she unbuttoned the front of her shirt, reached inside and removed each breast from over the top of her bra.

'Look at them, Roger, you ridiculous little man. Go on, take a good look. As you can see' – Sarah looked down and checked for herself – 'they are neither pleading nor panting to have you. In fact, like me, they simply find you rather a sad and silly fool. I feel sorry for you. My tits feel sorry for you. You must have such low self-esteem. So, if you don't mind, I'll take me, my pretty little head, my wadded panties and my deeply unpanting breasts back to the office and I'll let everyone there, verification or no verification, know just what a miserable berk I think you are.'

Sarah did up her blouse, to the disappointment of many a diner in the silent restaurant. After a moment of public embarrassment, someone started to applaud.

Soon the whole restaurant was standing and clapping. Taking a bow, Sarah grabbed her jacket and bag.

'Encore!' a voice cried.

'With pleasure,' replied the diva to her fans. She picked up Roger's glass of wine and slowly poured the contents from a great height onto what we shall discreetly call his lap.

The people in the restaurant went wild, cheering and stamping their feet. Someone brought her flowers from the vase on their table.

Sarah bowed graciously again. 'Enjoy!' she whispered into Roger's ear, before walking gracefully out of the restaurant, through the thunderous applause of her audience, waving her flowers at them.

What a show. What an exit. She'll pay for it.

Five

Of course Sarah didn't say anything when she got back to work. Roger was right: as far as she was concerned, it was his word against hers. As far as he was concerned, he had a whole restaurant of witnesses to testify indecency and assault. Roger, of course, didn't say a word either. The bitch had made a complete fool of him. He'd have to find a way of getting his own back.

For Sarah, life was now a slow countdown of the hours leading up to dinner with James on Thursday evening, with not a lot to look forward to until then except work and more work. That Tuesday afternoon, she had arranged an internal training presentation on the Internet for DFDDG staff. It was the kind of thing you did if you wanted to keep your name at the top of everyone's list: you got to be a bit of an expert on something and organised an internal presentation on it.

Sarah had caught on to the potential of the Net early; she was already mistressminding the latest technology back in the days when the rest of us were still working out how to put the extra seven in the old 01 London dialling code. Now everyone in the agency consulted her on it, she was pulled into client meetings to present on it, and it seemed only fair to try and share some of this wealth of knowledge with her less on-line colleagues.

Sarah loved this kind of thing. A sea of thirty or so

expectant faces looked up at her as she Joan Collins'd into the room.

'Good afternoon everyone,' she greeted her congregation. 'Oh, thanks so much,' she enthused to the hand that timidly proffered her a cup of coffee. She dialled through on her modem to Demon Internet, her local Internet connection provider. Once in, with the image on her laptop brightly displayed on the huge presentation screen, it was simply a matter of typing the modern abracadabra of 'http://www.ibm.com' and hey presto, she was into IBM's home page. 'Let's surf,' she announced with a triumphant smile.

You had to be there to understand why this was not as cringe-making as it sounds. Coming from Sarah, it was not naff; somehow it was just inspirational. She was so glowing in competence that your stance was never a critical one in her presence, just a desire to be as close to her and to soak up as much of her intelligence as possible.

That's why so many people had turned up for an optional training session in their already over-worked timetables. There were people in the audience, from the most junior just-joineds to senior staff who were brave enough to show their colleagues that they still needed to learn about this kind of thing. There was even Anita, who had seen *Working Girl* often enough to believe that anyone can make it in this life, and who made a point of getting herself as well-informed at work as the prejudice instinctively shown to all secretaries everywhere allowed.

Having handed out copies of the article in that month's issue of *Wired* which predicted the death of advertising as we know it, Sarah proceeded to show her colleagues, with consummate ease and total control, how the information superhighway could rise up to meet them.

Her words echoed round the huge, glass dome ceiling of the agency's presentation amphitheatre, and the laughter of her audience bounced around after it in response to yet another off-the-cuff anecdote, as James, on a post-lunch tour showing off the premises to a big new potential client, emerged from the lift on the top floor.

'Wow. She looks good,' said Mr Big New Potential Client.

'Yes, she does,' said James, being straight with the guy for the first time that day. James switched on the voice controls so they could hear what Sarah was saying outside the glass presentation room.

'She sounds good too,' added the client admiringly.

'She is. She is. She's an excellent example, in fact, David, of what I was telling you over lunch, of what DFDDG is really all about, and the unique USPs that we can offer our select client base. Come on, let's join in.'

'Join in?'

'Yes, go in there, give her a hard time.'

'We can't just barge in, she's obviously right in the middle of her talk.'

'Of course we can. You'll learn, David, that our agency is run along very open lines of communication. Our credo is one of dynamic interactivity. My staff know, for example, that my door is always open – and I expect their doors to be open too, literally and meta-phorically. I expect, actually I demand, freedom of expression; an environment in which new ideas can be voiced, quickly and simply, and, if valid, acted upon efficiently, effectively. No meeting in these offices is so important that it can't be interrupted. Let's challenge her views, hear where she's coming from. It'll help you understand where DFDDG is different from the rest.'

What a tosser, thought the client to himself as James flung open the double doors to the meeting.

'We're interrupting,' announced James what he hoped was dramatically, as everyone turned round in astonishment, 'to put this agency's interactive credo into practice. Sarah, this is David from United Distillers. We'd like to challenge your assertion that the Internet is a marketing tool of the future.'

'Actually I don't want to challenge – ' began David.

'Hang on, hang on, Dave. Let's just see where this leads us, shall we? Sarah, state your case.'

'Well,' said Sarah, blushing and coy and delighted, 'my case, I don't know, you mean summarise what this talk has been about, James?'

'Yes, come on, let's hear where you stand on this.'

'Me personally?'

'Yes – I want your own standpoint.'

Oh goodness gracious me. Her own standpoint; in front of everyone; he was exalting her, upholding and extolling her, there, in front of the client, in front of everyone. Sarah felt dizzy with the excitement of it all.

'Well, my view is – ' Sarah cleared her throat and lifted her chin – 'that the Internet is the medium which will create an entirely new structure for society, one based on expressed personal interests, rather than geography. The Internet enhances and reinforces individuality by allowing each one of us to explore and to communicate with the people round the world who share our interests. And I think that, eventually, gradually, and in the not too distant future, this will have a fundamental impact on advertising, which, as we know it today, is based on communicating to a passive consumer. No longer will we have a mass of couch potatoes waiting to receive advertising; they'll only see the advertising that they want to see, and that will force us to make our advertising more interesting, involving and entertaining.'

'Bollocks,' said James.

There was a gaggle of gasps from the audience, one of which was Sarah's. She was enthralled: the sheer forcefulness of this man staggered her. She was so thrilled that he was taking this explicit, public interest in her.

OK, so he was ridiculing her in front of all her colleagues. But that wasn't the point.

The point was, it was her he was ridiculing. He had chosen her as the focus of his interest. Don't you see? You don't see? Oh, well. So much the worse for you. You've obviously never known what it is to be publicly humiliated by a man as exciting, as invigorating, as brilliant as James.

'Er, why bollocks, James?' ventured Sarah.

'Because,' he said, walking deliberately – a man of his bulk can only ever walk deliberately – up to the podium at the front of the room to take centre stage, 'because the Internet is a con, a fad, a bluff. Advertising is about selling things to people. Listen to that. Selling things to people. Look after the product and the customers will look after themselves. The market bloody researchers, who told Sony that the Walkman would never sell, where are they now? You can bet that our Jappo friends are thanking their lucky stars that they took no notice of that bit of advice.

'In advertising, the customer is not king, the product is king, and the customer, the customer is his slave. Don't ask people what they want, tell them what they want.

'The Internet will bomb – it expects people to have preferences, opinions. People don't have opinions. They have money in their pocket and they want to be told, told how to spend it. That's how a good ad works. Don't expect too much from your customer, in fact, expect sod all from your customer, and you'll never be disappointed. Customers don't think, they buy. And ads sell. It's as simple as that.'

Is this the point where I tell you that James knows bugger all about the Internet, or indeed any technological development since the wheel, or is that something you'd kind of gleaned for yourself?

But the fact was, people knew this. His employees, his clients, his women – they knew he was full of shit, and most of them didn't give a damn. Because that's not what people wanted from James. They didn't really care what he was saying; all they cared about was how he was saying it.

With James, style superimposed substance. James had presence, he had authority. He was naturally, indisputably in charge. He was a big man, in every sense. He filled rooms and belittled people. Most people like to be made to feel small: they like to feel inferior to a superior who will take command, who will tell them what to do and where to go, who will absolve them of their guilt and fears, and show them the way to happiness and righteousness. They want to believe, and James was someone you felt you could believe in. He made you feel safe and secure and protected.

Confidence is power. As long as James could convince himself, he was able to carry on convincing others.

But lately, doubts had begun to trickle through his bravado. Increasingly, he had seen a mocking glint of disdain in the eyes of those obliged to listen to him; he had heard the hollowness of his own tired expressions and hackneyed ideas. People around him had begun to notice the strings on his puppets, the ace of clubs hidden up his sleeve, as slowly but surely they realised that their Emperor was wearing no clothes.

But Sarah, superwoman Sarah, she suffered no such dilemma. To her James was still the master, the autocratic ruler of her heart, dressed in all the finery of a king.

Sarah doesn't want to find her own strength, she wants to rely on someone else's. She doesn't trust her own judgement, she wants someone else to judge her. So the more he judges, the more he criticises, the more he humiliates her, the stronger she feels.

Now, as she listened to James's diatribe of twaddle, her eyes misted over. She felt such a fraud, such a novice. Of course, he was right. He had such commercial intellect, such profound understanding of his craft. His vigour captivated her. The simplicity of his ideas constantly quashed her own.

He was right. The Internet had come along – everyone started following it like sheep, braying and crowing (some sheep do bray and crow, actually) about how wonderful it was, simply because it was new, so it must be better. But James could see beyond that, he kept the wider picture; he *was* the wider picture, for heaven's sake.

'Yes, well, I think I can see what you mean. I mean, I think you may be right, really,' she babbled into the microphone that James had gallantly restored to her. 'I guess everyone's just got so caught up in the new technology. It's just that, well, we don't have your experience, your vision, James, to grasp the essentials, so we lose – '

'Anyway,' James interrupted benignly, 'I'm glad that we're all working in the kind of environment where these ideas are getting challenged, examined, where new thinking constantly questions the old. Excellent work, Sarah.'

Sarah's face shimmered with pride. 'Thank you James.'

James turned and walked back to escort the client down to his office. But the client had left – no doubt just too overwhelmed by the dynamic interactivity of it all.

As the session had obviously come to a close, Sarah's dazed audience started getting together their things and leaving, not sure whether their conclusion should be that the Internet was the greatest thing since white Hovis or a load of old men's genitalia. People slowly shuffled out in confused silence until there was only Sarah, and Anita, left behind.

Every office has its office bike and Anita was the Harley-Davidson of DFDDG. She disseminated her favours liberally throughout the company and men were happy to seminate her in return. At Christmas parties they practically had to form a queue to have their turn.

Anita is what the high street retailers call petite, i.e. short, and pretty in a pinched kind of a way. She has worked very hard to get to be the directors' secretary and now has five other secretaries reporting to her. She has an astronomical w.p.m. score and faster shorthand than anyone else in London – she won Secretary of the Year in 1992 because of it. Anita has always been good with her hands – no wonder she is in so much demand at the agency.

Sarah does not like Anita, because, successful as Sarah is, she is unfortunately also one of those career women who pulls up the ladder behind her, and has scant regard for others below her who are still trying to make it. One of Sarah's less endearing characteristics.

'Hello, Anita,' said Sarah pleasantly, patronisingly. 'Did you like the presentation?' Both women knew that what Sarah really meant was 'did you understand it?' but of course you never really say a thing like that directly to a secretary, you just intimate it five days a week.

'Yes, it was good entertainment,' said Anita ambivalently. 'I always think I've learnt what people are like, but then they go and surprise me. Anyway, I just wanted a quick word. I thought you'd like to know that James is on TV tonight, a documentary on BBC2 about advertising.'

'Is he?' said Sarah, delightedly and too quickly. Then, collecting herself added, 'Fine. Well, thanks for letting me know.'

'No problem,' said Anita and made to go.

'Anita, you stayed behind just to tell me that?'

'Yes.'

'Why?'

'Well, I thought you'd be interested.'

'Well, yes, I am.' Sarah wriggled a bit. 'But so would anyone at DFDDG.'

'Oh no, I don't think so. Not as interested as you.'

'Come on, Anita. Why should I be more interested than anyone else, for heaven's sake!' This came out rather defensively, rather squeakily.

'Not for heaven's sake, for your sake. I thought that you, in particular, would be interested in James being on TV and it looks like you are, so there you go, that's why I stayed behind, to tell you that, and now I have, so I'll go. See you later.' She turned to go again.

Sarah touched her arm to hold her back. 'Anita,' she said, 'you don't like me very much, do you?'

Anita looked unimpressed. 'I'm not that fussed one way or another about you, to be honest.'

'Well, I wish we could have a better working relationship, you and I. Sometimes I feel . . .'

'Yes? Sometimes you feel what?'

'Well, sometimes I feel you have a bit of an attitude problem.'

'You what?'

'Yes. I do. I try to be pleasant with you but I always get the feeling that you're being hostile and sarcastic with me, and I wonder whether it's because I'm a woman. You know, our training department has an excellent course on working with female managers. Would you like me to arrange a session for you?'

Anita's black eyes glowed under their heavy shelves of eye-liner. She moved her face very close into Sarah's so Sarah could smell the cigarettes and Juicy Fruit on her breath.

'Sarah, save your crap for someone else. I can see right through you. You might have the money and the title, but at the end of the day, you're no better than me. You go home to your lonely little flat just like I go back to mine. You might fool everyone else with your high and mighty ways in the office, but I've been watching you and I know what you're up to with James. You're desperate for him. I know what that feels like. The man I want doesn't want me either. At the end of the day, we're the same, you and I, both lonely women who can't have the man they want, and we both want the wrong kind of man. So save your lectures, and give me a break, OK? I may be a secretary, but I'm not stupid, not stupid at all. And I've got you sussed.'

She turned to go and this time Sarah did not hold her back. She watched Anita totter away down the aisle between the chairs and sighed. She always under-estimated how jealous other women must be of her. OK, so Anita had figured out that there was something going on with James. And if she thought that James wasn't interested, so much the better. What did she know. Just as well she was only a secretary, and hardly likely to cause any trouble.

Sarah quickly collected together her notes and her equipment, went straight back to her office and dialled her father's number. She was going to ring him anyway, I mean, she'd been meaning to ring him for a while now.

'Hello, Dad.'

'Hello, Twinkle. How's my little girl?'

'I'm fine, thanks. How are you?'

'Fine, just fine thanks.'

'Dad, I thought you'd like to know that my boss, you know, James, I told you about James, he's on the TV tonight.'

'Oh, he is, is he? What programme's that then, Twinkle?'

'The programme on advertising on BBC2 starting at ten. That's not too late for you, is it, Dad?'

'No, ten o'clock's not too late. Well, I'll look forward to that then. He must be a bit of a big shot to be getting on a programme like that. So how's the job going? How's the promotion?'

'Great, thanks. It's going really well. In fact I'm having dinner with James on Thursday.'

'What, James that'll be on the BBC?'

'Yes, that's it.'

'Oh. Oh, well, that's grand, isn't it? If he's taking notice of you, asking you to dinner with him and all. That's promising isn't it, Sarah, I mean the man at the top taking you under his wing and that?'

'I suppose so,' said Sarah coyly. She's seven years old and she's just come first in her class for arithmetic again. 'Right, well, Dad, I'd better let you get on. I just wanted to let you know.'

'Right, Twinkle. Thanks for that.'

'Speak to you soon then.'

'Righty-ho. Cheerio for now.' He hung up and went straight to get his address book with the telephone numbers of everyone he knew, at the Rotary Club, at the bowling club, at the Royal British Legion. His Sarah, going out with James, her boss, who was going to be on the BBC. They'd have to be told.

That evening, Sarah got home a bit earlier than usual, at 9.00 p.m., to be ready in time for James's show. She chucked yet another M&S dinner from the stack in the freezer into the microwave, put on her Muji bathrobe and climbed into bed with her supper and her laptop (just a quick final memo that needed to be ready for her 8 a.m. meeting the next morning). Her bedroom, like all the other rooms, had that rather minimalist, not to say unloved look about it.

The flat was OK, I suppose, big rooms, high ceilings and so on. But it was one of those places you would see and say it needed a woman's touch – that is, you would mean it was all a bit cold and functional and needed some jolly plants, some unnecessary cushions and a bit of mess to stop it looking quite so much like the set for *Alien 3*. Sarah, however, had no time to water plants, no time to choose cushions and no time to make mess.

At 10 p.m. she flipped the remote control on to BBC2 and sure enough, ten minutes into the programme, there were the smug features of young Jimmy. As Sarah watched her man on television in bed, she dreamed lazily that one day soon she might be watching TV in bed with her man.

Needless to say, James was in his element on the show. Loud, arrogant, not best-informed. While the rest of us cringed at the opinionated rantings of a well-groomed bigot, Sarah saw only the power and the glory, she heard only the vigour and the verve. Such is love, my friend.

Six

By Wednesday mid-morning, Sarah was in hypermode. Only thirty-four hours until lift-off. She arranged to meet one of her closest friends, Suzanne, for lunch at Soho Soho to calm her nerves.

Walking down towards Frith Street, she sucked in the smell of hot London pavements and felt super-human. She was working at the best agency in the best city in the world. Tomorrow she was probably going to begin an affair with one of the most powerful men in London. As she swanned past Groucho's she thought, yes, I'll probably be in there all the time with him now, at all the media events, all the dinners.

The heat of the concrete under her feet shot right up through her. This was life, this was exhilaration. The constraints, the inertia of Yorkshire, that was all a million miles away, thank God. This was her, this was Sarah, this was life.

She walked by all the other post-yuppy, post-modern, posturing executives taking their executive lunch breaks. They all wore the same too expensive clothes, the same gosh I'm a bit bored but I'm also terribly busy so I'd better hurry expressions on their faces. Mobile phones, shades, real tans, regular pay cheques in their pockets, company cars in their garages, equity shares in their portfolios and designer food in their stomachs. Life was sweet.

Suzanne was also very sweet, the kind of best friend

every girl should have. Pretty, but not quite as pretty as you. A love life that's always just a tad more problematic than your own. Successful, but successful in direct marketing rather than advertising, so not quite the same league. The perfect pal.

'Hello, my darling,' babbled Sarah affectionately.

'Christ, we're in a good mood,' retorted Suzanne. 'What's brought this on? Are you feeling OK?'

'OK? I'm feeling fantastic. In fact, you know, I think I've never felt better in my life.'

'Oh fuck. I get it. You're in love. You and Adam.'

'Adam?' Sarah suddenly realised that she had completely forgotten about him. From the moment she had walked into that directors' meeting, she had hardly thought of him. But she had been crazy about him for weeks. What kind of a woman was she?

'Yes, Adam. He is the man of the moment, isn't he? Or am I already behind in your romantic schedule? After all, it's four days since I last spoke to you.'

Normally Sarah would have told Suzanne everything. But today, today was such a special day, life was sweet, etc. She just didn't want to spoil it with the whole Adam story.

'Oh Adam, no, not him. This is much more exciting. Guess who I'm having dinner with tomorrow evening!'

'Come on, Sarah, just spit it out, you know how much I hate all that guessing games stuff.'

'James.'

'James? James? James as in your hero James? Or should I say, more to the point, James as in your boss James? Dinner? That's jumping in at the deep end, isn't it?'

'His idea. What can I do?' smirked Sarah.

'Say no.'

'What?'

'Say no. It looks bad, looks unprofessional. First date a dinner date, that's not good. He should have suggested lunch, not dinner. It makes you look cheap. It makes him look like he's not taking you seriously.'

Sarah heard her friend say her own thoughts out loud and she didn't like the sound of them. 'What are you talking about?'

'You know bloody well what I'm talking about. He's your boss. He should know better. More to the point, you should know better. Come on, Sarah. We've talked about this kind of thing a million times, slagged off all the other women we've known who've done something like that. You don't do dinner on a first date.'

'For fuck's sake, Suzanne, it's like having a conversation with my grandmother. To think I've got you of all people lecturing me about playing it cool with a man, after all that crap your charming Stuart put you through. Look, he's not exactly going to shag me on the dining table in the restaurant, is he?'

'Don't drag Stuart into this, Sarah. That's not fair. You're only getting defensive because you know I'm right.'

The two women stared at each other. Sarah swallowed hard. She liked her friend so much. And that dig about Stuart, Suzanne's ex, a character so ghastly he made Freddy Kruger look like Peter Rabbit, had been below the belt. But no one was going to stop her having her moment with James. 'Maybe. Maybe you are right. Look, I tell you what. Let's change the subject and not talk men any more, OK? Is that OK Suzie?'

'Sure,' said Suzanne. So they made polite conversation for a half hour or so, then Sarah invented a meeting and left to go back to the office. Outside, the pavements were hot, smelly and dirty. Sleeping body-bags of teenagers fell out of doorways. People around her looked pretentious and stupid. Life no longer seemed quite so sweet.

Seven

Finally. Thursday finally arrived. James displayed his usual indifference around the office, with no obvious signs or hints that they were about to start a great love story, whatever Sarah might have imagined these signs or hints might have been. Sarah, on the other hand, having accepted the inevitability of her situation (which is, after all, the situation she wanted in the first place, isn't it?) had been getting her ammunition ready for the manoeuvre.

She'd been to Rigby and Peller and bought new underwear in chantilly lace. You know the song: Chantilly lace and a pretty face and a pony-tail hanging down and a randy boss.

She'd visited the Face Place on Monday evening for various treatments.

Tuesday lunchtime she'd bought a new jacket in Browns which went very well with the trousers she took to the dry cleaners on Tuesday evening.

On Wednesday evening she went for a cut and blow-dry at Nicky Clarke's, even though it was only five and a half weeks since her last one and Nicky had told her she ought to leave it a good eight weeks between sessions if she wanted to grow her layers out properly. When a girl puts the future of her layers at risk for a man, you know it's the start of something big. On the way back from the hairdressers she bought a pack of condoms and vowed to use them whether James said his willy felt as if it was being strangled or not.

Finally, she was ready. Everything was in place for the big day.

Then, oh dear, disaster. When Sarah woke up that morning, she knew that the one thing she could do nothing about was about to happen.

Loony time was about to descend upon her. That monthly fling with dementia when every part of your body feels like it's a piece from another box's jigsaw that has somehow got jumbled up in your own. When your stomach is a lilo so pumped up that if you stuck a pin in it, it would burst in your face.

But the physical discomfort, the aches and the pains and the blood and the tiredness and the headaches and the more blood – this is nothing compared to the loony, loony, loopy-loop. The fairies at the bottom of the garden in your head. When all your little hormones decide they all want to play with the same toy at the same time and start beating the shit out of each other inside your mind. The ticket collector at Notting Hill Gate doesn't return your thank you: the very end of the world has come and big tears well up all over your face. None, none of your friends really likes you, that's if you had any to begin with. You are stupid, ugly and past it, except you never were it anyway, and if that man rings up once more to check what happened to his ad copy you're going to say to him, I took it and shoved it up my fanny you old git. Broken glass, jangle, jangle, more tears, loony.

And all because the great soggy mashed potato of womb inside you is shedding itself or some such ridiculous story. And it takes a week for it to do it. And you feel pretty odd all week before it arrives. And it takes a week for you to get your act together again afterwards, and ring up a lot of people and apologise for your peculiar behaviour. 'You know how it is! Once a month I turn into a loony!'

And then there's that joke, the joke that goes: what's the difference between a rottweiler and a woman with PMT. Answer: you can always reason with a rottweiler. Yes, that's a funny one. And meanwhile your fat squelching hormonal sponge of a stomach, full of soggy pain, full of slurching, bloated sadness sandwiched with clenched anger, that's a good joke too.

Well, blow me if, this very Thursday, it wasn't Sarah's time of the month. Never had times of the month in Dallas, did they? Sue Ellen never said to JR, popping down to the chemist now to get a stock of STs in, darling. Wilma never asked Fred Flintstone to back off because she'd just come on. And when Harry finally met Sally, it was all fireworks and moonlight, not Tampax and toilets.

No, in real life, Mother Nature – who must really be a bloke in drag given her lousy sense of humour and bad timing – often throws the proverbial spanner in the works of romance and says, here's a pint of blood loss, cop a load of that, sweetheart!

So our Sarah, just when she's hoping to look at her most formidable, is transformed into a bloated stuck pig who has to feel really good about herself while she sits just so on her seat so her nappy stays in place to soak up all the drip-drip-drips. Do me a favour.

Still, life must go on. She'd just have to explain to him when the time was right that she was bleeding. Perhaps he was the kind of guy who likes doing it with women while they bleed. A lot of them do, you know. Sarah spent the whole of Thursday morning worrying about it and trying to sort out in her mind how the scene would go.

At three, James gave Tony a going-home present of his framed marketing diplomas and his P45. When, at 3.10, James rang Sarah to say he'd booked supper for eight, she was still undecided as to how to break the news. Perhaps she should tell him there and then, while he was on the phone – look, James, I've come on, so if you want to save dinner until another day that's fine. That's how Sarah thought, I'm sad to say, and I'm sure you are too.

In the end, however, she said nothing.

James thought she sounded nervous. 'Are you OK, Sarah?'

'Oh yes, yes, just got a lot on my plate today,' she said, stroking the outline of her new bra strap to reassure herself, as if it were some kind of Amazonian lucky charm. (I know, I know – they don't wear bras in the Amazon.)

Anita came into her office to say that, while she'd been on the phone, someone called Adam had rung, no message other than would she please call him back as soon as possible.

'If he rings again and you take the call, please tell him to get stuffed,' said Sarah imperiously. With James now finally on the scene, Sarah had no more need for Adam. He was a very meagre coffee and croissant compared to the full English breakfast she would soon be tucking into.

'Yes, ma'am,' says go-tell-it-on-the-mountain Anita, itching to get back and give the others a blow-by-blow account. Blow-by-blows were Anita's speciality, after all.

At four, James sent her an e-mail which told her that he was going on to another meeting at five and she should wait until 6.30 for a call in the office. If no call came, it would mean that the meeting was dragging on and rather than get together for a drink beforehand, she should meet him directly at the restaurant. Well, it seems that even romance has to be organised.

At 6.15 the phone rang.

'Yes!' Sarah grabbed the phone.

'Um, hi Sarah, it's me, Ralph. Just ringing to finalise a time for Saturday.'

'Saturday?' said Sarah irritably. 'What's Saturday?'

Ralph was going to joke that it was a day of the week

but her tone, which had sounded so promising when she first picked up the phone, now suggested that the cute jokes were best left edited. 'Er, you know, the Portrait Gallery?'

Sarah did not know. At this point in time, it felt as if the end of civilisation, the very edge of the world, was that evening. Beyond those confines of time and space Sarah could not and did not wish to comprehend. Saturday! Saturday was another galaxy.

'Ralph, let's discuss it tomorrow. Sorry, I've got to go. I'm expecting a call.' She put the phone down angrily, convinced that James must have rung during that twelve-second call, cursing Ralph and his portraits.

By 6.45 no call had come. So she knew, following her instructions, that she had at least another hour to kill. Waiting patiently for her allocated slot on James's runway, Sarah started preparing herself mentally and physically for the jeux sans frontières ahead.

She was determined to take better control of this new relationship. Her recent track record had been a nightmare of unanswered phone calls and lonely misery. She was starting to tire of her constant trauma. It wasn't as if Adam was an exception.

She had met him just days after another on–off fling had finally petered out. That time it had been with an introverted (but internationally acclaimed) professor of English. The crunch had come one evening when she arrived to find him crying in his flat. In spite of her repeated questioning, the English professor could not find words to express whatever it was that was ailing his tortured soul, so he just carried on sobbing. She comforted him to the point where they ended up in bed, then he fell asleep and she left early the next morning. It occurred to her later that day that he had not spoken one word to her throughout. She never rang him again and he did not ring her.

Er, that's it. And what was really strange about this bloke, apart from just about everything, was that when he was in the act, he was one of the most passionate men she had ever received. He lunged and yelped and tore at her body like a dervish. As soon as it was over, he subsided back into his dormant, semi-comatose state where every word was an act of torment, every sentence had to be squeezed out like a deeply embedded blackhead.

As you can see, our Sarah isn't getting any of this right. Even though she seemed to end up spending a lot of time in bed with men, sex with them was not really what made her happy. She always resented the bit where they got inside her, which didn't help. What she really liked was a good cuddle, which was unfortunate, because with the kind of men she went for, she rarely got one, either before or after they had her.

Sounds like she's going for the wrong kind of man. What I want to know is, why does she keep doing this? Why are the rotters so appealing to her? You can't just keep blaming men for being gruesome: you have to start to wonder about the women who constantly seek them out, ferreting about under paving stones and down sewers to find their ideal bastard.

It's all a question of supply and demand, you know. Everything in this life is a question of supply and demand. Gosh, I wonder: if women stopped loving rotten men, would rotten men cease to exist?

It has to be said that an episode of *EastEnders* is usually more exciting than most sexual encounters with a bloke. So is a plate of beans on toast with a knob of butter in them. So is a really gritty glass of Rioja. Give me all three and I'd never need another man. But this story is about Sarah. She doesn't like *EastEnders*, so she's going to have to carry on regardless. Carry On Advertising. Carry On Bleeding. Carry On Getting It Wrong.

While Sarah was in angst over her menstruals, her ex-boyfriends and how late she should leave it before getting a cab to the restaurant, James had his own problems to sort out. Jayne, one of his regular diary dates, had rung him on the mobile at seven in a state of hysteria, wailing down the phone right in the middle of his meeting.

Jayne was also having period trouble. I don't know, these wretched women and their bloody periods. Jayne's problem was that she hadn't had hers and what was James going to do about it.

When Sarah arrived at the restaurant at 8.05, having waited five nonchalant minutes in the taxi, the extremely thin woman at reception told her that her friend had rung to say that he was most unfortunately not going to be able to make it. His meeting would be going on into the small hours. Would she like a table for one?

The extremely thin woman put her extremely thin lips together and smiled. A smile which said, tough titties sister. Sarah got another taxi home to Notting Hill, picked up a curry and stuffed the Chantilly back into its box.

Back home in her designer pad, the only things on TV were a documentary on sperm whales and a sitcom on an unmarried mum and her three kids. But of course the telly's always bad when you really need it. Her curry tasted like a spicy combination of ear wax and tarpaulin, not that I've ever eaten either, but you know what I mean.

She put on a CD – the song was about that boy, who's broken my heart, who's made me start, to wonder why, I ever try, while I sit and cry. Sarah turned off the CD.

She picked up her book. Samantha is just getting into bed with David, the high-flying City executive we know from Chapter Three is already doing it with Tanya. Bullshit. Who was going to believe stuff like that? No woman could be so stupid to ignore all those warning signs, to begin to put up with someone as obviously horrible as David. No wonder the novel was written by a man.

Sarah put down her book and looked vaguely through the *Evening Standard*. Di has a new hair-do. Some actor's died. Dwing-Dwing the panda's died. The prime minister is thinking of getting rid of MIRAS. Some dotty female columnist has filled a whole page with an article on the ins and outs of the female condom. London life went on its weary way and Sarah was feeling blue.

Just then, dring, dring, you've guessed it, it was the telephone and the person at the other end – you can't guess this so I'm going to have to tell you – was her sister Caroline, calling from the Big Apple where she now resided with her extremely wealthy and extremely dull husband, aptly enough called Edward, who, by interesting coincidence, was also in advertising. Small world, eh?

Caroline is the other side of the coin to Sarah. Heads and tails, if you get my drift. Caroline took no interest in school, which was just as well, because with her IQ school was hardly likely to take much of an interest in her. Then she chalet-girled her way through the Alps until the let-me-not-set-the-world-alight presence of Edward turned up at Chalet Les Calecons one day, took a shine to her banoffi pie and, after a few months' courting back in London, told her she could share his bank account – every girl's dream really.

Caroline is an old-fashioned kind of woman; she likes men to hold doors open for her, in every sense. She's easy-going, trusting; I guess I'm being polite here for dull and gullible. But take no notice of me – easy-going and trusting are admirable values in some people's books. Everyone likes Caroline because no one feels threatened by her, unlike her steamy, thorny sister who makes everyone feel in some way deficient.

Caroline, especially, is in awe of the mighty Sarah, who started bossing her around from the day she turned up, six days old, from the hospital ('No, Mummy, she's not hungry yet, I'll tell you when she's hungry'). Growing up alongside Sarah was like living in the shadow of Mount Kilimanjaro. No wonder Caroline gave up trying to compete – she'd have gone bonkers otherwise.

Now, as adults, and such different adults, they have learnt to be friends. Caroline has Edward to protect her and giggles nervously but with some relief when Edward refers to his sister-in-law as the drag queen (i.e. man in woman's clothing – Edward thinks that any woman with a career is a freak).

Caroline admires Sarah's lifestyle from a distance but thinks that, whatever Sarah says, deep down all she really wants is a nice man to settle down with. Sarah thinks that her sister has married the human equivalent of what the cat sicked up and is destined for a life of diapers and Prozac. No wonder they're so nice to each other nowadays.

Caroline and Edward have never had a particularly jolly marriage because, right from day one, there not being many other prospects in life open to Caroline, they started trying for The Baby. That's when the problems began. About the time Sarah was at Unilever doing the business for promoting their fishfingers, Caroline was at home in Clapham, cooking them for Edward, wondering where The Baby was. Where's The Baby, not a new board game from Waddingtons but Caroline's constant dilemma.

Caroline and Edward always thought that the moment you did it without the wellington boot (that's the kind of vocab you use if you live in Clapham and you're called Caroline and Edward) you got The Baby. But The Baby did not come. They did it a bit more. And still it did not come.

Edward told his mother that he thought Caroline might not have been the right girl after all. Caroline told Sarah that she wanted to die. So Sarah told both of them to go along and see a GP, and guess what, Caroline was fine. It was Edward who had fewer spermatozoa (such a revolting word) in his knick-knacks than I've cooked hot dinners.

It took four and a half years, that's fifty-one months of tears every twenty-eight days, for the doctors to finally extract something vaguely resembling yeast from Edward in sufficient quantities and of sufficient quality to get a bun in Caroline's oven to rise. All this while, Edward thought it best if they told his family that it was Caroline who had problems down under, otherwise his mother would have been upset. After much such antipodean bullshit, one of Edward's tadpoles finally made it, panting and gasping, up the junction; Edward could finally ring his old school and book a place (naturally, it was going to be a boy); for Caroline had finally seen that blue line squinting out at her one Sunday morning, praise the Lord. Caroline was pregnant. She was going to have The Baby. Two weeks later, Edward and Caroline flew off to Edward's new job in New York with a daily dollar salary bigger than my daily calorie intake.

Now they do say that a pregnant woman's hormones make the Niagara Falls look like a mill pond and Caroline was certainly producing a lot of hydro-electricity at this happy time. From the day Caro found out that she was to be blessed with a mini-Edward, calls to her sister upped from a once-weekly to a once-daily basis.

While Sarah truly loved her little sister, even the best of us can only take so much in-depth chundering analysis of each movement of a six-month-old foetus, of piles and vaginal discharge, of nipple rash, *et al.* So when she heard her sister's plaintive voice this particular evening, Sarah's heart sank.

'Hello Caro, how are you feeling?'

'Waah.'

Good heavens, Evans, thought Sarah, was this The Baby already? Or had the US telecommunications giants developed a device which enabled you to chatter transatlantically with your as-yet-unborn nephew?

'Caro, is that you?'

'Waaah.'

'Caro, you haven't had it, have you?'

'Waaah. No, it's Edward.'

'That's Edward making that noise?'

'No, it's me. Edward's left me.'

'Edward has left you?' Sarah repeated unhelpfully. Edward had left her? Steady Eddy? This was incredible. Edward's idea of taking the initiative was telling the waiter, ten minutes after placing the order, that he would, in fact, after all, rather have the beef than the chicken for his main course, not walking out on his wife and sprog-to-be.

'But you're six months pregnant, Caro,' exclaimed Sarah, telling her sister something she probably already knew.

All Sarah could hear was loud crying coming from the other end of the phone, the end that was located in the very plush apartment on the upper 57th up-town NW east side or whatever other ridiculous name it is that New Yorkers like to call their streets by.

'Caro, do you know where Edward's gone?'

There was much waahing. Through the snot and tears Sarah more or less made out that Edward had moved in with a colleague, sorry, I mean co-worker, from the office – a guy called Larry – because he couldn't cope with the idea of a baby.

'But you've been trying for a baby for ages! Surely he's had time to get used to the idea of it by now?' said Sarah. Well done Sarah. Remind me to give you a call next time I've got a crisis on my hands. Have you noticed how women, even when they're really trying to be helpful, always specialise in stating the bleedin' obvious, which is not always a great help?

While her sister continued to sob, Sarah had a sudden and terrible thought. Eddy – Larry – Larry – Eddy. She'd read about this kind of thing. Would it help her sister at this point in time if she were to suggest that Eddy and Larry might be an item? Would that stop her sister crying and make her feel better, to know that it was not her femininity which had driven him away in the form of an impending baby, but Larry's masculinity which had attracted him out of the family nest?

After much rapid reflection, Sarah wisely concluded that this would not, after all, offer much consolation.

'Come home,' said Sarah.

'What!' shrieked her sibling. 'I can't come home! I can't leave Eddy!'

'But Edward's left you!'

'But what if he comes back?' Caroline wailed, with real desperation.

Sarah felt a rush of anger in her chest.

'What if he comes back? What if he does come back? Fuck him! Leave him! He can make his own meals! You're six months pregnant and he's walked out on you. He's never had any respect for you and you've just lapped it up, lapped up all his pompous, patronising ways, treating you like a cross between a maid and a chef, preparing his corporate dinners, washing his corporate shirts. He's spent the past decade telling anyone who would listen that you're as barren as the outback when we all knew that he didn't have two sperm to rub together! Caroline, how much bullshit are you going to put up with?'

Caroline did not speak, but the waahing had stopped.

'There comes a point where you have to say, no, no, I'm sorry – either you show me more respect, or that's it, I'm out. Do you see, Caroline? I've told you all this before. You're caught in a spiral of low self-esteem. You have no confidence in yourself, no respect for yourself, and so you're attracted to people who reinforce your own lousy feelings about yourself. Why don't you come home, you can stay with me, I love you, Mum and Dad in their own strange ways love you, you can have the baby here and see how you feel after the birth. You're not at the mercy of this man, you do have options, if you put up with his shitty treatment of you, it's because you want it, it's because you think that's all you're worth, do you see? But you're worth so much more, you don't have to sink to his level, you don't have to let his insecurities become the barometer, the yardstick for your own self. You can have your own values, your own expectations, your own identity. You don't have to live through this shit with him to show him you love him. First of all, you need to think about yourself – and the baby – and then decide if he's worth having, if he really represents what you think about yourself, or whether you decide you deserve better.'

Sarah stopped for breath. She was red in the face and her heart was beating fast. Her sister could hear the heartbeats down the phone.

'Give me a week or so to get my things together and organise everything,' said Caroline. 'I'll ring you when I know the day and time of my flight. Will you meet me at the airport?'

'Of course I'll meet you at the bloody airport. I'm your sister. I love you.'

'I love you too,' said Caroline, without a trace of waah in her voice.

Somewhere just round the corner from Central Park, a woman put down the phone and started packing bags, ringing airlines, making plans to take control of her life.

Somewhere just up the road from Kensington Gardens, a woman climbed sadly into bed, and wondered whether the man who had stood her up that evening might ring.

You see, that's the way Sarah's cookie crumbles in matters of the heart. She can preach to everyone else about their low self-esteem while she drags her own along the bottom of the ocean. She knows what's wrong. She knows what's right. She can think right in her head, she can sense right in her heart.

But when it comes to actually doing right in her own life, well, that's when she fucks up.

Eight

The next day, Sarah happened to see James through the glass window of one of the meeting rooms. His still-thick thatch of dark hair hung crumpled around his ears. His tanned and toned complexion now looked merely tired and sallow. He had an altogether dejected and hang-dog look about him. With a pang, somewhere where you get those kinds of pangs, Sarah thought that he must have been genuinely sorry to have missed their date, he looked so miserable.

She was right. He'd been really looking forward to putting his cork into Sarah's rather handsomely shaped bottle, rather than re-shafting poor old Jayne who was more the shape of a carton of orange juice nowadays.

To be fair, he had not lied in the message he had left Sarah at the restaurant: his meeting had indeed gone until the small hours – three in the morning, to be exact. That's how long it had taken to persuade Jayne that, in the interest of her career, she ought to get rid of 'it'. As Jayne sold jumpers part-time in a store in Oxford Street (they'd met while James was buying something in yellow cashmere for a weekend away with Lucy), the career angle was pushing things a bit, but Jayne bought it, so who was James to care.

He wrote her a cheque for the abortion, then they had sex, then he told her he would always have a special place for her and then he legged it.

Confucius must at some stage have said words to the

effect that, as long as men behave like poodles, there will always be women to follow them around with pooper scoopers. If he didn't, you read it here first.

So yes, he was sorry about blowing Sarah out. That's why around lunchtime that day, Sarah got another e-mail which read 'Sorry. Dinner next Tuesday?'

She wanted to say no but of course she didn't. All she could think of, the only flash to pierce the brain of this very intelligent person was that by the following Tuesday her period would be over. Great, Sarah.

She e-mailed him back, 'OK, but only because you're my boss!' It seemed like a witty reply at the time.

Just then, Ralph popped his head round the door. 'I've heard the news,' he said.

'What news, Ralph?'

'About Tony.'

This was all she needed right now. 'Oh. Yes.'

'A woman who takes no prisoners, eh?'

'Ralph, it's not like that.'

'Come on, let's go and get a sandwich. You can tell me what it is like. And I'll tell you about an idea I've got.' OK, she thought. It would be a relief to talk this through with someone, even if it was only Ralph.

'OK, but I've only got half an hour. I'm up to my ears.'

'We'd better hurry then, hadn't we?' he laughed.

He took her to a small place near the agency which she'd never been to and would certainly never have gone to on her own.

To be honest, it wasn't much of a place. Whoever had last decorated it obviously had a formica fetish, as that's what covered every available surface. A pale green formica with black bits in it that looked like so many millions of squashed flies. The café was full of taxi drivers and shop owners from the clothes whole-salers round the corner, middle-aged, short and stocky men munching on salt beef sandwiches. It wasn't exactly a greasy spoon, but it wasn't the kind of Soho eaterie that Sarah frequented. Sarah was more ciabatta and mozzarella than bagel and cream cheese.

But everyone in this little place seemed to know Ralph by name. Especially the woman behind the counter who seemed to think she was his mother.

'Raphael, Raphael, you're looking pale today. Sit down, I'll bring it all over to you.'

'Thank you Helen. But today, I've got company.'

The whole place hushed. All eyes gaped on Sarah. Helen's were on the brink of their sockets. 'Is this your girlfriend?' she asked in wonder, like it was Princess Diana he'd brought in for a sandwich.

'No, Helen, we just work together.'

'Well, she should be your girlfriend,' said Helen emphatically, approvingly, examining Sarah's intelligent brown eyes and her elegant face.

'Yes, yes,' chipped in one of the old men at the table behind them. 'It's about time, Raphael. About time. Make the girl a serious proposition. Do you know the family?'

Ralph laughed. 'Leave it, Sidney, leave it. We're just here for lunch.'

Helen was by now in a feverish state of excitement the other side of the counter, manically wiping down the already spotless glass as her only outlet for her uncontainable emotion. 'Today just friends. Tomorrow, who knows, who knows?' she was muttering to herself and the rest of the café who all nodded in agreement.

'A nice girl like this, you should snap her up, start a family. You two would have beautiful children. Don't waste your time. At her age, I already had three kids, Raphael.'

Ralph grinned, not totally displeased by this scene. 'Helen, are you going to give us something to eat or just advice on how we should run the next twenty years of our lives?'

'Eat. Eat. Yes, you young people need to eat. What's her name, Raphael?'

'I'm called Sarah,' said Sarah a tad irritably, worried that the next question to Ralph would be did she take sugar. Who were these people? she thought. Beam me up, Scotty.

'Sarah?' cried Helen. 'Excellent! Sarah. My father's cousin was a Sarah. A beautiful woman. Beautiful like this Sarah. So, Sarah, what can I prepare for you?'

Sarah looked at the array of morsels in their steel platters under the glass counter. This place hadn't changed since the fifties. With so many wonderful little restaurants in the West End, why did Ralph come here? Ralph watched her looking around at everything with an unattractive expression of incredulity and disdain. 'Right, well, if you're still making up your mind, Sarah, I'll have my usual, please. And a coffee.'

'Of course, my darling,' said Helen. 'Now, Sarah, what takes your fancy?'

'Yes, I'll have a coffee too.'

'A coffee, good.'

'And for my sandwich' – she surveyed the shelves under the counter – 'some chicken, I think.'

'Chicken, yes, chicken, a nice piece of chicken, my darling.'

'Could I have it in some of that rye bread there.'

'Rye bread. Yes, of course, in the rye.'

'And do you have any crispy bacon you could put in with it?'

Helen stopped in her sandwich-making tracks and frowned. The diners put down their salt beef and turned their heads to look again. 'No bacon,' Helen said.

'No bacon?' said Sarah in loud surprise. Sorry, she thought to herself, is this a sandwich bar or is this a sandwich bar: no bacon?

'No bacon,' Helen said, her eyes burning.

'Try some coleslaw with your chicken,' said Ralph helpfully, 'the coleslaw here is delicious.'

Sarah looked round the restaurant. The initial

expressions of delight at her presence on their faces had wilted into disappointment. What had she done wrong? 'Yes, I'll try some coleslaw,' she whispered.

Ralph led her to a table at the very back of the restaurant. 'Don't worry,' he said, 'They're a really friendly crowd when you get to know them.'

'I can see that,' retorted Sarah sarcastically, feeling as if she'd just walked on to the set for *The Munsters*.

Presently Helen waddled over with the food. She seemed to have a bosom that went all the way from her neck to her knees. She plonked the food at the table, looked mournfully at Ralph and then backed away.

'Well, I've obviously made a big impression on her,' said Sarah. 'I shouldn't expect she'll be including me on her Christmas card list this year.'

'No,' affirmed Ralph. 'I don't suppose she'll be doing that,' he said kindly.

They started eating.

'So,' said Ralph, 'poor Tony.'

'Yes. Poor Tony.'

'Did you ask James for the job?'

'No,' said Sarah. 'I did not. He offered it to me. I suppose you think I slept my way into it?'

'No, I didn't think that, Sarah. I know you're good at what you do. But I'm surprised. It all happened very suddenly. It makes us look like we're some kind of hatchet firm. The minute you start treading water, you're out.'

'Ralph, Tony wasn't treading water, he was drowning.'

'But aren't you supposed to throw a drowning man a lifebelt, not push him further under?'

'Ralph, did you ask me here to slap my wrist? I thought you told me you were impressed by what I said in the meeting?'

'I was impressed, Sarah. I am impressed. Don't be so defensive. I'm surprised by what happened, that's all.'

They chewed on their food for a while in silence.

Ralph reached out and took her hand. 'Don't look so glum. I'm not blaming you. On the contrary, I just wanted to have a chat, to show you you've got a friend. Is that OK?'

'Because I'm a woman, I suppose you think I need a friend, I need my hand held?'

Ralph took back his hand. 'No, you obviously don't need anyone, Sarah,' he said and finished his sandwich.

Sarah swallowed hard. That last remark had been a bit aggressive. But she had to stand firm. After all that business with Roger, she didn't want Ralph thinking she was a soft touch. 'So what's this idea you mentioned?' she said, to break the unease.

Ralph looked sad. She was brittle. She looked so soft. She was all brittle and sharp. 'My idea is something I'd been discussing with Tony for a while, but he seemed in no hurry to take it up. I thought you might want to think about it, now that you've taken over.'

'Now that I've drowned him.'

'Yes, now that you've drowned him.' God, thought Ralph, she's hard work.

'Go on then.'

'Well, the product that your lot are most interested in at the moment, of course, is their muesli flakes Brekky Chunks concoction. They think they've got a good market for it in all those middle-class, nearly middle-aged executives who have nothing other to worry about than their cholesterol levels and their bran intake.'

'I know all this, Ralph. I've done my homework.'

'Right,' said Ralph. Talking to her was like caressing a hedgehog. She had always looked lovely to him from a distance, but now he was getting to know her, all those dreamy projections of loveliness were bouncing back sharply in his face, like hailstones on a windscreen.

He battled on bravely through the storm. 'The point is that their target market is the same as mine. My charity. The above-average-income people worrying about what polyunsaturates will or won't do for them are the same above-average-income people feeling guilty about not saving the whale or the panda. It occurred to me that some kind of promotion on your cereal packs for my charity would position the product with exactly the right kind of values. So people can feed themselves and their consciences at the same time. Over breakfast. What do you think?'

'Not bad,' said Sarah tepidly. 'Why didn't Tony take it up?'

'I don't know. Why didn't Tony take anything up? Inertia? Lack of confidence?' Ralph shrugged his shoulders. 'But it's a good idea. It would help me if it happened, but right now I think it would help you even more. Think about it, and let me know if you want to go ahead.'

'OK,' said Sarah, benevolently. 'We'd better get back, I've got so much to do.'

'OK,' said Ralph. He was unnerved by this conversation. He hadn't thought she would be like this. So tough and thorny. 'Are you happy at the agency, Sarah?' he asked, as one final bid for some friendly dialogue.

'Happy? Sure I'm happy. What kind of a question is that? Why shouldn't I be happy?'

'I'm not. I think the whole place is going downhill fast. James is going through some kind of mid-life AWOL. He's sitting on talented people instead of letting them grow. He's doing things for the wrong reasons. It's all starting to disintegrate at the edges. Quite a few people are thinking of leaving.'

'Are you?'

'Kind of.' He wasn't sure he liked her enough any more to trust her.

'I think you're wrong,' said Sarah haughtily. 'James is the best this industry has got. I think I'll learn a lot from him.'

'I'm sure you will,' said Ralph. 'Let's go.'

He wanted to remind her about the visit to the Portrait Gallery the next day. She hadn't mentioned it. He couldn't decide whether he wanted to suggest it to her again or not.

He paid on the way out. Sarah opened her purse to offer her share. 'No, that's OK. I'll get this one, you can get it the next time we have lunch.'

Dream on, thought Sarah.

Helen was wiping down the counter as they went out, still looking as if the pot at the end of the rainbow had turned out to be full of sand. 'Goodbye,' said Sarah to her politely.

'Goodbye,' said Helen, 'you can always convert, you know.'

'Convert? Convert to what?' But Helen had already disappeared to the other end of the counter.

'That's why I love London so much,' said Sarah as Ralph shut the door of the café behind him. 'It's full of nutters.'

'I'll see you later,' he said to her. 'I've got a couple of things to get before I go back.'

He walked off in the opposite direction. He had decided not to mention their ghost of a date. He might fancy the pants off this woman, but he sure as hell didn't like her.

Nine

Weekends are lonely things when you haven't got a regular relationship in tow. Although Sarah hardly ever used to see Adam at weekends when the two of them were supposedly an item, there was always a chance that she might, that the phone might suddenly ring and Adam might say, darling, slip into something sophisticated, I've got tickets for the opera tonight and a cosy dinner afterwards. You know that kind of might.

This might, tenuous as it will appear to those of us not living in Warp Factor Nine, somehow made those forty-eight hours of limbo between the end of one working week and the beginning of another more bearable. Now, not even that might was an option.

Ralph, she seemed to remember, had mentioned something earlier in the week about meeting up on Saturday but hadn't referred to it since, which was just as well as he really was a bit of a sanctimonious bore. All that dressing down about Tony had been too tiresome for words, it sounded like he was beginning to confuse the agency's business with the charity he worked for.

So now there was no Adam and no Ralph, and it seemed that the hours of Saturday and Sunday were piled up ahead of her like shirts in an ironing basket. (Naturally, Sarah has a woman who does all her ironing and cleaning for her, but if Sarah could remember what it was like to iron a pile of shirts, that's what it would be like.)

Usually Sarah worked one day each weekend, which soaked up a lot of the white space; this weekend in particular she had her new cereals clients to prepare for, which meant plenty of hours of work and very few hours in which to wonder what her life was really all about.

By Sunday afternoon, her laptop had steam coming out of its ears and she knew she had a presentation which would have them chomping at the bit. It was four o'clock. When it's four o'clock on a Sunday afternoon and there's no man in your life, there's only one thing a working girl can do: visit her grandmother.

Sarah's grandmother, Bessie, was in an old people's home in Kew, very near the Gardens, although no one ever thought to take any of the 'residents' across the road to see them. Bessie was in this place not only because her daughter, Sarah's mother, was incapable of looking after herself, much less her eighty-five-year-old mother. She was there because she had always wanted to be in a home. Bessie liked institutions; she had lived her life in hotels and the progression from hotel to old people's home seemed a natural one.

Bessie's body was no longer doing what her head told it to, which made her look old and incapable and incontinent and all those other old things. But her mind was not old; on the contrary, Bessie could hear the pin of an idea dropping in your head. While you were still talking to her in megaphone monosyllables, she had got you sussed down to your last lost marble.

Sarah is the only one who comes to visit Bessie, for which fact you might think that Bessie would be unendingly grateful. But Bessie has scant regard for her rather strange granddaughter and for the rather odd and lonely executive life she leads.

Sarah sat down just as Bessie was being served her tea. This was not a good thing to do.

'I've told you Sarah not to bloody come at tea-time,' said Bessie, who, unlike Sarah, had practised neither the split infinitives out of her grammar nor the native twang out of her voice.

Sarah had grown up two streets away from her grandmother in Yorkshire or anyway somewhere very north like that; north of Islington is about as north as my experience goes. Her village, as I imagine it, not having been there myself, is one of those chilly and weather-beaten places where people still go round shouting for Heathcliff, where the soap is still all coal tar and costs 2d a bar and where the Hovis boy looks radical chic.

For some reason, people from those kinds of places have enough chips on their shoulders to supply McDonalds for a week, which is silly: they ought to be glad they grew up knowing what a field is and not spending their lives aspiring to become jaded and surly Londoners like the rest of us. But aspire thus they do; they get out as soon as they can, they change the voice, they buy the clothes and get the image and hope to God their parents never visit when friends are round. That's until they succeed in life, when suddenly their culture, their ethnic diversity, are hauled back out of the closet, dusted up and given a good airing on the inside cover of their book jackets.

Sarah smiled nervously. 'I know, Granny, I'm sorry, I mean Bessie, but it's the only time I could come and I haven't been for a while.' Sarah was slightly ashamed. Notting Hill Gate is twenty minutes' drive away from Kew on a Sunday: she could visit far more often but keeping up with her workload just didn't allow it.

Bessie was unimpressed. 'Yes, well, hang on to your hanky, sweetie, because it's you who needs these visits more than I do. It makes no odds to me whether you turn up or not. I've got all the company I need, it's you who has to trawl along here on a Sunday because you need to hear a human voice that doesn't come out of a television.'

'Don't say that, Bessie. I thought you liked seeing me.'

'I'm happy enough to see you, Sarah, but you're the one who needs the sympathy, you funny woman with your funny little life, not me.'

'Don't keep going on about my life, Gra, I mean Bessie. It's my life not yours. You're so judgemental when you know so little about it. And eat your soup before it gets cold.'

'You know I don't like you coming when it's teatime. I don't like people sitting and watching me try and shovel this stuff into my face while they feel all superior.'

'Come on, you know I don't feel superior to you.'

'Too bloody right.' Bessie aimed a spoonful of the tomatoey slush towards her mouth and only missed by a couple of inches. 'Your life, Sarah, your life is a mess.'

'Oh dear, here we go again.'

'Well, if you don't like it you can shove off, but as you keep coming back I can only suppose you know deep down that what I'm saying's right.' A spoonful of soup hit her left ear.

'Shall I wipe you down, Bessie?'

'No you bloody shan't. It's you who needs putting in order, not me. I suppose it's all over with that Adam fellow?'

'Well, yes, that really didn't work out.'

'What a surprise. So who's leading you up the garden path now?'

'No one's leading me up the garden path. In fact, if you're interested, I'm very happy, I'm doing very well, I've recently had a promotion at work and – '

'You're very happy?' demanded Bessie, wiping the soup from the few strands of hair she has left which are combed, sports-presenter-like, over her crown. 'You're happy? You come in here, pale as a ghost, no smile on your face, tired as a bluebottle. If that's happy don't show me sad.'

'Well, yes I have been working hard, but that's just this weekend, it's a special job.'

'That's not just this weekend, that's you, Sarah, that's how you fill up your life. You're all work and these funny men who aren't nice to you. Why do you always like the ones who aren't nice to you?'

'I don't just like ones are aren't nice to me, it doesn't work out, that's all.'

A nurse came to wipe down Bessie's face and blouse. She brought with her a plate of spaghetti, which she then started mashing up so it resembled as closely as possible the tomato soup mush which had preceded it. 'Would you like me to feed you, Bessie?' asked the nurse.

'Sod off,' growled Bessie.

The nurse rolled her eyes at Sarah and walked away.

'It doesn't work out, Sarah, they never work out. What is it in your head that makes you want to be with the men who treat you bad? You've always been the same, such a pretty little girl, such a bright little girl, but the minute you found men, you went for the bad ones. I can't understand what makes you do it and what it is that keeps making you go back for more. You want to watch it, Sarah, one day one of these men is going to do you in, I mean hurt you proper.'

'Please, Bessie.'

'No, I mean it. You get what you want. The trouble with wishes is they come true. You aren't interested in the easy types, you want the ones with sharp teeth. Well, those ones bite and they leave their mark. Why do you do it, Sarah, why do you like the ones who hurt you? You know who you remind me of, don't you?'

'Yes, I know, I know.'

'Your mother. Just the same. Beautiful little girl she

was, my pride and joy. But the minute she met your father, she lost all her self-respect, let him treat her like a dog. Seeing you is like watching the same film in a different cinema. It breaks my heart, it really does.'

Sarah winced at the mention of her mother. Unlike her father, her mother had never really understood Sarah's need to succeed, the importance of her ambitions. Sarah's mother was a failure, a drunk, a punch-ball for her husband's frustrations at his own inadequacies. Coping with her mother as part of her life, as a part of herself, had always been difficult for Sarah.

However many other members of the family thought it, no one other than Bessie would have dared to suggest to her that, for all her apparent achievements, Sarah was really no more than an updated version of her mother. It was not something that Sarah liked to hear, because in her heart of hearts, it was her own greatest fear. But now was not the time to argue.

She reached across and picked the strands of spaghetti from her grandmother's nose. 'I really appreciate you caring about me, Bessie. I know you think I work too hard, and I know it must seem to you that my life is just one bad affair after another.'

'Yes, that's how it seems, now how are you going to tell me that that isn't how it really is?'

Sarah looked into her grandmother's yellow, fragile face. She looked at her grandmother looking at her and saw what she saw.

'Go on, bugger off and let me eat my tea in peace,' said Bessie, with irritation but not without affection. 'Come back when you've learnt how to be nice to yourself. Come back when you've learnt to say to them, go away and stop hurting me. You just have to say it and mean it and stop it.'

'All right, then,' said Sarah, 'I'll let you get on with it. I'll come back and visit soon. You take care.'

She walked back to the car-park, reflecting that the old woman's mind really was starting to go.

Daft tart, thought Bessie as she watched her granddaughter walking back to her fate.

Ten

On Monday morning, Sarah turned up at the offices of her new clients. She was ready to impress. All five directors who had anything to do with deciding the company's advertising had assembled to meet this new girl and tell her they were putting the account up for review. As far as they were concerned, this agency was running out of steam and they needed fresh blood to inject their cereals with the necessary snap, crackle and pop.

They'd put up with Tony for long enough. Now, all of a sudden, he was gone and they'd got the news that some girl they'd never heard of was coming to run the account in his place.

The gathering of old farts sat in their resplendent boardroom awaiting her arrival. The upside of being located in Slough was that you could spend a lot on space and design, to make up in architectural éclat what you lost in geographical kudos.

Sarah entered the awesome marbled reception atrium: I believe atrium is currently the correct term for the place where you leave your anorak in today's modern office environment.

Land-of-the-giants-sized plastic models of their awful orange and blue Brekky Chunks packs adorned the sophisticated reception area, and Sarah shuddered at the thought that her agency had been responsible for this. All up the magnificent stairwell someone –

probably someone called Tony – had arranged a vast cardboard frieze of huge smiling faces of happy families, that's families as in all white people and all dad-at-the-top-of-the table kind of scenes. Each family group was clustered around a different one of each of the company's best-sellers, grinning deliriously at the prospect of a bottle of ketchup or a tin of soup or a packet of instant potato. It looked like a scene from consumer hell.

'Can I help you?' chirruped a woman who had obviously learnt to talk from listening to her pet budgerigar at home.

'Yes, thank you,' smiled Sarah with some disdain as she surveyed the orange wall-to-wall deep pile carpet of foundation on the girl's face, her sweetheart nylon neckline, and the gold necklace charm at her throat, the kind which reads 'I love you' when you spin it round. Sarah explained who she was, where she was from.

'Shall I say it's Miss or Mrs?' tweeted the budgie.

'I'm sorry?' said Sarah.

'Shall I say,' tweetie-pie re-trilled, head cocked to one side with only mild, obvious irritation, 'that it's Miss or Mrs?'

'Well, don't say either.'

'Well I have to call you something when I tell them you're here!'

'Fine, and I've told you my name.'

'And I've said, is it Miss or Mrs?'

'Why does it matter?'

'Why does it matter what your name is?'

'No, why does it matter whether I'm Miss or Mrs? You wouldn't ask a man if he came here whether he was married or not, would you?'

'Of course I wouldn't! What do you take me for! I'm fiancé'd and I would never do that kind of thing at work!'

Sarah gave up. The millet brain had exhausted her.

'Oh, it doesn't matter. Tell them what you like. Just tell them I'm here, would you? Please.'

As she went to sit down, she could see the receptionists flapping their wings and hear the word lesbian being exchanged in loud twittering whispers.

Meanwhile, up in the senior boardroom, Sarah's prey were pluming their own feathers.

'I've rung James,' said Old Fart Number One. 'Told him I'll be happy to give her the once over to see if she'd look good in a swimsuit. Never say no to checking out a good pair of legs. But as for having some overgrown Girl Guide run our account, no way. I said that to James. He said to see her anyway. He rates her. Nice way to waste half an hour, I suppose.'

'Have you organised coffee?' said Old Fart Number Two. 'Or shall we ask her to do that for us when she gets here?'

Guffaw, guffaw.

'Perhaps she can give the boardroom a quick dust and polish while she's here,' quipped O.F. Number Three.

Snigger, snigger.

'You still got that French maid's outfit in your office from the Christmas party, Tom? Could come in handy.'

Smirk, smirk.

'Well I just hope you lot do the gentlemanly thing and leave us to it if I decide to take her here on the boardroom table.'

Titter, titter.

'No, we'll all stay and watch while you – '

Wham! The double doors to the boardroom were thrown open.

Bam! Sarah threw her briefcase onto the table.

Gasp! The five men stared at her. Is it a bird? Is it a plane? No. It's Sarah ready for business.

'Good morning, gentlemen! I'm here to tell you what we need to do to make it happen for your muesli flakes. Lights, please!'

She flung her carousel of slides onto the projector that she'd asked in advance to have ready in the room, and nodded to one of the men to switch off the light. He shuffled over and turned it off. He happened to be the managing director of the company, but at that moment he was too terrified to do anything except obey her command.

Off went the lights, on came Sarah's slides. Her slide suppliers had worked overtime on treble rate all Sunday evening to get them done in time.

The first one showed a photo of a little kid standing somewhere in Africa, flies eating his eyelashes, his stomach distended like he'd stuffed a football up under his skin.

'This charity does more for the Third World than any other in Great Britain. A year ago, they found this little boy in this state, orphaned, starving, illiterate. Today' – click, new photo showing same kid, well-fed, clean, clothed, with his hand up answering a question in a classroom – 'he's a different little boy. This is the charity, gentlemen, that will sell your muesli flakes for you.'

Stylishly and articulately, the story unfolded from here. Image by image, Sarah talked them through their product, told them home truths about their customers, what they read, where they went for their holidays, what else they ate, what cars they drove, what they thought about the price of fish. Amazing what a few phone calls can do on a Friday afternoon if you know who to ring.

'Think about your customers as real people. Think about the hearts and minds behind these statistics. All these above-average-income people worrying about what polyunsaturates will or won't do for them are the same above-average-income people feeling guilty about not helping the Third World while they're living it up in the First. They've got consciences to feed as well. Let's feed them.'

(Getting that *déjà entendu* feeling? It is at this point we may quietly take note that our heroine appears not to be over-burdening herself with compunction about snitching Ralph's idea. Well, you know what they say, all's fair in love, war and advertising.)

'This campaign will combine an on-pack promotion for sponsorship of the charity with a door-to-door distribution of product samples using pre-paid envelopes for donations in areas of greatest potential around key retail catchment areas analysed by ACORN consumer type.

'Let's keep away from TV and invest in below the line strategies that reinforce the product as the only choice for caring individuals who really care, not only about themselves but about others as well.'

The end. Sarah flipped the lights back on. The directors closed their mouths from the gaping Os of admiration that had accompanied her every word in the darkness. 'Well?' she said, taking a seat. 'How about it?'

Cor, yes please, thought the MD. What a chest she had on her. It had silhouetted against the screen for the entire presentation and he had gazed at it so intently that now, when he blinked, he still had the image of her bust against the bright light etched into his eyes.

The men shuffled in their seats. 'Thank you. That was very impressive,' said Michael, the marketing director and poor Tony's ex-golfing pal. 'However, I'm afraid that we've already – '

'Hang on,' said the MD. 'Hang on. No rush. Would you like some coffee, my dear? Nip out and arrange some coffee for us all would you, Mike, there's a good chap. Let's think this one through, shall we? Why don't you come on over here and sit next to me, Sarah?' He patted the seat next to him that Michael had just obediently vacated. 'That way we can talk better.'

Sarah smiled her smile. They never said no.

Eleven

Things sure move fast in the racy world of advertising.

By 4 p.m. that Monday afternoon, Sarah had got Anita to fax a press release on the client's exciting new plans for an innovative charity sponsorship campaign to every marketing correspondent on every national newspaper and every trade and marketing journal in the country. By the following morning, everyone was talking about it; there were press cuttings like confetti on it. Come lunchtime that Tuesday, she was almost an hour on the phone with their MD, who was asking her how she'd feel about taking on another one of their accounts as well. How does she feel? She feels good.

She put down the phone; it rang immediately; it was Adam again. That bitch Anita had put the call through deliberately; she was probably the other side of the door now with her ear up against a glass. Adam was saying fretfully that he'd like to see her and did she want to come round.

God, how Sarah loathed men who grovelled. She asked why it had taken him over a week to realise that he wanted to see her. She also asked whether he realised what a shit he really was. The exact wording, for reference, was: 'Adam, do you realise what a shit you really are?' Then she put the phone down.

Ha! Getting real tough now! Let's hope Anita picked up that one through her glass hearing aid! (She had: she often listens in on Sarah's calls from the switchboard.)

This being the Big Day, or, to be precise, the Big Evening and, who knows, possibly even the Big Night with James, Sarah stayed very late at work and made sure that, this time, she arrived at Langan's a good twenty minutes after the appointed time, so that if James wasn't there when she arrived, she could always pretend to herself that he had been there but had assumed she wasn't coming and had left. It's called kidding yourself, but what the hell. One less pebble to cut your foot on along the stony walkway of life.

James was there all right. A little flushed from the wine and scotch at lunch, the beers in the pub after work and the two bloody Marys he'd already knocked down the porthole in the ten minutes he'd been waiting for her, but he was there.

That day he'd had lunch with Frank, the marketing director at Birksomes. Birksomes made toiletries; Birksomes was DFDDG's biggest account, and Frank was in charge of it. James had become quite pally with Frank, as you do when brown-nosing your way through billings of £25m a year, and made sure that he gave the Birksomes account his personal attention. So next time you spray on your deodorant, think of James. It's his livelihood, and the largest toiletries account in the country.

Winning that account a decade back had been one of James's truly golden moments, and to be fair, he had built it up significantly over the years. But James had made the old mistake of putting almost all his agency's eggs into that one basket of hairsprays and aftershaves. This single account represented almost a quarter of the agency's entire revenue.

Frank had called James at home that morning, just before he set off for a new business pitch, to suggest they have lunch.

'Frankie!' exclaimed James. 'You know my lunch diary's booked up weeks in advance. I won't have a lunch window again until next month.'

'Sod your windows, James,' advised Frank, cheerfully but ominously. 'I'm doing you a favour.'

He refused to tell James what it was about. James is a man who doesn't like surprises. He could tell from the tone of Frank's voice that the news, whatever it was, was not good news. Just thinking about it gave him the jitters all the way through the meeting, where, fortunately, he wasn't doing much.

The pitch that morning had been an important one, an account which could, single-handedly, have restored equilibrium to the agency's toiletry-heavy figure. So two of the agency's most creative hotshots, Angus and Bill, had come up with some wacky ideas to whet the client's appetite. These two worked as a pair and just to say you had them on your account gave you infinite street cred at any adperson's dinner table.

The pitch was for a luxury four-wheel-drive. A & B (yes, A & B) had used special effects to get the car building itself from a tiny black speck in the middle of the PC screen into the shining black car into a shining black panther into a shining black leather sofa into a shining black woman wearing a shining black evening dress. Like, everything was shining and black.

It spelt speed, comfort, elegance. The images slipped seamlessly one into the other. It was wordless, it was stunning. It used the latest visual technology to make it happen so effortlessly.

James had not been involved in any of this. He knew nothing about visual technology. He'd been wheeled in as the big name, the Experience.

This seemed to be happening more and more often. He'd make the introduction to set the scene. The clients would look distracted, anxious to get on with the creative stuff. His people would look bored, eager to show off their lovely new widgets. The jokes, the coined phrases which they once used to lap up now appeared to irritate them. The brand managers were all half his age and treated him like a friendly pet dinosaur. They had cheered at the end of Angus and Bill's show.

James knew that his performance had been merely an optional accessory. He made a mental note to have a word with those two smart-arse creatives who were clearly getting too big for their boots. And he'd heard that they were being wooed with offers from some start-up agency to go in as partners. James fretted and worried his way through the presentation. Twice, when the clients asked him something, he'd been staring out of the window, chewing on his preoccupations, and hadn't heard them. Time for new batteries in that hearing aid, James, chirped Angus to relieve the general embarrassment the second time it happened.

James was glad to get out of the meeting. Hardly waiting to say goodbye to the clients, he'd dashed out to grab a cab and find out what this business with Frank was all about.

Bloody computers, he ruminated grumpily in the taxi. Nowadays it was all fancy footwork with a PC keyboard. As long as it looked high-tech, people bought it.

James had watched advertising grow from housewives in whiter-than-white aprons preparing something really special for when their husband got home, from an industry you'd be embarrassed to tell your father you were in. Now it was a force that shaped people's lives and lifestyles, a force that obliged manufacturers to change their lousy products into better ones, that gave consumers the right to vote with their hands and wallets. There was nothing James didn't know about advertising, about the right size and shape for an ad, for a typeface, for the angle of a model's head, the glint in an eye, the comma in a strapline. And he knew everything about every consumer type, about every twitching instinct of the 25–34 year old women walking down the catwalk between the supermarket shelves, about the aspirations of the C2DE men choosing their cigarettes in the local newsagent's, about the purchasing preferences of a five-year-old.

But these fucking computers. He didn't know how to switch one on, didn't want to. Now multi-media technology was running the show, and he was the warm-up act nobody wanted any more.

All those big-shots you think are thinking that they rule the earth, most of the time they're bricking it. And fragile egos sure are tedious things.

Poor James. When he got to the restaurant that lunchtime and heard what Frank had to say it set his gout off again in a twinkling.

As a friend, Frank was letting him know that there were mumblings from Frank's colleagues about the quality of James's work. As a friend, Frank was telling him that – and he quoted – James's 'megalomaniac hubris' was starting to piss people off. His last TV campaign for their new shower gel, Glisten, had shown, from discreet angles, a couple fiddling about ambiguously with each other in the shower. This had not appealed to their middle-of-the-road, middle-age customer base, who didn't want to be reminded that they had given up things like that with their partners years ago. The joke going round was that James had insisted on personally interviewing all the models for the girl-in-the-shower role.

As a friend, Frank layed it on the line for him. The word on the street was that James was an eighties man who couldn't cope with today's consumer. He thought they were still buying the hype. They weren't.

Frank rammed his bolt home. 'James, I think my team at Birksomes has decided they're looking for a younger man. A fresh approach. You know it's my call on whether you ultimately stay or go, but I've got MDs and FDs and a whole host of others that I've got to think about as well, and, right now, you just haven't got their vote of confidence. You're the master, the guru. Everyone knows that. But perhaps the time has come for you to go into consultancy. Do the conference route. Concentrate on the books.'

James felt his bowels tremble. He was only forty-six, for Christ's sake. Here was some thirty-three-year-old prat telling him to pack it in and sign up for crochet classes. 'Frank, come on, Frank. Give me a break. The agency's had the account for over nine years.'

'Exactly,' said Frank with a sympathetic smile, like James had just confessed to having warts. Nine years in the fast-track world of advertising is like the ice and bronze ages wrapped together.

'Frank, help me out here. You know that it would only take your say-so to change their minds and keep us on.'

James heard his words and went pink with embarrassment. Two years, a year ago, he'd have told the guy to bugger off if he didn't like it, confident that there'd be plenty more punters where he came from.

Frank heard his words and went pink with nerves and excitement. He'd thought the conversation might go something like this. It was time to put his plan into action. 'Well,' said Frank. 'I've got an idea that you might want to consider.'

Frank left ten minutes later. James finished off the wine, ordered yet another double scotch and stayed at the table for another half-hour, drinking, sweating, thinking about his life, his age and what's it all about, Alfie. When he finally got back to the agency, he tanked up on a few shots from the drinks cabinet in his office. He joined some of the boys for one or two rounds in the pub before he met Sarah. By the time she appeared at the restaurant, he felt like he had the Rovers Return throwing a party in his stomach.

He stood up and gave her a Chuck and Di style kiss into the air beside her ear when she got to the table. She noticed and thought it was nerves. He noticed and thought he'd better slow down the drinking, as he had been aiming to plant the kiss on her cheek.

'Hello, Sarah,' he said, with a voice that sounded like the voice of the Mysterons. 'You look absolutely wonderful. There's a Bloody Mary here for you and I've ordered champagne – I hope that's OK with you.'

Zing! Sarah's nipples stiffened into two little diamonds. First the dinner date, then she looked wonderful, now he's ordered champagne.

As far as she was concerned, this was it. Fanfare of trumpets, roll of drums. This is the moment when David Cassidy suddenly jumps off the stage, fights his way to the back of the crowd, grabs you and says: 'I think I love you'. This is the moment when you win the competition for a dinner date with Donny Osmond and he says 'Can I see you again?'. And now, this is the moment when James, advertising supremo, the cream of the media crop, says 'Sarah, you look wonderful. Champagne?'

No doubt about it. This was it. Give it just another couple of hours and the cameras will move to a shot of white waves breaking on the shore. I've never quite understood why crashing waves stand in as the PG film certificate interpretation of a good bonk, but there you go. Someone somewhere must have a good imagination. Or think that having sex smells like seaweed.

So: spotlight on James. It's not all bad news about James, you'll be glad to know. For starters, he's not married. Sarah will not be his bit on the side. She will be right there in the bosom of his harem. He's forty-six, divorced, still got masses of hair. Especially, recently, in his ears. He goes places, sees plays, watches films, knows people. He's not a snob and doesn't smoke a pipe. Doesn't cut his toe-nails in bed, knows how to use a toilet brush.

Not bad, not bad, I hear you saying. There must be a catch though! I hear you cry. There is! There are! Less fragrant aspects of our Jim are that, first of all, he's got a bit of a problem with the old percent proof stuff. It started as social drinking, then it became business drinking, now it's just drinking.

Recently, there have been more than the average number of hiccoughs at the agency. In fact, there have been some bloody awful problems which James just can't seem to sort out. Notwithstanding the agency's past glories and its roaring reputation, in adland you're only as good as next quarter's billings. Your hands that wash dishes might feel as soft as your face, but when you're in the red with the bank manager breathing down your neck, what use are soft hands, I ask you? And when business is looking wobbly, James drinks himself wobbly. To make all the nasty bits go away.

Second of all is the way James uses women. James uses women like toothpaste. A couple of squeezes at least twice a day, maybe more at the weekend, make sure all the bristles are nicely covered, get it right up there in the nooks and crannies right up at the back, lick your tongue round it, swill it around a bit, spit it out. Things are fine for a while, then you get that furry feeling again and it's time for another go. James needs a lot of women lined up to get his regular ring of confidence.

So Sarah needn't flatter herself here. She is one of the chosen many. And with her taste in men, it sounds as if a rat like James is going to suit her just fine.

There's no obvious reason why James should behave so badly. He's a bright boy, got all his fingers and toes and bits in the right place. No dire childhood to trace it back to, no history of abusive nannies, depraved schoolmasters down country lanes, no father with a big brass buckle on the end of his belt.

I know business is not going too well for him right now. I know that the world has most irritatingly moved on while James would have liked it to stay conveniently as it was in the seventies when men wore Old Spice, women wore Playtex and we all knew what we were doing and what class we were in and what sex we were and there was none of this weird and wonderful nonsense about customers also being consumers whose needs had to be recognised, acknowledged and fulfilled. But can a spot of professional frustration justify the hanky panky he gets up to?

Anyway, the issue is not why men like James are scum. The issue is why women like Sarah like scum like him. James is just not a nice man. He hurts his women, he needs to hurt his women: emotionally, professionally, any which way he can. I can't be doing with that. I want to know why Sarah can. She's not poor, she's not dependent, she has no red-eyed kids with snot running down their faces howling and clinging to her designer skirts. There is no excuse. So why someone like her hangs on for more is what I want to know.

Why he does it in the first place? – Well, who gives a monkey's. Asking why men treat women badly is like asking why trains are always late. No one knows, no one really cares and it will always happen anyway. Why women allow it to happen, that's the question.

Anyway, we digress: back to Sarah's thudding heart and itching nipples in the restaurant. James sensed her excitement and felt the natural dick-jerk reaction. Under the table, his battered old codger, worn out through constant over-use, had been happily planning to use this meal-time as a moment of brief but welcome respite to take forty winks. Now it peeked its nose out from under the Calvin Klein duvet and sniffed the air. It could detect, wafting through from somewhere at the top of Sarah's talcumed thighs, her oestrogens asking his testosterones if they wanted to come out and play.

But old Dick was just too knackered after all the alcohol to even pick up the ball and throw it back to her. It snuggled back into its den and carried on snoozing.

'How did the presentation go today?' Sarah asked. She looked disarmingly into James's eyes and hoped that her new thick'n'lush mascara was doing what it said it would do on the packaging. James's eyes were very bloodshot and bleary. He could just about make out her outline opposite him, but was having problems working out where her face was on it, much less whether her lashes looked thicker, fuller and suddenly lovelier than ever before.

The waiter handed them both the menu and James felt his stomach lunge at the prospect of food. 'Presentation? Oh yes, the presentation.' Somewhere back in what seemed like the distant past he remembered the meeting he'd had earlier that day. 'The meeting went well. Very well.'

He looked at Sarah's expectant face, like that of a three-year-old waiting for something wonderful to happen. Women always expected something wonderful from him. He knew that at this stage he was expected to say a few seminal things, and jump through three burning hoops on a unicycle. Cue James the performing seal. He took a deep breath to steady his swaying mind.

'Actually the meeting went bloody well. It's going to be a three-way pitch, and that's not counting BDCB, the incumbents, who are stalking round with their tails between their legs ready to throw McMannon any deal he wants. The other two are KGN and MCPP. KGN don't know their arses from their elbows at the best of times, and since Steadman left MCPP they've gone to the wall. Although Collins is still hot stuff; but knowing them they've stuck him on some two-bit piece of business doing press ads for holiday brochures. This account is worth megabucks, and we could do with a tasty piece of car business. I had Angus and Bill working on a concept. They're great kids and I think they could go a long way, but for the time being they haven't really got the understanding of automotives that this account demands. I can see I'm going to have to take over on this one.'

'Sure,' whispered his awed audience.

'My concept,' he blasted on, both he and Sarah hearing these sprawling vine-sodden ideas for the first time, 'which still requires some development work and which is completely confidential of course, is to bring the culture of sex and cars to its ultimate, shuddering conclusion. I mean, cars are sex. Sex is cars. The first time you did it was in the back of your dad's chevvy. The gearstick as phallus, the whole bit.'

'Right,' murmured Sarah, a bit lost.

'In the good old days, they draped a blonde with a decent pair of bristols over a motor to get that little line on the sales chart erect. If you were to do that now, you'd get shot. No way can you exploit a woman nowadays. But what is OK now is to exploit men. It makes the dyke brigade happy because they see it as revenge, it makes normal women happy because they always like to see a bit of chipolata, and it makes men happy too, because – well, because most men are half nancy anyway, and those who aren't are quite pleased to think of a car as male.'

James paused for breath and another slurp of his drink. Although Sarah could follow very little of what James was actually on about, she was in ecstasy. Here she was, with James, her boss and her mentor, confiding in her about his secret strategy for an important new account. Could ever a girl's dreams have been so fulfilled?

But she didn't want him to realise how he overwhelmed her. With great self-control she kept her composure, stifled her veneration and said in a rather haughty way: 'Yes, I think you're right, James. Consumers are ready to handle the open fusion of sex and cars in a way that, say, ten years ago, would not have been possible.'

Neither of them were quite sure what she meant by this, but her deferential tone suited both their needs at that moment, so it wasn't questioned. Meaningful content was somehow superfluous, as is so often the case in a relationship, don't you find?

I know you might be disappointed by Sarah at this point in time. But give the girl a break here: this is her big night and she needs to make it work.

'So how will this actually look in the ads?' she continued gamely.

'Well, that's what I'll ask Angus and Bill to work on, it's only fair to keep them involved, I can't hog all of the limelight all of the time. I want to set up a debriefing on today's presentation to consider the concept in its strategic context, then we'll get together in another couple of days to see what they've come up with. Of course, and just between you and me, I'll probably end up having to do all the creative work for this anyway. Bill and Angus are full of promise, but they're still so inexperienced. This is a heavyweight account.'

They both smiled politely at each other. Given James's not insubstantial girth, this was perhaps a less than felicitous choice of word to describe his input. If they'd known each other better they might have made a joke about it. As they didn't, there was now an unattractive lull in the conversation.

James drank his drink. She looked significantly at her fork as if it held all the mysteries of the universe.

Tick, tock, tick, tock.

After what turned out to be rather too pregnant a pause, Sarah thought it might now be a good time to change the subject, to get things maybe on a more personal footing. She launched forth bravely. 'I wanted to say that . . .' she began.

But the alcohol had caused James to slip his siding; his mind had become the Cannonball Express, careering down its own little track, its engine fuelled by the sound of his own voice. There was no stopping him now.

'I've got this image in my mind for this campaign, you know,' he interrupted her, so we shall never know, as long as we live, what it was that Sarah wanted to say. 'It's the image of a car in a field full of poppies. Forget all the macho crap of the cars speeding up and down through mountain crevasses that are always served up to us in ads, like some hangover from a James Bond movie. No, this car is going to be in a very quiet, very beautiful field of poppies and a man, wearing nothing, a dream of a man, is polishing it, rubbing it, smoothing a chammy over the bonnet, wiping the glass, caressing the mudflaps. It'll be carefully done so you don't get his willy splashing all over the place, but you might see a touch of buttock pressing against a window here or a bit of muscled chest reflected in a wing mirror there. It's hot sun, in the middle of nowhere, in a field of red steamy poppies, and there's a naked man alone with his car, polishing and pleasing the object of his desire.'

Pause for effect. And a slurp of wine. Not in that order.

'Sounds good,' said Sarah merely, straining to be cool, sitting on her hands to stop her flinging them round his neck with happiness that James is sharing his creative inspiration with her, no matter that my nine-year-old niece could come up with something better if you said to her 'You've got thirty seconds to think up an ad for a car'. As far as Sarah is concerned, she is in the presence of seminal creative thought in action; it has not clicked that these are little more than the ramblings of a beer barrel.

James waited for the laud. Usually, by this stage, any advertising skirt he graced with his 'I've got an image' speech, recounted in the tones of 'I've had a dream', is flailing about in her chair, practically begging him, demanding him, to take her there and then, on the restaurant table. But Sarah, desperate to appear nonchalant and therefore what she imagined was mature and desirable, looked distant, as affectionately interested as you might be in next door's cat.

Christ, thought James, doesn't anything impress this

tart? By now his head felt so watery he was sure he would see a posse of goldfish riding by any minute. All he could comprehend was that she was looking distinctly indifferent to his outpourings. Perhaps she had seen the three hoops on the unicycle act before.

James had a quick feel of his apparatus. It felt like it was in deep coma and not even Elle Macpherson with knobs on could do anything to resuscitate it. But he wanted to keep his options open. OK, he wasn't up to much now: that's because he was pissed as a fart. But he might perk up later on. He'd recovered from worse situations than this before, and he'd had nothing since the weekend.

In his alcoholic stew, James suddenly felt a stab of desperation. Couldn't he pull a bird any more either? Was he too old for the clients and too old for the crumpet as well? Suddenly, Sarah's attention was paramount. He had to know he could have her if he wanted her. Had to get her adoring him. She had to adore him. Adore him with adoration.

She was looking vacantly round the restaurant, as if she wanted to see if she knew anyone there who could rescue her from him. Maybe she was looking for Angus and Bill, maybe they'd give her one on their sodding little mouse mat. Fuck it.

'Of course, all this is nothing compared to the other deal I'm working on at the moment.' A voice somewhere back on the shoreline was shouting, shut up you stupid bugger, but James was so far out to sea by now, there was no going back.

'What deal's that?' asked Sarah, forgetting her play-it-cool, intrigued and incredulous.

Aha! Got the bitch now. Got her now. Got the cool-as-a-fucking-cucumber bitch interested in me now. 'Yes, yes, the other deal,' he blurted on thickly. 'No one's supposed to know, Sarah, so don't tell 'em, will you?'

'Tell who?'

'Bloody anyone, who d'you think, you daft cow!'

Now she looked hurt. Oops. Slow down, James, calm down, slow down. Be nice. Remember your plonker. 'Sorry. Sorry. I didn't mean to say that. I'm a bit touchy about it, that's all. We're re-pitching for the Birksomes account. You know the one.'

Sarah was baffled. 'What do you mean the Birksomes account? Why on earth are we re-pitching for that? We've been working with that account for years.'

'Right,' improvised James. 'Er, because it's company policy to have regular reviews.'

'What, regular reviews once a decade?' They both sat in silence for a few moments. 'Weren't they pleased with the Glisten campaign? I know there were some comments that the creative side was a bit, well, strong, and all that stuff about the first nipple in a TV ad, but I thought generally it was OK, wasn't it?'

'Oh sure, yes, great. Glisten was a great campaign, superb AB consumer awareness,' James babbled incoherently.

'My God,' continued Sarah, still in shock. 'If we lost that account, it would be a disaster. So many brands, so much business, and so many people at the agency working on it.'

'No, no, don't you worry your pretty little head about it, Sarah,' said James. 'No, we won't lose it.'

'How can you be so sure?' she asked.

'Because!' barked James before hesitating. The man on the shore was screaming now, waving his arms wildly at him. No! No! Don't do it! he was crying.

'Because?' parroted Sarah.

'Because,' repeated James with a voice like Peter Cushing in the catacombs, his pupils dilated on the little creases at the top of Sarah's cleavage, 'because I've told the marketing director who has the deciding vote that I would make it worth his while. His personal while. We'll pad out a few invoices and make sure he gets the difference, straightforward stuff. No one will ever know. It'll get lost in the big numbers.'

Sarah gasped and held her hands to her cheeks in horror.

'No need to make that face,' said James, irritated. 'We need this business. It's too important to lose. We need this business. And you may have saved Tony's account for us, but there are rumblings from two other clients, rumours I've heard, even today, just now, in the pub, I don't know.'

His voice trailed off mournfully and disintegrated into a strand of mumbles. Something about business and computers and fucking kids running the show nowadays.

'Sorry, James, I can't understand what you're saying.'

'Anyway,' he said, jolted by her voice back into the land of the living. 'This is all secret squirrel. Can't tell a soul. This is just between you and me, OK? Can't tell anyone about the re-pitch, much less about the other little business. So bob's the word.'

'You mean mum,' Sarah said reassuringly.

He wondered why the fuck she was bringing her mother into this. He'd just told her something which he should have kept entombed in his breast to his dying day and now she wanted to talk about her mother.

He finished off his drink and reached out for hers, which she didn't seem to have touched. 'So what do you think to that then?' he concluded triumphantly, wretchedly. He should never have told her. But he'd done it now. Might as well get maximum mileage from it.

Now Sarah was truly enthralled. Sorry, but she was. She should have been appalled but, the way James told it, she was just enthralled. Whatever revulsion she may have felt for James's plans was lost under the heap of wonder and gratitude that he should have confided in her in this way. She could contain her awe no more. 'James, that's amazing,' she whispered.

Thank God for that, he thought. James was exhausted by this monologue. He needed another drink quickly.

But at least she looked satisfied that his credentials as Superman were still in order. Should be no problem getting one up her at the end of the evening if he still wanted it.

There's a natural break here, folks, so you can pop out and put the kettle on if you like. James ordered two more Bloody Marys and a bottle of claret. The champagne that he had supposedly ordered had not materialised and James seemed to have forgotten about it. Sarah didn't mention it. She also didn't mention that she doesn't like tomato juice when he ordered the drinks.

She's behaving like a real half-wit at the moment, a real amoeba-woman. This must be love.

They studied the menu. Sarah chirruped, 'Langoustine — my favourite,' and James clutched at his stomach. They ordered. They ate. Throughout the meal their conversation was forced, patchy, uneasy. Just a bit of polite chit-chat about work.

James was starting to feel really very ill. It was all he could do to get intelligible sentences out. Sarah was getting worried. He was hardly talking to her and he looked green. He ordered another bottle of wine even though she had only drunk one glass from the first one and it looked to her as if he'd certainly had enough.

Perhaps he's drinking so much because he's bored, she thought anxiously. Perhaps she wasn't capable of keeping a man like him interested. He was so clever, so successful.

Sarah felt a slow panic coming on. Even though she was only half way through her food, he had started looking round for the waiter, having informed her that they wouldn't want any pudding, would they, so he'd better get the bill.

Is that it? Does he find her conversation that dull? What about the big romance? What about the scene when he reaches across the table and murmurs, softly, 'I've been thinking about you a lot recently, Sarah,' or other such dribble that she's been churning round in her fantasies for the past few weeks? What about the bit where they go back to his place and discover that they've been looking for each other all these years? She can't just let the evening finish like this, without more intimacy, without making more of an impression, without forging a bond that will form the basis for a truly loving and committed relationship that will sustain them throughout the years.

'I've just ended an affair,' she blurted out.

'Have you?' he enquired, nonplussed. Oh God, what's this. A nice little meal followed by a nice little shafting would have been just right. His brain was doing the butterfly stroke in a swimming pool of vodka. He was in no mood to do a Claire Rayner for the next hour.

'Yes. I have. And it's left me feeling a bit bruised.'

'Like a banana?' James quipped inanely with a lop-sided grin. 'Sorry, Sarah.' Even he could hear how pathetic that had sounded.

A tiny gobbet of spittle had now appeared twinkling at the corner of his mouth. For the first time, Sarah clicked that her guru was well and truly pissed. So automatically she assumed, as doormats do, that it was her fault, that the reality of an evening with her had proved to be dreary enough to drive the poor chap to dipsomania. Her head began to knot with nerves. They both sat in silence. Which became embarrassed silence again.

'So you're really cut up about it?' James continued thickly. He was doing his best, although his stomach was doing the lambada and he thought he might soon want to die. 'Anyone I know?' If he was going to have to sit through a heavy session of 'My Last Boyfriend', essential reading for every woman he went out with, perhaps he could at least get some decent gossip out of it.

'No, no,' said Sarah. She already wished she hadn't

started this, but it had seemed like the only thing to get his attention and get the mood of the evening on a slightly more personal footing.

You can't blame her for this. She wasn't to know that James didn't need to be in any kind of a mood at all to whip his ding-a-ling out and dial a number. He could do it in any mood, any time and any place, and indeed often had done it on his desk, in the office car park and, *naturellement*, in the photocopying room. James had served up so much spunk in the photocopying room into poor Anita's little mouth that it was surprising the photocopier wasn't in therapy, having been forced to witness such a scene so often. So Sarah needn't have worried, but how was she to know?

'No, it's no one you know. Do you remember that I was late for last week's directors' meeting?'

'Yes,' said James. He had no idea what she was talking about. Last week seemed like a previous incarnation. His mind had imploded to the size of the little black dot on Angus's bloody presentation. But that was the least of his worries. The most of his worries were all the bits and pieces in his gut and liver area which were now re-enacting the scene from *Saturday Night Fever* where they all dance in synchronised ghastliness on the disco floor.

'I'd just lived through a terrible scene with some PR nerd who I'd been seeing. He dumped me that morning.'

Why am I telling him this ridiculous story? thought Sarah. Why is she telling me this ridiculous story? thought James. By now, he could feel the vomit rumbling at the pit of his throat.

'You know, I really thought I liked him, otherwise I'd have ended it long before. Sometimes it just takes a while to get to know men.'

James looked at her blankly, biliously.

'I mean, they take a while before they open up to you.'

The good news for Sarah was that James was going to take no time at all opening up to her. The waiter came and took Sarah's plate and hovered with the half-eaten langoustine right under James's nose. 'Has sir finished?' he enquired.

The sour stench of the fish caught James's nostrils. 'Sarah' he managed to utter. 'I've got to go.'

He made a funny noise and thrust his napkin to his mouth. He leapt from his seat with heavy, sticky strands of sick trailing down from either side of him and reaching out to diners at the closely packed tables as he stumbled through them towards the exit.

Sarah was left at the table. All that was left of her romance for the evening, of what she had hoped was going to be the beginning of the rest of her life, was a tiny pool of puke of half-digested goats cheese and venison on the tablecloth opposite her.

She waited patiently for James to come back from the loo. She ignored the hostile looks of the people round her, especially those who were wiping down their shoulders or their hair. She tried to look calm. She tried to have an expression which said, hey, no problem – didn't you know it's fashionable nowadays to have your partner barf all over himself and everyone else in the restaurant – it's all the rage in the States.

After fifteen minutes she asked the waiter if he could check the gents to see whether James was all right in there. The waiter returned to say that James had left in a cab a quarter of an hour before.

'Oh. OK,' said Sarah. She paid the bill. She went to the loos and put on make-up over the sad bits of her face. Then she took a cab, straight round to Adam's flat.

There are plenty more pebbles on the beach, you know.

The taxi arrived in Holland Park. She got out and looked at the graceful white Victorian mansion flat in front of her. Adam had the top flat there, complete with roof garden.

Even Adam, bastard that he was, seemed normal, desirable after what she had just sat through. She should have given it more time with him, she thought absurdly as she doled out the contents of her purse to the taxi driver. Although he (Adam, that is, not the taxi driver) had always been so detached with her, this behaviour might really have been a call for help, a call for love from someone who found it hard to communicate. After all, he was in PR.

Women always go psychological when they can't face up to men's shortcomings, have you noticed that? I mean, what is wrong with admitting to yourself, the guy's a shit, he'll always mess you around, you'd be better off taking up bungee jumping without the string if you really want a hobby which guarantees you're going to hurt yourself.

The truth of it is that Sarah was all primed for her next fix of being treated badly, and if James wasn't going to give it to her, Adam would have to dole her out a dose to slake her addictive itch.

Sarah saw a light on in Adam's bedroom window, right at the top of the house. That light, a light that was calling down to her, Sarah, Sarah, I need you, I want you. She'd put the phone down on him. Put the phone down on him when he'd rung her to tell her he needed her. God knows what courage that must have taken on his part. What a cow she'd been. Adam, Adam, my darling. I've come back. I've come back to you.

She tapped in the code he'd taught her and let herself in the main front door. She started up the long staircase. Every step (and there were quite a few) was a penance. Every step led her, Dante-like, up through purgatory towards heaven. Every step was a renunciation of her act of sin, a lightening of her load, a movement of proximity towards her beloved.

When she got to the top of the stairs, she saw that the

front door to his flat was open. It was almost midnight. Her first instinct was to run and call the police. Her second instinct was to go in and check that Adam was all right, that he wasn't lying on the floor with a knife in his back. That would serve her right, wouldn't it? The only man who had ever really loved her, whom she had loved without even realising it, would be lying there in a pool of blood.

She tiptoed in. There were quite a few lights on, so it wasn't hard to see. A CD was playing some melancholy jazz. No one was in the kitchen or dining room.

Then she heard muffled noises from the bedroom. She took an iron from the fender and walked up the corridor. The moans got louder, like an animal in some kind of pain. A floorboard squeaked.

Sarah stopped, too scared to breathe. The soft grunting continued. Had he been bound and gagged by an intruder? Well, er, yes, kind of, Sarah.

She crept forwards. Peering round the door frame into his bedroom, she saw Adam, face down, sluiced in sweat. Slowly and rhythmically, a man was pushing himself in and out of Adam's backside. The room was glowing in a rich pink light. On both their faces there was a look of slow, sweet bliss. Their eyes were shut. Their flesh was pink like the light. Pink, warm and hot. These men looked like they had heaven in their heads. Their hands were locked together as if they were playing that children's game where you sit on the floor and rock each other back and forth. Only Adam was playing it upside down. Upside down and inside out. They were moaning and groaning with delight.

Have you ever seen snakes making love? They slip and wind themselves round each other and slither their entire lengths over and under each other, like they cannot bear to have any part of themselves which is not adhered to the other. Hot, greasy, rich, thick. Slow. Rhythmic. Dripping. Sarah had never seen sex like that. She had never felt anyone want to have all of her like that. She knew she ought to leave. She left.

Twelve

On Wednesday, Sarah took the day off work. A girl can only take so much before she has to take time out to recover. Of course Anita didn't believe her story about a migraine when she rang in with it, but it hardly mattered what Anita did or didn't believe, Sarah wasn't going to worry about her. She had some stuff she could work on at home later anyway, so her conscience was clear.

She got up early and spent the morning wandering moodily around the cosmetics departments of Harrods to de-stress, as you do. She ended up buying nothing – until they brought out something new, there was simply nothing in the Clarins range left for her to buy – and sitting moodily in Richoux across the road, drinking an enormous cup of hot chocolate and an even larger plate of cheese on toast.

James: it was obvious that James had no real interest in her. She'd let her over-fertile imagination overtake her. He was showing no more than due interest in her as a new director. If she'd thought it was going to be any more than that, she'd thought wrong. He'd drunk himself literally sick with boredom at dinner with her: this did not indicate that he would soon be asking her to bear his children. How stupid she had been.

Adam: the Adam incident was too difficult for her to deal with just yet. She was jealous, jealous of that raw red meat love she had witnessed but never experienced. For Sarah, sex was only ever a cerebral activity of nerves, a tense and loaded exercise for the mental measuring of commitment and fidelity. A good fuck, full of fun, just for the sheer physical pleasure of it: this she never allowed herself. It would have been too easy, it would have been too much.

Ralph: oh, God, Ralph. Ralph was a really nice guy, but you know how it is. Nice means interesting. Interesting means wet. You can leave the nice guys for your next life.

Her mind was fuzzy with confusion and a vague depression. She rang Suzanne from her mobile and arranged to meet her for a meal that evening.

She got home, gloomier than before she set out. A single message winked out at her from her answering machine. Probably work. But no. It was Adam again. She flipped with fear. He'd obviously seen her in his flat the night before.

'Hi, Sarah, I know you're angry with me but I think we should meet. Please call.' His tone was pally. It seemed he hadn't seen her, which was, on reflection, not surprising given his circumstances at the time.

Sarah was numb. But somewhere within that numbness, a flicker of hope flickered when she heard Adam's voice. This was the third time he'd rung. He wasn't giving up on her that easily. She squirmed with doubt: what were these calls all about? He obviously still cared for her, but what about last night?

She wanted to ring him back and shout abuse at him, but she had no right to do that. No right to accuse him of his infidelity. And no right to accuse him of doing it with a man because she had always very nobly told herself that it was people who were important, not their gender. She'd have to stand by her theories, now that they were standing in front of her, hands on hips, asking her what she was going to do about them. No right to accuse Adam because she had no right to know about it in the first place, having trespassed on his property. And, finally she reasoned, if you think reasoning has anything to do with any of this, no right to accuse him when he had rung, three times now, to say he wanted to see her and she had always rejected him.

But it was clear that Adam wanted her back. And, now that she thought about it, with this extra dimension to him, he was suddenly more attractive to Sarah than ever. Who knows the hurt that kind of triangle of human relationships would inflict! She rang him at work. Felicity, Adam's PA, with whom she had almost become a bosom pal, given all Sarah's unrequited phone calls during their affair (I won't say love affair, because I can remember how things were with Adam even if Sarah seems to be suffering from emotional amnesia at this time), seemed surprised to hear from her.

'Hi, Felicity,' said Sarah cheerfully. 'I'm returning Adam's call.'

'Are you really?' said Felicity, as if Sarah had just said something highly improbable.

When Adam came to the phone, Sarah found that her well-prepared speech, for which she had jotted down just a few notes, did not come out like what she had intended it to.

'Adam, hi, I got your message, I had no plans to ring back but I thought it might be something that wasn't you know about us but maybe another thing that you had to say so I rang but I am glad that you rang and I'm sorry I put the phone down on you which was incredibly childish of me and I just want to tell you to let you know that I am really glad you rang and in fact I also want you to know that I never stopped thinking about you.'

There was a dreadful silence. Could she cope with being married to a bisexual? she was wondering. She remembered reading an article about it once in *Marie Claire*. About a woman who was married to a guy for twenty years, who had three kids with him, before she realised that he'd had a steady male mistress (master?) for the last fifteen years of those twenty. This woman had been devastated.

But it would be different for Sarah. She would know about it right from the start. It was the deception that was the worst thing, and Adam would not be deceiving her. She would have to remember to pop into Waterstone's and see if they had a self-help book about it.

'Adam, are you still there?' she asked, coming back from her reverie of preoccupations.

'Yes, Sarah, I am but I'm at work, you know, it's kind of difficult to talk.'

Of course. How stupid of her. He couldn't pour out his heart, his angst, his commitment to this other man versus his yearnings for her over the phone in the office.

'Sarah, we really need to talk.'

'Yes, we do need to talk,' echoed Sarah urgently. 'I really do feel such a fool having put the phone down on you and ignored your call. I've behaved like an idiot. Adam, I want you to know that I'm really pleased that you've called again so we can make a fresh start.'

'It's not going to be that easy,' Adam said in a semi-whisper.

'Relationships never are easy,' said Sarah, wise like the old hermit who lives at the top of the hill. 'But we can sort it out, don't worry. It'll take time and we'll both have to work at it, but we can sort it out. When do you want to meet?'

'Today, lunchtime today.'

God, he really is keen, thought Sarah with a lick of pleasure. It was already gone eleven. But he was right. No more games. No more pretence. He wanted to see her. She wanted to see him. 'How about L'Escargot at one, OK?'

'No, not there, let's go to that sandwich bar in Covent Garden.'

Where we always used to meet, thought Sarah dreamily over her irritation that their Great New Relationship was going to be baptised in a sandwich bar rather than the glamorous setting of her favourite French restaurant.

She had less than two hours to make herself look amazing and by God, she was going to meet that challenge. Nicole Farhi came out of the 'best occasion' end of her wardrobe. Something greasy in a little pot made her look as if she'd just flown in from the West Indies without the jet lag or the mosquito bites. The Carmens were whacked into her locks.

Sod James and his shenanigans, she muttered to herself as the mascara got caked on. I've always thought that Adam would come round eventually, she's thinking. I've always know that it would take him time to face up to his real feelings about me. OK, so there's this problem with his thing about men, but he could well grow out of that. Come to think of it, perhaps last night had been just a final farewell to that guy before he made a real commitment to me.

Female intuition.

She arrived at one and Adam was there, but, significantly, not at their usual table. She was dressed as if she was going to a first night at the Opera House round the corner, not for a diet Coke and tuna sarnie in Donato's.

'Adam!' She flung herself into what should have been his arms, but as he didn't reach out to her, she ended up nuzzling his chest and chin in a peculiar way.

'Adam! Adam! Adam!'

This is Sarah demonstrating joy at seeing him.

'Adam!'

Hang on a sec, I think there's a couple more still to come.

'Adam! Adam!'

Some of these sounded like she was about to come,

114

some like she was his headmistress and had just found him tossing off in the toilets, some like he'd just stepped on her big toe. Quite a range.

'Hello, Sarah,' said Adam, without range. 'Do you want a drink?'

'Yes, I'll have a cappuccino thanks. And have you ordered food yet?'

'No, I'm not eating,' said Adam curtly. 'I'll get you your coffee.' He jumped up and returned a few moments later with her drink.

'Thanks, Adam,' Sarah gushed on. 'You're looking well. How's work? I saw your article in *PR Week* – not bad!'

Adam stared into his Coke can and gulped. 'Sarah,' he said, 'I've got something to ask you.' Omigod, she thought, he's not going to propose now, is he? 'Sarah, I want to meet you to ask you if you will . . .'

'Yes, Adam . . .'

'. . . go and have a check up. Don't be alarmed, I had an AIDS test recently, so I don't think you need to worry about that. But I've got a few other complications and it's just as well that you get yourself checked out. I've got the name of a really good doctor if you need one.'

The taste of coffee turned foul in Sarah's mouth. 'Is that what you wanted to see me for?'

'Yes,' said Adam, with obvious relief that his speech was over. 'I'm ringing round to all my old partners and I'm taking the time to see them face to face. It seemed like the right thing to do,' he added, as if, should you wish to pin a medal on his Armani jacket, he wouldn't mind as long as it didn't leave a pinprick. 'I think it's better that I leave now, Sarah. I hope one day we can be friends. I've paid for your coffee.'

Just then, the Nancy Sinatra song came on the radio in the café. What do you get when you fall in love. You get enough germs to catch pneumonia. After you do, he'll never phone you.

Those DJs, I swear they're psychic.

Thirteen

Dinner with Suzanne that evening no longer seemed like the best of ideas. Much as she cared for the woman, another detailed analysis with her of the intricate failings of the male gender was no longer appetising. But by the time she rang to cancel, Suzanne had already left.

When Sarah and Suzanne met for dinner, they always met at the same, up-tight Italian restaurant just off the New King's Road. Forget the classless society: life in this restaurant had only one rule of social status: were you in *Hello* or weren't you?

If you were, this restaurant deemed you a Favoured One and all manner of manna from heaven would be showered on your head as you entered its Tuscan portals.

If you weren't, things were not so *bello*. You had to give up your table by 9 o'clock; any attempts you made at a suitable pronunciation of the dishes listed on the illegible designer menu were greeted with the same snooty snarl of contempt – 'Tagglitelly? Aah, you mean tahliatelle' – your plates were snatched away from you before you had quite finished; your bill was thumped on the table with equal alacrity just as you were beginning to dare to relax at the end of your meal; and the frothy bits on your cappuccino were of highly dubious origin.

Selections started the moment you walked through

the door. Favoured Ones were greeted with the full force of the manager, Alfredo Gambetta from Napoli (*né* Colin Dugmore from Croydon) who missiled his ample self at the celebs as they entered, prostrating and salivating in sycophantic ecstasy, practically coming with delight at the prospect of having one of their famous bums on one of his chairs for the evening, exclaiming in the broken English which is *de rigueur* for Italian restaurateurs, 'Marvellous, you looking marvellous. Younger every time I see you. So come, come, we have the best table prepared just for you.'

You can tell who the Favoured Ones are because their photos line the walls behind you, almost putting you off your pastasciutta, lots of grinning faces with too much make-up and black ink scribbled oh-so-casually all over their rhinoplasty saying meaningful stuff like 'To Alfredo – grazzi for the best carbonara in London.'

Frequent as Sarah's visits were, delectable as were her charms, she had failed to tell the world via the pages of the aforementioned journal about the heartache of her last divorce, or to display her newly born twins, conceived only after years of anguish, or to invite readers into her stately home, now lovingly restored after many wanton years of neglect from her titled husband's first wife.

Sarah was not, therefore and alas, eligible for this lavish treatment. Like all the other non-VIPs, grateful to be able to fork out sums well over the odds for the privilege of being able to enter this gastronomic temple, she was no more than tolerated by all the staff.

Unfortunately, Suzanne wouldn't hear of going anywhere else. Her ex, Stuart, often came to this place, and although she would never admit to it, she always went there in the hope that she would bump into him again and he would realise just what a mistake he had made by dumping her for his personal trainer a week before their wedding.

'So what's up?' said Suzanne, stuffing a Marlboro

into her dewy lips while surreptiously scanning each table for a Stuart red alert.

'What's up?'

'Yes. What's up. I saw you a couple of days ago and I quote "life had never been better". Now you look like shit.'

'Thanks, Suzanne. Now I remember why you're my best friend.'

'That's right, and don't you forget it,' said Suzanne, letting her stomach out again under the table. Stuart wasn't there. 'You're still as gorgeous as ever, of course, but you look sad and blue. I assume the dinner with El Boss was not a success, or is it more problems with golden boy from the PR agency?'

'Well, yes.'

'Yes? Yes what?'

'Yes both of those things. Especially Adam.'

'Come on, Sarah, you know I don't speak Klingon fluently. What does especially Adam mean? Do you mean it's over with him?'

'I hope so.'

'You hope so?'

'Well, I hope he hasn't left any lasting mementoes of his affection in my bloodstream. We met today. He told me he thinks I ought to get a check-up.'

Suzanne dropped her fork. 'It's not what I think it is, is it?'

Sarah shrugged impatiently. 'No, not that. I don't think so, anyway. Look, I don't know. I don't want to think about it right now.'

'Well, have you at least arranged to see your doctor?'

'Not yet. I think I'm too scared to know what it is. I don't know. I'll think about it. Anyway, enough about me, I'm sick of talking about me and thinking about me. What about you? You're looking absolutely wonderful. I guess you're well and truly over Stuart by now. How long has it been, three months?'

'Yeh, something like that.'

'Have you ever been tempted to get back with him?'

'God no!'

'I suppose that stint he pulled with the woman from the gym was the last straw, right?' Suzanne shrugged. 'Well, anyway, I must admit you're right, Suzanne. I am feeling low. I'm feeling . . .'

'Yes?'

'Well, I'm feeling that what I really want in life now is just the closeness of a really loving friendship with a man. You know. A man I could ring in the afternoon to tell him what I'd had for lunch, how work was going. A man I could cook a nice meal for every so often, who'd want to cook a nice meal for me sometimes too. Someone you can just go out and see a good film with, then have a meal and have a chat about it. Go to a dinner party with him. Give a dinner party with him. It's funny, isn't it? Have you ever had that feeling that you're only thinking something for the first time when you hear yourself saying it, like I'm talking to you now, hearing myself say all these things, and I know that this is the problem, this is what I really want. To have a man get to know my friends and my family, become part of my life. Now, to me, these seem like they're very simple things, but of all the men I know and I have known, there just aren't any who are capable of just that kind of, you know, simplicity. Do you know what I'm going on about, Suzanne? The older ones are weighed down by their hang-ups, their work, their ex-wives, their current wives, their mortgages, their kids. And the younger ones are even worse. They're so bloody analytical. All they want to know is – What am I really looking for in myself? – In life? – Why do women never really understand me? – Am I gay? – And has *Match of the Day* started yet? Do you know what I mean, Suzanne?'

Suzanne had started crying.

'Oh, God, Suzanne, I'm sorry, I'm being terribly depressing aren't I?' Sarah felt the tears welling up in her own eyes. It was good to have a friend who cared so much about her, who understood her so well. Suzanne had certainly enjoyed her own share of problems with Stuart. Sarah's outpourings must have hit a nerve.

Suzanne was sobbing loudly into her napkin.

'Darling, I'm sorry, cheer up. I've upset you with all my tales of doom and gloom, haven't I?' Suzanne's sobs slowly crescendoed until they had an edge of hysteria. 'Come on, Suzie, I was only thinking aloud, surely what I said hasn't upset you that much, has it?'

Suzanne held her head up just long enough to howl 'Stuart' before submerging it again in the folds of her napkin.

'Stuart. Of course. I guess you're still really cut up about him, aren't you, Suzie? I'm sorry. Did all that stuff I was saying bring it all back?'

From deep in the depths of her wailing, her head still buried in its white cotton shroud, Suzanne's arm slowly rose up, the finger pointing towards the entrance of the restaurant.

Sarah turned round. It was Stuart. Stuart who has walked in with – well, I won't say, but if I just tell you she's rich, she's famous and she has been on the, wait for it, cover, repeat cover, of *Hello!* – well, I think you'll get my meaning. Most Favoured of all Favoured Ones. Taking Favoured One status to new dizzy heights. No wonder no one believes in God in heaven any more when there are gods like these roaming around on the face of the earth.

Alfredo/Colin-to-his-mum was going delirious, making himself dizzy running round in circles on the spot, forgetting the accent, mentally preparing a new space on the wall for the signed photo, wishing the folks back home in Shirley could see him now.

While their centre court table was being prepared, Stuart and the woman were embracing – you know, as one does when one is casually waiting for a table in a restaurant – and when I say embrace I mean serious embrace: a full, clinched snog with copious oral fluid exchange.

Suzanne could not cope. Her sobbing mutated from a stifled gurgle to a tribal holler. She jumped up from the table and pounced on the object of her desire, flinging the frenzied Alfredo to one side. 'You bastard, Stuart. That tongue was down my throat last night.'

Graphic, explicit, somehow an odd thing to say. But let's face it, people do say odd things when they get upset.

'Come on,' said Sarah grabbing her by the arm. 'We're going.' It was unfortunate that going meant brushing past the entwined ones to get to the door.

'You shit. After everything you told me, everything you promised me,' yelled Suzanne. Stuart was unperturbed. Hey, this kind of grief is kinda what you expect when you're Chelsea's answer to Tom Jones.

'Suzanne, let's just leave,' said Sarah.

'Yes, Suzanne, listen to your friend,' said Stuart, casting an appreciatively greasy eye over Sarah and wondering why Suzanne had never introduced her to him. Sarah finally managed to shove her way out of the door, shove some Japanese tourists aside just as they were getting into a cab and shove Suzanne into it.

'I thought you told me it was all over with him,' she said. But Suzanne buried her head in Sarah's lap and refused to speak. 'It's OK, it's OK. I understand,' said Sarah, stroking her friend's hair. 'Come on, we'll go to a club, have a dance, have a few drinks and just forget about men for a while. How does that sound?' Suzanne carried on tie-dying Sarah's skirt with her mascara, but as she didn't say no, Sarah, knowing her friend, concluded that this was a yes.

By the time the taxi drew up at the club, the smudged make-up on Suzanne's face looked like she was ready for a walk-on part in *Worzel Gummidge*. Fortunately the club was very dark and it was the kind of place that was desperate for anything under forty in a skirt. Sarah administered cosmetic first-aid to her friend in the loo and then dragged her up to the bar for a large G&T.

'You know, Suzanne, I thought we were friends. I thought you felt you could talk to me about anything. What was all that stuff about not caring about Stuart any more? Why aren't you more honest with me? Why didn't you just come straight out with it and say you were still hurting over him?'

'Oh Sarah, don't lecture me, I don't know why I didn't tell you, sometimes it's difficult to talk to you, you seem so prudish about men, you never want to go out with anyone, you're so critical of them all the time and frankly the ones you do go out with are all jerks who treat you like shit. How come such a smart woman like you ends up with pricks all the time?'

'OK, OK, now who's lecturing. I'm sorry I asked. I'm just trying to show you I care about you, Suzie. I know I'm not exactly perfect myself.'

'So are you going to answer my question?'

'What question?'

'Why someone like you always ends up with bastards.'

'Suzanne, I suppose it's because—'

Just then, a hand plonked itself, Dixon of Dock Green-like, on Sarah's shoulder. It's Ralph.

'Ralph? What are you doing in a place like this?'

'Why? Do you expect me to live in a cave when I'm not in the office? I've come along with a group from work: we found out that we won that press ad award today. I tried ringing you to ask you along but Anita said you weren't in work today, you weren't feeling too good. From the looks of it you've made a speedy recovery!'

'No, well, I was feeling bad, but—'

'Hey, don't worry, it's none of my business, I was only winding you up,' he laughed. Noticing Suzanne, Ralph held out his hand. 'Hello, I'm Ralph, a colleague of Sarah's from the agency.'

'Well, hello, Ralph,' says Suzanne, with a look to her friend that decoded as: you could do a lot worse than him for starters, sweetheart.

'Can I get you both a drink?' said Ralph.

'Oh no, thanks,' said Sarah, 'we were just . . .'

'She means, I was just going. The babysitter goes mad if I get back late. Goodbye, Sarah darling. Have a lovely time, I'll ring you.'

'But Suzanne!' squealed her pal. As Suzanne kissed Sarah goodbye She whispered into her ear: 'Shut up and go for it, will you? He likes you! He's nice!' Then Suzanne disappeared into the crowd with a smile and a wink at Ralph.

'She looks nice, is she a good friend of yours? She seems young to have a kid.'

'Suzanne doesn't have a kid.'

'So what was that stuff about a babysitter?'

'Oh, well, you know, I think she was trying to be kind.' God, does everything have to be spelt out to this dork, Sarah wondered.

After a few more seconds, the penny dropped and Ralph got quite excited. Sarah must have been telling her friend she liked him. That's why she made up the babysitter story. Perhaps tonight was the night, then. 'So, how about that drink,' he said enthusiastically.

'OK,' said Sarah with gracious indifference, watching the silk-clad cellulite of her friend bobbing away into the crowd.

If only Sarah weren't so vain, she'd wear her glasses more often. Then, as she accepted the glass from Ralph, she would have seen that her friend didn't make it as far as the door. She would have seen a tall and sweaty guy grab Suzanne by the arm and ask her to dance. She would have seen him, a-huffin and a-puffin, gyrating round like one of those nerdoids in the crowd on *Top of the Pops* in the sixties, drinking champagne from the bottle to the delight of his companions. She would have seen him muscle up to Suzanne on the slow dance and start licking the insides of her ears and stuffing his hand up her skirt on the dance floor. Then she would have seen them leave together.

Perhaps it's just as well Sarah is so vain. She wouldn't have wanted to see her hero James behave like that just yet, otherwise she might never have considered going out with him, and we'd have no story.

Fourteen

'So,' said Sarah haughtily and defensively to Ralph, 'I suppose you're going to ask me why I didn't get back to you on that charity business. Look, I'm sorry, everything's a bit hectic at the moment. I had meant to come and talk to you but I just didn't . . .'

He looked at this woman, the woman he'd already decided wasn't that nice a woman anyway, the woman he couldn't stop thinking about.

'Well, yes, OK. Look, I'm not keen on talking about work out of work, but let's just get this one out of the way. I'll admit that I'm a bit surprised you went ahead and used my idea but not my charity. And that you didn't feel you could talk to me about it, before or afterwards.'

'No, Ralph, that's not true, I was going to come and discuss it with you but I've just been, well, really snowed under recently.'

'Come on, Sarah. We're all busy. There's only two floors between us, and a telephone extension number if you haven't got the guts to see me face to face.'

'Ralph, calm down, please. I was going to talk to you about it, but I've been busy, I just told you. And you must realise that I made the right decision, that whales and ozone layers just aren't the right kind of thing for this project.'

They glowered at each other. They both knew she was right about the choice of charity. Hers was better.

But she could have made it happen with his. Or at least given it a try. Or at least talked to him about it. Ralph's head ached. His heart ached. He wanted her.

'OK, OK, look I'm not going to argue about it. It's academic now anyway. Why don't we have another drink and make friends, what can I get you?'

'No, Ralph, thanks, I want to leave. It's late, look it's almost midnight, and I've had too much to drink already.'

'Come on then, Cinderella, I'll drive you home.' (Geddit? Cinderella – almost midnight – our Ralph's a hoot, isn't he?)

Sarah was surprised when she saw the sporty Mazda MX5 – she'd expected something much more pedestrian, if you'll pardon the choice of epithet, from Ralph in his choice of car. She got in, sat back and shut her eyes. She really was feeling exhausted: first the scene with Adam at lunchtime, then with Suzanne in the restaurant, now the telling off from Ralph, of all people. What a day – it was like living through an episode of *Brookside*.

When she opened her eyes, she saw that, instead of heading west, they were going south towards Battersea. 'Ralph, what are you doing? I told you I live just off Notting Hill Gate.'

'I know. But I thought we might take a short cut there via Brighton.'

'Brighton?'

'Yes, why not? It's not that late and we'll be there in half an hour. We can go for a walk along the shore and I know a place where you can eat oysters until 4 a.m.'

'Ralph, cut the crap. I have no desire to go to Brighton. I hate oysters.' Even so, she was not unimpressed by this act of initiative from the Milky Bar Kid. It was a rather lively idea, to banter off to Brighton in the middle of the night. Methinks the lady doth not protest enough.

'Don't worry, you'll love it when we get there. Why

not have a sleep on the way down if you're really tired? I'll wake you up when we arrive.'

'Ralph, I feel as if I'm being kidnapped.'

'You're no kid, Sarah. Admit it, you quite like the idea. Do you want some music?'

'No, that's OK. We can talk.'

Ralph breathed a silent sigh of relief, and the little car sped off due south.

'What did you mean, in the club, when you said it was academic?'

'What was academic?' said Ralph, playing for time.

'You know. About my not using your charity.'

'Oh, that.' He might as well tell her. He had nothing to lose at the agency, and it was beginning to look as if he might have something to gain with Sarah. 'Well, this is still strictly hush-hush, but I've accepted the offer from Mark and Paul to join their agency. I'm going to tell the Colonel next week.'

'Who's the Colonel?'

'The Colonel? You know, Colonel Sanders. James. You must have heard people call him that.'

'No, I haven't, actually. Why Colonel Sanders?'

'You know. Finger-licking . . . Oh well, it doesn't matter. What matters is that I'm finally out of that place.'

'I had no idea you disliked it so much.'

'Yes, the job is really getting me down. I'm stressed out, hung up, miserable. I'm thirty-three and just not making it. If you're not making it when you're thirty-three, you've got very little chance of ever doing it.'

'But you've got a great account.'

'Great, what's so great about it? The charity account in an ad agency is just a gesture. My life's beginning to feel like a gesture in that place. I can't stand being at the agency any more, the politics, the bullshit, those endless directors' meetings like the re-creation of some feudal court where we all sit in a circle round King James and suck up to him in turn. I can't bring myself

127

to do it, that's why I'm not going anywhere in the company. I sit through those meetings in abject silence, angry at them, angrier at myself. I hear them make ridiculous decisions based on ridiculous judgements. I could make a real contribution, helping them avoid countless fuck-ups and grasp countless more new opportunities, but instead I just sit there week after week, listening to myself saying nothing. I just can't be bothered to get involved in any of that shit. Especially James, I mean the guy is an embarrassment.'

'Ralph!' cried Sarah, as if he had blasphemed.

'What?'

'James is not an embarrassment, he's the best man in the business.'

'Which Moonie centre have they just let you out of? A few years ago I'd have agreed with you, but not now. He's got stuck in a time warp, no new ideas, and absolutely no inkling about people management and how to run a business. Have you noticed how many people have left DFDDG in the past couple of years? And even professionally, did you see what he made the creatives churn out for that new Glisten product for Birksomes? You can't take a guy like that seriously. You certainly can't spend fifty hours a week working for him.'

'If you have such a low opinion of James and the agency, why did you ever take the job on?'

'Because it was a time in my life when it seemed important to me to be doing something more important. I was thirty, I was running my own business, doing on-pack promotions, for Christ's sake. Which means crap like free tea towels when you collect ten tokens on your sweet wrappers, or a chance in a million to win a trip to Australia if you send in enough plastic margarine lids.'

Sarah laughed. Omigod, she thought. Ralph's said something and I've laughed. Ralph, the man with less personality than Spotty Dog has said something that I've enjoyed listening to.

'Whose company was it?'

'My own. I started that business up myself, from scratch, at twenty-five. The archetypal eighties bloody whizzkid. I made Gordon Gekko look like a Boy Scout.'

'You started and ran your own company?'

'Yes. Is that so amazing to you?'

'Well, yes. I mean no, but I had no idea you'd done that.' Sarah is, after all, like all women, a bit of a snob and finds something irresistibly appealing about a man who owns his own business. Suddenly she found herself wishing she had touched up her make-up before they left the club. For Ralph? Yes, for Ralph. 'Was it very hard work?'

'God, yes. I never slept, about ten hours of sleep in five years, or that's how it felt. I worked every inch of the day and then some. And when I wasn't working, I was partying off my exhaustion. I was making a dosh of money, enough to show everyone – friends, women, parents, me – that I was in with the in-crowd, whoever the hell they were. I had the car, I had the flat, the paintings, the holidays, and always, of course, the pretty girl, lots of pretty girls.'

Sarah was amazed. Was this really Mr Blue Peter talking, the man with all the sex appeal of Postman Pat, going on about partying and cars and women? She could tell from the tone of his voice that this was genuine stuff, not some chat-up bravado-speak. She just wished there was some way she could run a comb through her hair and get thirty seconds on her own in front of a mirror.

'Lots of pretty girls, eh?'

'Yes, but never a decent relationship with any one of them. Lots of meaningless, empty one-night stands, you know what I mean?'

'Well, er, sure.'

'And it caused such grief, this lifestyle, always tears, always traumas. I just couldn't understand how women worked. I couldn't understand where I was going wrong. When I slept with them, I thought it was what they wanted and what I wanted. But women are so dishonest, with themselves and with others. Sorry, Sarah – do you mind me ranting on like this? Only I really feel like I can talk to you.'

'No, no,' said Sarah, whose ugly duckling of a date has suddenly turned into a glamorous swan. 'No, I'm interested to know what you think.'

'Well, I'll give you an example. There was this one woman, some kind of TV presenter, you'd know who she is, but I won't name names.'

Sure, nodded Sarah, her I-am-impressed dial shooting up silently into the red zone.

'I was pissed out of my head at a party after some first night do at a theatre. She'd been following me around all evening. It was late, almost dawn. I wanted to leave, but, you know, I didn't fancy going home to bed on my own, so I asked her if she wanted to come back with me. Her face lit up like a Christmas tree, she seemed so pleased. All I said was, do you want to come back with me, and she said yes.

'Pretty simple communication, you'd have thought, I offered and she accepted. I didn't exactly have to half-Nelson her into the taxi. And when we got back, I said, would you like a drink and she said no, so I said, right, well, shall we go to bed then, and she said OK. All straightforward so far, wouldn't you agree? So I wait for her to warm up the bed a bit, and then I got in after her. But just as I started to get stuck in, I felt my head sobering up, just that tad too early, I mean just as I was about to do the dirty deed. Give it another three minutes, it would have been all over and I'd have gone to sleep and everything would have been all right.

'But my head starts to clear, faster than I could have ever wished it would, and I look down and I think, Jesus Christ, what am I shafting here, as I see this sad small white face peering up at me, with a look that seems to say, go on, you wicked man, puncture me, wound me with your Black & Decker, you know, the true victim stuff. And I'm thinking, sweetheart, if you're here, it's as much because you want it as me. In fact, it's probably more.

'So I look down and I think to myself, shall I stop, shall I go on, and my old man's peering up at me and asking, so, are we stopping or are we starting, Ralphie baby? and I can't decide whether it's too embarrassing to stop or too gruesome to continue. And as I'm not one for embarrassments of any kind, I shut my eyes, think of Michelle Pfeiffer and Ian Wright holding the Cup Winners' Cup and I forge ahead and poke my confused willy into her.

'She looked as if she was hating every minute, although she couldn't have been enjoying it any less than I was. And I swear, I'm panting my way to some kind of conclusion inside her, thanking God for my fertile imagination in the face of such dire reality, and she's lying there with her back to me, completely immobile, and I think God, maybe she's dead, so as much to check whether this is the case as to be polite, I say are you OK? and she says, not really no, and I say, what's wrong? and she says she feels cheap. She feels cheap? She feels cheap! How does she think I feel? Well, since they never ask, I'll tell you. I feel lonely and frustrated and unhappy. I feel like a tart that I've done that stuff with such a cold and miserable and mixed-up woman.'

Sarah was riveted. She was transfixed. How could she have been so wrong about this man. What a lad! What a boy! He was going to first nights, getting drunk, picking up women, generally getting a life in a major way. 'So what happened then?' said the born-again Ralphite.

'Well, the next morning, I invent an urgent business meeting (even though it's a Saturday) and she goes. She leaves me her phone number on my kitchen notice board – I guess that's in case I ever want another wild and crazy evening of fun-packed sex with her some-time. Of course, I don't ring her, and a few days later some woman I've never met calls me to tell me what a shit I am and how I've used her best friend. And I think, what's to use? And the friend tells me that I should buy myself that month's *She* magazine because there's an article in there about hit and run lovers like me, men who aren't capable of any kind of real relationship with women. The friend advises me that I might be able to learn something from it.

'I look at the phone in disbelief – is this woman serious, I ask myself. She tells me that the article explains how most men find it very hard to communicate with women, and use sex as a cover for their inadequacy. Well, I say, you learn a new thing every day. I'm glad to have confirmed *She* magazine's no doubt extensive and very thorough research into this matter, I say. That's right, sneer, says the friend, cynicism is always the best defence for fear. Fear? I say. Like, I'm completely lost now. She starts talking me through what I'm supposed to be afraid of, but I hang up.

'You tell me, Sarah, where I'm going wrong. Things always seem to start off OK. The first few dates are fine. You get little packages arrive on your desk which contain a CD with a special song highlighted in dayglo pink highlighter on the songsheet, and when you play that song, the lyrics are all along the lines of baby, baby, never thought it could be true, that I could love someone so much as I do you, doobee doobee doobee doo. You get cuddly toys of little pink pigs or tigers sent to your home, with notes that say "To my little pork pie," (great line to send a Jewish guy) or "To my little tiger – ggrrrrr!! wait till I get my claws in you," and you think to yourself, my God, is this crap from that incredibly sophisticated and intelligent business-woman I chatted up last Tuesday?

'Then, one day, out of the blue, you're no longer a porky pig, or a naughty tiger, or a doobee doo. You're a first-class bastard, and you've messed up her life and she's in despair, all because of you. And all this because you've been up-front, open, honest, yourself. You've had sex with her when you've had a hard-on, and gone to sleep when you haven't. You've rung her during the day if you thought of her and not rung her if you didn't. Perhaps one night you mentioned that you'd like to see your mates for a drink – you haven't seen them for a while, you've been on too many dates with her. And wham, it's: do you prefer your male friends to me? Er no, as well as. Are you just taking me for granted now? Er no, I'm going for a few drinks with my mates. Suddenly the tear-ducts become waterfalls and the time has come. You are a bastard. You weren't yesterday, but you sure as hell are today. Her life is a mess and it's your fault. Help.

'Then there are the other victims, the ones who, after a few dates, decide that they're going to move in. One evening she turns up at your flat with more stuff than she needs. Just in case. In case of what, you dare not ask. Next evening, she's brought round even more things – no reason given this time – and she's had a copy made of the key you stupidly lent her, and she's in. Fair enough, you think.

'But pretty soon, things start to turn sour. She wants you to change the colour of the towels in the bathroom. You keep too many cans of beer in the fridge (your fridge). If you cut your toenails in bed (your bed) one more time, you can go and sleep on the sofa (your sofa). Suddenly your flat is not your own, your things are not your own, your life is definitely hers. Your diary is scanned avidly for uncensored appointments while you get dressed to work, on the pretext that she's got to find an evening when you can go round to visit her mother.

'Suddenly it's: "Emma? Emma? Who the bloody hell's Emma?"

' "Oh," you say casually as you get your tie just so in

133

the mirror, "she's a girl I used to see, we're having dinner on Tuesday."

' "What, we're living together, and you expect me to wait here at home for you while you spend the evening chatting up your ex-girlfriend?"

'Bravely, you try to explain that you certainly weren't expecting her to wait at home for you. Less bravely, you don't get as far as suggesting that she could always go and spend the night back in her own place for once.

'There's a bit of silence and you think it's settled. How wrong you are. She was only gathering up energy, stoking up the engine for the real onslaught. "How dare you flaunt your ex in front of me. I suppose I'm meant to be challenged by it, threatened by it??"

'Feebly you start to explain that you've known Emma for years, that she's one of your closest friends.

' "Does that mean I'm not your friend, I'm just someone you shaft every night? Is this your way of saying that you aren't happy with the relationship any more?"

'Exhausted, you open your mouth to answer, to explain. Then you think, what's the point, and you just leave to go to work. By the time the teddy wearing the little T-shirt that reads "Sorree" is biked over to your office later that morning, you've had enoughee.'

'So Sarah,' concluded Ralph, 'what's your diagnosis? Where am I going wrong with women?'

Wrong? Who said anything about wrong? As far as Sarah is concerned, this man has just taken his finals in How To Get Sarah Interested In You and passed *summa cum laude*.

'No, well, I don't know Ralph, I think it's just a question of meeting the right woman.'

'So you think there's hope for me yet?'

'Sure,' said Sarah, suddenly finding hope, faith and charity well up inside her for this man, the ex-Pilsbury Doughboy, this new Lorenzo El Magnifico.

For the rest of the journey, they made amiable small

talk, until they got to Brighton and found Ralph's oyster bar. She tried a couple of oysters, only to do him a favour, and found she actually quite liked them. Ralph said he loved oysters because they reminded him of women, the salty, tangy taste made him think of women's sexuality.

By now Sarah's hairdryer speed was on maximum volume, maximum heat and she was almost audibly whirring to make up for lost time with this man before she blew a fuse. After a while, people pushed the tables back in the café and started dancing – hey, it's that kind of a place.

Suddenly Ralph grabbed her by the waist and was leading her clumsy feet through a sequence of some very expert rock and roll. Sarah was flushed and breathless, and that's even before she started the dancing.

After a while, they decided to go out on to the beach for a walk along the shore to cool down.

'So there's never been anyone special in your life?' said Sarah, about to present him with her CV for the job.

'Yes, since you ask. There has. Once there was a woman, a very special woman, but it ended badly.'

Oh, goody, just the sort of thing Sarah loves.

'Very badly?' she asked hopefully.

'Yes,' nodded Ralph. 'Very badly indeed.'

Wunderbar.

'Did you end it?'

'It's more complicated than that. This was one woman I actually asked to move in with me. Begged her, would be closer to the mark. Her name was Sally. Sally was lovely. She was going out with a good friend of mine when I met her. A good ex-friend,' Ralph added quietly and bitterly. 'Anyway, he and Sally turned up half way through a dinner party given by mutual friends. I was the spare man that they were trying to pair off with the spare woman – neither of us was interested. When Sally arrived, I could see her walk through the front door from where I was sitting in the dining-room. I can remember the very first second I saw her, and it was like someone had slogged the back of my head with a brick. She hadn't seen me – she and my friend were making their excuses for their late arrival to our hosts in the hall. Sally and he were red in the face, giggling. Whatever nonsense they were coming up with, it was clear that they were late because they'd been giving each other a good shagging somewhere.

'Right,' says Sarah. The night sea wind was chipping round them but she was not cooling down.

'The moment I saw her, I felt a belch of heat in my chest and in my groin. The chest was envy, the sourest envy of my dear friend, a man who had been through some shitty times and who deserved a break. I'd never seen him so excited, so animated, so totally happy and all I could do was hate him for it. Some friend I was. The groin was Sally. A hot flush of the groin. I thought my dick was going to explode. My knees were knocking together under the table. And you know what. She turned her beautiful head round and saw me sitting there, and it was the same for her. She still had my friend's sperm squelching away inside her, the tracks of his saliva all up her thighs, but when she saw me, she was mine.'

'Right,' said Sarah, fanning the hot flushes with her hand.

'That dinner party was such a nightmare, my God. My friend introduced her to me. I took her hand and held it. I felt like saying, look everyone, I'm sorry but I have to leave with Sally and have sex with her now. I couldn't let go of her hand. I felt the blood in her fingers and it felt like it was my blood. Eventually someone, my friend I think, had to prise us apart and try to make a joke of it. But it was no joke. They sat her next to me at dinner. I drank myself silly trying to stay

136

sober so I wouldn't do anything stupid. My friend was, at first, ecstatic, post-coital, gurgling on with lots of stories about Sally and him, him and Sally. Our hosts laughed obligingly. Sally and I were silent, we did not laugh. All we wanted to do was to rub bodies, exchange fluids, stick as many parts of ourselves into each other as was possible.

'By the time coffee arrived, I gave up and reached for her hand under the table. We sat there, holding hands, as my friend grew quieter and quieter, like one of those battery operated toys whose battery is just about to run out. He wasn't stupid, he could sense something was up, even if he couldn't see us clutching each other under the table. The only people talking were the woman I should have been holding hands with and the hosts. If this woman, sitting to my left, could see what Sally, sitting to my right, and I were up to, she was too considerate, probably too appalled, to say anything. I left as soon as possible and shoved a piece of paper with my phone number and address on it into Sally's hand when we said goodbye. My note said – I'll wait for you. Real C-movie stuff, eh?'

'Tee, hee,' giggled Sarah obligingly and reverently, putting her arm through Ralph's.

'Sally left, with my friend, and – she told me later – they had a terrible and obvious row in the car even before he'd turned on the engine. She arrived at my place in a taxi ten minutes after I did and I have never fucked anyone the way I fucked Sally that night. I mean, it really was fucking, you know, it wasn't sex, it wasn't making love, it was just real fucking. Each time I felt myself coming, I panicked that it was soon going to end, so I'd have to do it again straight away.

'The next morning I was two hours late for work. My dick was raw, my balls felt like marshmallows. I rang her once every hour, more if I couldn't help it, to tell her I was thinking of her and to check she still existed. Is this boring you, Sarah?'

137

Boring her? She's transfixed. 'No, that's OK,' Sarah whimpered, as Ralph put his arm round her burning shoulders.

'I went on like this for weeks and weeks. Once I almost fainted on the tube on the way to work after a particularly robust weekend. I knew that I ought to try and make an effort to put the relationship on a more non-physical footing, do normal things like go out to the cinema, see friends, have a proper conversation with each other, all the stuff you're meant to do. But we kept putting it off, like a diet, till tomorrow. I'll start tomorrow. My boxers developed a nervous tic thinking about her when I wasn't with her. I grew lean and muscular doing press-ups, sit-downs and God knows what other physical jerks all over her. I began skipping meals because shopping, cooking, even sitting up to gulp down a take-away, meant too much time in a vertical position away from her.

'We hardly spoke to each other, and then it was usually only fairly anatomical stuff, not much about the world outside our personal gymnasium in my bedroom. A couple of times she told me a bit about her job, she said she was a designer for some corporate design outfit. Sometimes I'd tell her about mine. But it was just small talk, to punctuate the end of one sweaty session and the beginning of another.

'I couldn't get enough of this woman. I'm not sure why I had this demented passion for her. She was very attractive, but then all the women I have been out with have been very attractive. I don't know. When I think of Sally, I think of her smell. The hotter she got, the more smell there was and it's like I was addicted to it. I gave up taking a shower in the morning so I could still smell her body on me during the day. I'd sit and sniff at my hands at my desk, run my forearms up and down under my nose while I was on the phone. When I shook clients by the hand, it annoyed me that I had to deface the odour of Sally's dried juices with their greasy palms.

'I was twenty-nine when all this happened and still unendearingly naïve. I thought it would go on for ever. No, that's not true. I didn't think much at all about it, about anything that wasn't screwing her. I lost touch with my friends and I guess she did the same. It didn't worry me much; I spent all day with people at the office, and was just happy to get home to the flat at the end of each day to be with her, be in her.'

'Right,' dribbled Sarah. 'So what went wrong?'

'In retrospect, I can see that she must have got very isolated over those four or five weeks we were together. She was spending all her time with me, we didn't really speak to each other. It was only much later that I found out from her mother that the agency had made her redundant one week after we'd met.

'I don't know if it was coincidence. I suppose going into work late, clearly shagged to pieces, didn't help much. But Sally didn't tell me any of this. Her mother said she had been too ashamed to tell me; she thought I would have ended it with her if I'd known she didn't have a job. So she spent her days walking round shops, sitting in libraries and coffee bars, too scared to go back to the flat during the day in case I came home by chance.

'She got in a bad way pretty quickly. I know that now. But when I came home that Thursday evening, when I came home and found her there, I knew none of this, so remember that. God, I'll never forget seeing her there, sitting on the bed, drunk out of her head, all gob and spittle coming frothing out of her mouth like she'd had a fit, with the letters and the empty wine bottles all over the duvet.

'I sat on the bed and took her hand. Sally, Sally, I kept saying. I tried taking her in my arms but she pushed me away. I just sat there stroking her hand which had cuts all over it. I have never seen a woman, or anyone, cry like that, cry, cry, like she was impaled.

' "My God you bastard," she suddenly starts screeching out of her foamy mouth. "How could you?"

' "How could I what, Sally, my love, how could I what?"

'She throws the letters into my face. "That's fucking what," she screams.

'I look at the letters. They're from Jocelyne, my girl-friend when I was twenty-one, twenty-two, twenty-three, my pen-pal who became my lover when I spent time in France in my third year at university. It had petered out, but I had kept those letters as a memento in a box under my bed, along with all my papers and bank statements and God knows what other trash. I'm not sure what had prompted Sally to look under there, under the piles of under-the-bed dust and old pubes and junk, to fish out these letters and make herself so upset.

' "Sally," I yell, grabbing the letters, stuffing them under her dripping nose to show her the dates of the postmarks. "Look! These letters are from six, seven years ago. Look. Look!"

' "That's not the point," she sobs.

' "Why isn't it the point?" I yell. I'm going mad. She's going mad.

' "It's not the point. I thought you loved me."

' "I do love you." I realised then I had never said that to her. As I said it, I wondered whether it was true. "Why do these letters mean I don't love you?"

' "Because you loved her."

' "Yes! I loved her. Loved her. Seven years ago – not now."

' "How can you love me if you loved her, you bastard!"

'I knew then that there was no sense in trying to reason with her. I hoped it was because she was pissed. It wasn't. She was very depressed. She'd been cutting her arms up with the corkscrew, doing all kinds of shit to herself. I called a doctor at five the next morning, she was getting steadily worse, tearing at her skin with her fingernails when I took the corkscrew away from her, and I couldn't cope. She was seeing things, hearing things, talking to people who weren't there. It was a relief when they took her away. They asked me who her next of kin was, the name of her parents, their phone number. I said I had no idea. They asked me how long we had been living together and I said about five weeks. They gave me a filthy look, like I was a criminal.

'When she'd gone, I felt icy. That bedroom, that cubicle of steam and sweat for so many nights, went chill.

'A few days later I got a call from Sally's mother to let me know that Sally was in a clinic and they thought she was going to need months there to help her very severe depression. Her mother was more direct than the ambulancemen. She told me that it was most probably my relationship with her, the way I'd treated her, that had left her like that.

'The way I'd treated her? I didn't remember whipping her into submission. I tried telling the mother that Sally was a grown woman who could make her own decisions, that Sally had wanted the relationship as much as I had. Then I got a barrage of abuse, telling me that Sally was very ill, on heavy medication, suicidal, and it was my fault, my fault because I had treated her like a whore. Sally's mother said she was taking legal advice. I told her I didn't think you could be sued for having an affair with someone. I felt sorry for Sally, but even more pissed off that it was, as a matter of course, My Fault – again.

'I suppose I should have sent flowers, visited or something but I thought that, given the circumstances, it was probably best that I stayed away. So I did nothing. Nothing definitely seemed the best thing to do.'

Now there was silence, with only the crunching of shore gravel under their feet. Sarah shivered. Ralph thought it was because she was cold. 'Come on,' he laughed, hugging her closer to him, 'you must be freezing and I've ranted on for long enough. Let's get back.'

Sarah was already trying to remember what state the flat was in and how clean the duvet cover was. Wow! What a catch. He'd give her a lift home and she'd ask him up. This guy was bad news and she wasn't going to let him get away that easily.

'So, what do you think about my little story, Sarah?'

'I think you can't hold yourself responsible for other people's actions,' she replied inanely. 'It's a two-way street. Women get what they deserve; I mean, like that story you were telling me earlier about the TV presenter, there's no point leading a man on and then crying wolf, is there? Women have to be responsible for themselves, and if they end up getting hurt, somewhere they must have wanted it to happen.'

Read my lips. Straight from the horse's mouth. Which makes the mess that happens to Sarah at the end all the more poignant, don't you think?

'Well, maybe you're right, all I know is I felt very screwed up after that. The whole thing got to me. If I'm going to be honest, not because of Sally's misery, but because of my own. For over a month, I had carried on like a rabbit in overdrive, and I had never stopped to ask myself what I really thought about the woman I was bonking every night and every day-time at the weekends. What did that say about me? I looked back on previous relationships and the pattern seemed pretty much the same. Engage dick – imperative. Engage head, heart, mind – optional. Unlikely. I was burrowing my way through all this female flesh and never creating any kind of rapport with the head at the top of it. Perhaps the magazine survey had got me sussed out after all.'

How was she going to get this guy to shut up and get physical with her? It would be nice to get a bit of a kiss in before she invited him back to the flat. She was going to wait until they get to that next lamppost, so he could see her eyes in the moonlight, and then just turn and grab him.

Ralph was still babbling on. He's not to know he's got twenty paces to screw up in.

'Anyway, after all that happened, I decided to change my lifestyle completely. I gave up the business and got the job at the agency. The experience with Sally was driving me into some kind of mid-life crisis at bloody thirty. It was either the agency or back-packing through the Himalayas until I found a monastery that would have me. Somehow working for James on the con-science-soothing charity account seemed like the more comfortable option.'

'What about girlfriends since then?' teased Sarah, excitedly anticipating a new catalogue of horror stories. Only five paces to go to the lamppost; then she was going to turn to him and say: so how about me as your next candidate?

'Girlfriends?' said Ralph, as the seconds ticked away to his doom. 'Well, since then, I've basically given up women.'

Sarah stopped and looked at him in jaundiced horror, her face in the full glare of the yellow light. 'Given them up?'

'Yes.' Ralph plodded on, head down. 'You know, I was so hung up about women, and me and women specifically, that I preferred to avoid them. I'd go out with my single male friends, get thoroughly slaughtered and go home alone. In a way, this period was quite a good time for me. When I did see women friends for dinner, I stopped assuming that at the end of the meal I was going to sling them over my shoulder and carry them back, caveman-like, to my place as pudding. And here's the nauseating, new man bit, so steel yourself. I actually started to like women. I really liked them, which was great, but I thought that by liking them that also meant not sleeping with them. How could you do that to someone you really liked? You fucked the ones you fancied. The ones you liked you had a good time with. A couple of them suggested, more or less, that they would have been happy to be liked by me and screwed by me as well, but I couldn't cope with that. That kind of concept was way over my head. Only now, now it's different.'

'It is?'

'Yes. Since I met you, Sarah.'

Oh, no Ralph! You're not going to ruin it all by getting nice again are you? Hang on in there, kiddo, don't spoil it! She was mentally smoothing back the duvet for you, she was putting that extra dab of perfume behind her ears, don't blow it all now!

'Not till you met me?'

'Oh, it's all right, Sarah, I know every bloke in the agency wants to pin your knickers to his chest. I know I'm only one in a long queue, probably towards the back of the queue, with the Big Daddy Jimbo at the very front of it. I know you're not really interested in me, so I can confess to you.'

By now they were back at the car. Sarah was visibly upset. What had happened to Darth Vadar?

'That time I asked you out,' Ralph cruised on self-effacingly, with his shipful of tea receding ever more rapidly back towards China as he drove gloomily up the road, 'to the exhibition, and you said yes, I thought I was going to burst with joy.'

Christ, Ralph, we're not back to this, are we?

'I thought that maybe things were going to take a new turn. Maybe, these past few years, I'd been stalling everything, never committing myself, only because I'd been waiting for someone like you to come along. I felt happy for the first time in a long time. This is embarrassing but I tell you what – I stopped outside a jewellers on the way home. I looked at the rings and – I'm dying here – I thought about marriage, babies, the whole works. With you.'

Ralph – get a grip on yourself, boyo.

'I just felt that you were the right one. Everything else had been merely a prelude. You were right for me. Smart, beautiful, confident, you know how to handle men.'

Yes, men, not veggieburgers.

'Then I took you to that sandwich bar. I'd never taken anyone in there before and I suppose, if I'd thought about it, it was a stupid place to go. I should have rung and warned Helen in advance. Helen thinks I'm the son she never had. I like it in there, there are real people doing real jobs and having real conversations, not comparing the costs of poster sites with the precise size of the letter B in a drinks commercial. But the moment we walked in, I knew it was a mistake, with Helen practically asking you what we were going to call the children. She was over the top, I know that – '

– right, so not restrained like you Ralph, my old son?

' – but you, Sarah, well, you were just not very nice really. In fact, I thought you were rather snooty and patronising, and then asking for bacon in a very obviously Jewish sandwich bar, that was a bit crass. When I tried talking to you about the Tony business, you were so defensive. When I tried being friendly, you thought I was being patronising. As we talked, I realised that the real Sarah was not anything like what I had expected, what I had dreamed up. You are really quite a tough and hostile person. I suddenly felt a twinge of panic. I really wanted to make us work. I didn't want to lose you, I didn't want to lose that dream. So I talked you through my idea for integrating our accounts. I thought it was a good idea, I thought it would give us the opportunity to work together. Even though you only seemed

145

half-interested at the time in my suggestion, a few days later I find out that you'd gone ahead and used my idea with your clients, the idea you'd been so apparently indifferent to, you'd gone ahead and done it with another charity, not mine.'

'Oh God, we're not going to dredge up all that again, are we?' said Sarah with total irritation, moving away from him. 'We've been over that. We've dealt with it. We agreed, I did the right thing.'

'No, you agreed. I'm sorry, Sarah, but I've got to sort this one out with you. I just couldn't believe it when I heard it. I've met some tough business types in my time, but you're incredible. No conscience, no sensitivity at all. You didn't bother to come and talk it through with me, explain in advance. I just found out through the office grapevine. Why did you feel that you couldn't discuss it with me, as one colleague to another, if not as friends?'

'Have you finished?' said Sarah.

'Come on Sarah, don't get upset.'

'Don't get upset? You bring me down to this godforsaken place, you slag off the agency, you slag off James, who, by the way, is a better adman than you'll ever, ever be, then you start haranguing me about my professional business practice. Why did you drag me all the way down here to give me a telling off, wouldn't Hyde Park Corner have been just as good a stage for your amateur dramatics? How dare you criticise the way I run my account?'

'Sarah, if it hadn't been for me and my idea, all you were going to do was tart up the packaging. That wouldn't exactly have had them dancing in the aisles, would it? Don't you think I deserved a little more from you?'

'If I'd come to talk to you about it, all you'd have wanted to do was to dissuade me from doing what I had already decided to do. That's why I chose to avoid you. Ralph, I had to do what was right for the business, that's what they pay me for. I'm not here to give you a leg-up when you need one.'

Ouch.

'I've heard some shitty stuff in my time in this business, Sarah, but that takes the biscuit. It's rich enough that you just snitched the idea without giving me any credit for it, but the icing on the cake is using another charity for the sponsorship and the sodding cherry on the cake is not even bothering to tell me about it. You're becoming too callous, too ruthless. You're turning into a media monster. I'd watch out before you go over the edge.'

'Thanks for the analysis. Send me the bill. Meanwhile, you can stuff your biscuits and cakes and cherries, and, if you wouldn't mind stopping the car right now, I'm going to get a cab back to London from this hotel. I suggest you just fuck off back home.'

To her surprise and his, Ralph stopped the car.

Well, you know what they say about the path of true love. But the really sad thing is, as Ralph stormed off alone back to London in his little Japanese number, he thought it was the telling off about the charity business that had blown it for him. But that was the least of Sarah's concerns: what had repelled her was all that lovey-dovey bullshit about wedding rings and liking women and treating them like friends. What kind of man worth his salt does that, I ask you?

Fifteen

When Sarah got back into the office the next morning, a rather agitated Anita advised her that James wanted to see her immediately. Sarah shivered. This was no doubt going to be the Dear John speech, in which he explained that he liked her, admired her, and all that, but he wanted their relationship to be strictly professional, as a polite way of saying she had bored him silly on Tuesday evening. She wasn't surprised. She'd had her chance and blown it. Telling him all that stuff about Adam – she cringed at the thought of it. James must have found her so completely naïve. Fine, we'll keep it professional if that's what he wants, she told herself bravely, let's just get this one over and done with.

When Sarah appeared at his door James scowled and asked the accountant who was in with him to leave them. 'Shut the door and sit down,' he commanded.

'I'll stand, thanks,' said Sarah.

'I said sit fucking down,' yelled James.

She fell with shock into the seat next to her. Like a big grizzly bear, James ambled round the desk and placed himself right in front of her. He looked better than the last time she'd seen him, but still pasty and red-eyed. All that clubbing the night before and other activities ending in ' –ing' with Suzanne afterwards had worn him out.

'So, let's talk about Tuesday, shall we?' he growled.

Sarah shrugged her shoulders and looked down at the ground, waiting to have her sentence read out to her.

'On Tuesday night I was ill,' he announced defiantly. 'I was so ill that the manager at Langan's wanted to call me an ambulance. I was so sick that the cab, instead of taking me home, insisted on driving me round to Charing Cross to make sure I was OK. And you, all you can do it sit on your bum in the restaurant, finish off your coffee, no doubt, and go home! You didn't come out to the reception desk in the restaurant to see if I was all right. You didn't call me at home that night or in the office yesterday to see if I was OK. What sort of a . . . a . . .' – he struggled for words here – 'woman [i.e. monster] are you?! I was suffering from terrible food poisoning. I only came in yesterday, against my doctor's advice, because I had meetings I simply couldn't get out of. What I want to know is, are you always that ruthless with people when they're sick, or is it just me you decide to treat like a leper?'

Good old James, a sort of latter-day Wife of Bath. His philosophy was always to get the telling-off in before others might think to do so. Timing could always outwit justification.

You don't reach the kind of salary that James has without the skill for giving a fairly adventurous interpretation of the facts of any matter when required. It's true that the taxi driver hadn't taken James home. After James had thrown up again all over the back of the cab, the cabbie had booted him out just fifty yards up the road. By then the combination of fresh air outside the restaurant and the lusty purification of his innards meant that James was starting to feel a lot better. He must have puked up the worst of the alcohol, or it just felt like he had. Dick was correspondingly re-animated and so the boys decided to make a night of it.

First of all they dropped in on a friend who by happy chance lived just round the corner from where he been kicked out of the soggy cab. After a happy hour there, they grabbed another taxi and dropped in at Francesca's, shagged Francesca on her leather sofa and borrowed one of her husband's shirts for work the next morning. Good job hubby was in Bahrain. Good job too that he also took a sixteen-and-a-half shirt collar. If there's one thing James can't stand, it's a tight collar.

Sarah was mortified. It hadn't even crossed her mind to ring him afterwards; she'd just assumed he'd had far too much to drink and that he'd gone home to sleep it off. It had never occurred to her that he might have been ill. 'I'm sorry, James. I don't really know what to say.' She stood up and put her hand on his arm. 'I'm really very sorry.'

'Well, all right,' he snarled petulantly. 'I was just a bit put out, that's all. Look, we still need to have a chat about a few things. I'm off tomorrow afternoon to spend the weekend in a place I know out of town, one of these country house hotel jobbies with a pool, tennis courts and all that nonsense, only a couple of hours' drive from here. I've got some work to catch up on, a few ideas to crunch over. How about you joining me and we do a bit of unwinding and brainstorming, get a few things sorted out?'

All the blood went to Sarah's head. He did care about her after all! 'I'd like that, James,' she said, breaking into a big, girlish grin. Girlishness being of course a synonym for foolishness: Sarah's certainly living up to its stereotype here.

'I'll pick you up from your place at around four tomorrow, then, shall I?'

'Fine,' she simpered. She looked deep into James's eyes. In a way, she was thinking, that whole episode has probably done us good. It feels as if we've already formed a kind of bond; an understanding that a meaningful relationship comes with both the rough and the smooth. And James was wondering whether he could wait till Friday evening to get himself up her. Then he remembered that he'd got Mandy coming round that evening, and the panic subsided.

Sarah went back to her office and tried to settle down for the day. It's hard putting up the business-as-usual sign when you've got Cupid doing press-ups in your head, but just in time, Sarah pressed the little work button in her mind and Cupid evaporated.

Sarah flicked impatiently through her post. In the internal private and confidential bag there was that month's set of company accounts, which were also the half-year figures. They made for gloomy reading. With her head immersed in all the little numbers with minus signs in front of them, Sarah did not notice Anita come into her room.

'Shit, aren't they?' opined Anita.

Sarah squealed with shock. 'What are you doing in here? How long have you been standing there? Have you been looking at these figures over my shoulder? You have, haven't you?'

'Don't be daft,' said Anita, settling back on Sarah's executive couch as she lit a ciggy, 'I typed the bloody things, I'm sick of the sight of them.'

'Oh,' said Sarah, peeved. 'I suppose you did.'

'You suppose I did? My bet is that you smart-arse, have-it-all, no-expense-account-spared types never really suppose – you never really think about anything. You think you know it all, you think you're the ones with all the power, but I tell you what, no one knows more than me.'

Oh, dear, secretary's bile, reflected Sarah. 'Of course they don't, Anita,' said Sarah patronisingly, in the tone that one uses to a being with fewer than nine O-levels to their name.

'Look, I tell you what, Sarah,' suggested Anita, carefully dropping her ash on a conspicuous spot in Sarah's deep pile, 'why don't you make an effort, and obviously I mean a real effort, to treat me like a normal person for a few minutes? I mean, I know I'm only a secretary, I know I'm not worthy to wipe the shit from your shoes when you arrive in the morning, but why don't you consider it for once, think about the advantages that it might bring you?'

Sarah had no time for this. 'Look, Anita, I can see you're upset, but I'm not quite sure what it is you're wittering on about. The advantages? What advantages?'

'Right, well, let me spell it out for you. Have you ever considered the fact that, as James's PA, I get to type every document that he sends out? That I get to read every document he receives? That I can switch on the intercom to hear what's being said in his office at any time? I see a lot of things, I hear a lot of things. I know things you just don't know and never will.'

'Oh yes?' said Sarah.

'You see, you're at it again. You just can't help it, can you? Just can't stop treating me like I'm the hair down your plughole. But you need my help.'

Sarah raised a cynical eyebrow. Anita took another drag of her cigarette.

'Oh yes. You don't know it yet but, believe me, you do. So why don't you cut out the snotty looks and listen to me. I'm going to try and help you, try and make it easy for you, OK? I'm going to give you a way of helping James, of helping the company, and, most of all, Sarah, of helping yourself.'

'Anita, what are you going on about? You come in here, start smoking in my no smoking office, chucking ash all over the floor, talking in riddles like you're Mata Hari. I fully respect your role in this company. I certainly don't look down on you because you're James's PA, I think it's a highly important and responsible role. So if you've got something to say, please will you come right out and say it, and cut out all this speaking in forked tongues.'

'With pleasure,' said Anita. She got up to close the door. 'Now it looks like I've got your attention, I'll begin. Sarah, what you need to know is, you're about to get the push.'

'I'm sorry?'

'I bet you are. What with the mortgage you've got on your flat, I reckon I'd be sorry too. I remember seeing the forms from the building society when you sent them through to James to get him to sign them off in case they didn't believe it possible for anyone to earn the amount you do. Oh, I suppose sooner or later you'd be able to find another job to keep up those monthly payments, but in today's climate, it's anyone's guess really, isn't it? Could take weeks. Months. And you've got no insurance on that mortgage, I seem to remember. And these clothes, Sarah.' Anita started running her raspberry pink acrylic talons through the folds of the linen jacket hanging up by the sofa. 'Must cost you a bomb this kind of thing, not exactly British Home Stores, is it? Must take a bob or two to keep up this kind of a wardrobe.'

'Anita, I'm flattered that you take such an interest in my personal life, my personal finances, not to mention my personal taste in clothes. But you need to explain yourself pretty fast. I'm not keen on people coming in here and making threats to me about my job. I hope you do have a good explanation, otherwise I'm going straight round to James to report this incident to him – you can listen to that on the intercom if you like, or you can come right into his office with me.'

'Fine,' said Anita. 'Fine by me. You won't be telling him anything he doesn't already know. He's the one who's going to give you the old heave-ho, anyway. Go ahead. Go and tell him. It'll be a laugh.' She makes to get up and go. Sarah realised then that Anita meant what she said. A pain entered her forehead somewhere on the right side and started drilling hard.

'Wait a minute. Wait a minute. Look, I'm sorry. Don't go. This is all a bit of a shock. I don't understand. Why are they doing this, Anita? What have I done?'

'Done? Nothing. You've done nothing. That's the point. You've done nothing and Roger's not happy about it. That's why he's going to get James to give you the chop.'

Sarah wiped her thudding head miserably with her hands. 'I'm completely confused. Roger . . . James . . . Why does Roger want me to go, what say does he have over James?'

Anita smiled. 'Questions, questions, and it's good old Anita who's got all the answers. I'll tell you why. Because James got himself in a fix over the Birksomes account. It seems that Frank has threatened to pull out unless James agrees to cream off a little something on our invoices from now on and bung it into Frank's personal account. James, who is a desperate man, agrees. But he can't do it on his own. He needs Roger's help, because Roger is FD and he's the one with his hand on the purse strings. Roger acts all shocked when he hears this and starts making demands, giving James terms and conditions. Of course James can't win by now, he can't say no; either he says yes or Roger shops him. Are you all right?'

Sarah had gone a whiter shade of pale and felt the head drill coming in at several different points of her skull.

She cannot believe that Anita, Anita the secretary, knows all this. She cannot believe that James has told Roger. She cannot believe that Roger is now threatening James. In short, Sarah is finding it hard to believe anything right now other than she must be dreaming, but it sounds like Anita's not stopped yet, so Sarah had better pinch herself pretty soon.

'Yes, I am, but I don't know, I'm shocked,' she mumbled.

'Of course you are,' clucked Anita maternally, proprietorially. 'There's no way you could be expected to know any of this. Anyway, one of Roger's terms is that you go. Now that's one thing I don't know, I have to admit. I'm not quite sure what you've done to upset him, but I suspect it's because at some stage you didn't make Roger a happy boy when he asked for it. You turned him down, didn't you? Now my guess is that he reckoned it was because you had bigger fish to fry with James. Am I right?' Sarah just stared at Anita, O-mouthed in horror. 'Right, I thought as much. Anyway, whatever the detail, the fact of the matter is that now he's getting his revenge, and you've got to go.'

Sarah got up and looked out of her executive window onto her executive view. Her stomach was bloated with anger at the foul Roger. But more than that, her heart was filled with love for James. Yes, her heart! Yes, love!

My God, here's James, trying to save the agency, trying to save all their jobs, and all this shit Roger can do is make demands and threats. There are so few decent men in this world, gushed Sarah's bosom to itself, but James, her James, was one of them. How could she help James? Her mind raced. (I know, I know: stomach, head, bosom, mind – but all of Sarah's organs do get very involved when she's upset.) She had to help James, had to help him to damn that bastard Roger for ever and get him out of this mess.

'You're asking yourself, how can I help James?'

Sarah spun round. 'Yes. Yes, Anita. That's exactly what I'm asking myself. Because, well, because I care about the agency.'

'Sure, the agency. Come on, I've told you, I know you've got the hots for James, you don't have to pretend with me. Anyway, you've asked me how you can help. And now, I'm going to tell you how we can sort it all out, sort out the agency, sort out James, sort out Roger, and, of course sort out you, Sarah.'

'You mean, you've thought of a solution?'

'Of course, why else do you think I've come in here and told you all this? Of course I know what to do. The only thing is, I need your help, that's why I've told you everything.'

'Right. OK. Well, what is it we need to do?'

'Haven't things changed since I first walked in here? Well I never! So, anyway, here's what we do. Well, you, not we. You're going to drop Roger in it.'

'Drop him in what?'

'In the shit, love, the shit, that's what. You get him to go round to your place, you get him to do what comes naturally to Roger, I video the whole thing and he's done for. He gets a copy of the video through the internal post with a note telling him to keep his gob shut, or we'll send another copy to his wife. There's no way Roger will risk anything after that – his wife's the one with the dosh and she's given him one last chance once too often. This would be the straw that would break the camel's back, and Roger knows it.'

'But what would I have to do, actually sleep with him? I couldn't do that.'

'No, no, don't get your knickers in a twist. You just invite him round to your flat, suggesting that you'll make it worth his while if he does, and when he walks through the door, while the camcorder's churning away, you start saying things, in a nice loud clear voice for the microphone, I haven't got that fancy a model, things like: so you told me you wanted to come here to discuss an urgent business matter? Meanwhile you'll have come on so strong when you first asked him over that, by the time Roger gets out of the taxi at your place, he'll have a codger so stiff that the taxi will charge him extra for the heavy load. He'll think you're just playing about and go for you, and we'll get it all on tape while you fight him off. Don't worry, I know it'll work, I know what I'm talking about. I know Roger.'

'It certainly sounds like you do. But how do you? How do you know all that stuff about his wife? And anyway, Anita, why are you telling me all this? Why do you care what happens to me or to Roger or James or anyone else in this place? Why do you care?'

For the first time, the smug look dribbled away from Anita's face. She stared at Sarah for a long time, then fished a photograph out of her bag and handed it to Sarah. It was a photo of a three-year-old boy, with chocolate down his *Thunderbirds* T-shirt. 'He's called Scott. His dad's promised me for four years that he'll leave his wife for me, and now he's told me he won't and that he can't justify the money he gives me any more. I'm going to get him, get him through the courts. But I want to do this first. This way I really get him, get him where it hurts. I suppose you can guess who the father is?'

'Yes, God, he looks like a mini-Roger that's been reduced on a photocopier.'

'Funny you should say that, Sarah, that's where he was conceived. Anyway, do you understand now, will you help me now, help yourself?'

'Yes, yes, of course I will. The stinking bastard. I'll do exactly what you suggest. And let's do it sooner rather than later. My God, the shit, we're going to get him.'

'That's the spirit. And we have to do it sooner than you think. We have to do it tonight.'

'Tonight! You must be joking!'

'No joke – when it comes to Roger my sense of humour takes the day off sick. It has to be tonight because he's told James that you've got to go tomorrow.'

'What?'

Anita drew her hand across her throat. 'El choppo. Roger's given James a deadline of tomorrow or no go with the Birksomes arrangement.'

'I find that hard to believe.'

'Why?'

Sarah was about to say, because James has invited me away for the weekend tomorrow, but if this was one piece of information that had escaped the agency's equivalent to Kate Adie, perhaps it was best to keep it that way, however confusing it made matters. 'OK, OK. Tonight, then. How do I know he's free?'

'He's free, don't worry, I know his diary better than he does. Just make sure you get him there for six-thirty; I'll get there half an hour or so before to take a recce and get to know your place so I can get all the best angles. Right. I'll see you then. Just make sure you get him to compromise himself loud and clear. It shouldn't be difficult. Good luck. Way to go, Sarah, eh? Sisters are doing it for themselves, right?'

'Right,' said Sarah, eyes and brain blurred with rage and anticipation. She was going to make that man suffer for what he'd done to James.

Anita headed for the door.

'Hang on, Anita,' said Sarah, 'don't you need to know my address?'

'What?' said Anita with a smile. 'As well as your bank account number, annual salary and rate of income tax?'

Still grinning, she left Sarah's office, exhausted but satisfied after her performance. She looked again at the photo of her sister's son Paul and placed it carefully back in the envelope in her handbag. Of course there was no Scott; of course she had no kid. Of course James had never told Roger about the deal – she'd only over-heard James talking to Frank about it on the phone in hushed tones late the night before. Roger had never known anything about it and had certainly never threatened James.

But Roger had bonked her when he'd felt like it since the day she'd joined the agency, and he had always promised to leave his wife for her. No man does that to Anita and then changes his mind without living to regret it – big-time.

Sixteen

It was already 11.30 a.m. Sarah needed to think of something quickly to get Roger to agree to go back to her flat. But she didn't have to think too hard; after all, this is a man we're talking about.

She picked up the phone, dialled Roger's personal extension and hoped the sound of her hand shaking couldn't be heard at the other end.

'Yes?' barked a Mr I'm Irritated Whoever You Are.

'Hello, Roger, it's me, Sarah,' cooed Sarah.

'Sarah? What the hell do you want?'

He had not spoken to her since their love scene at The Ivy, but he had not stopped thinking about her. Her feisty response to his advances had been a very red rag to his bull, and thanks to her little demo, he'd been able to confirm that, al fresco, her bosom delivered even more than it promised. He had been restlessly racking his brain to think up a smart way to find an excuse to contact her, without success, so this unexpected call warmed the heart of his cockles, but he knew he shouldn't act too keen too soon.

'Well, Roger, basically, I want you to give me a chance to apologise. I've been thinking about it and I feel like I behaved ridiculously in that restaurant. I think I was a little overwhelmed by you, to be honest, and I just really want to show you how sorry I am.'

Keep going, keep going, sweetie-pie: your words are rubbing Vicks into his chest, dribbling rose oil down his temples, wafting scented jasmine past his nostrils. 'Do you wanna come and bang me?' would have been just as effective in terms of net result, but why not indulge in a little poetry every now and then?

'Are you having me on?' said Roger eagerly. He wanted to hear more where that came from.

'No, Roger, no I'm not. I feel so young, so inexperienced, so foolish. You, you, finance director of this entire agency, you ring me up out of the blue and ask me out and I just, well I just couldn't cope, although that's no excuse for my absurd behaviour and I really wish I could turn the clock back and start again with you and so I was wondering, if you really wouldn't mind, if you could find the time to pop over to my flat in Notting Hill Gate this evening for a quick drink and, well, to discuss that helping hand you said you might be able to offer me, you know . . .'

That helping hand was already perspiring with excitement.

'Sarah, I don't think that's going to be possible. I'm a very busy man you know,' lied Roger, whose idea of a busy day was remembering to floss his teeth.

'Oh. Oh.' Her 'oh's sounded most convincingly like a cross between a cat in pain and a cat on heat. 'So, no chance, at all, not even for a quick one?'

Sarah babes, watch out, you're starting to use his language. Roger's not on heat, he's on bloody fire. 'Well, if you're really that desperate, I mean if you really can't wait . . .'

'Oh, Roger, I don't think I can . . .'

Say no more, white sugar, the phone's melting in his hairy hand.

'OK, I'll be there by seven. Leave your address with my secretary.'

'Oh, thank you Roger!'

'And Sarah.'

'Yes, Roger?'

'After what you did to me, your apology had better be good.'

'I don't think you'll be disappointed, Roger,' she sniggered.

'That's all right then,' said Roger, putting down the phone while he fished in his pocket for a handkerchief to wipe the wet from his upper lip.

I think if I were ever asked, what do you personally find the single most disgusting object in the whole world, it would have unconditionally to be a man's handkerchief. My own view is that men's handkerchieves should not be allowed into the washing machine with the other whites. They are too foul to be mixed with other clothing, and should either be washed quite separately or thrown away altogether after one day's use.

I'm not really sure how washing machines work, and I don't know how you feel about this, but the idea of putting in my delicate little lacy bras and dainty knickerettes, items which adorn my most intimate parts, in with yards of germ-rich cotton impregnated with bogies, ear wax and other sundry male facial excrement, is just unacceptable. I would rather wash my underwear alongside a used baby's nappy.

Men have this thing about their handkerchieves. They can't use paper tissues like other normal people, I've asked why but never really had a meaningful answer. A man's hanky is an extension of him, of his personality, it has to be accessible at all times, it bulges smugly from a pocket like a spare set of goolies, it is inherently the ultimate male accessory. And every morning, he has to take a virgin white handkerchief from the drawer, which, by the time it gets chucked on the floor at the end of the day, or discovered weeks later, stiff and encrusted in a trouser pocket, is etched in a swirling psychedelic pattern of browns, yellows and greens, looking like it has been deflowered in ways too vile to imagine, full of snot, phlegm and mucus and other tawdry expellations the origins of which no one has ever been brave enough to ask after.

When I think of the awfulness that is men, I invariably think of their hankies, and how, each time they blow their nose, they diligently examine the contents, as if the pattern of their nasal faeces might somehow reveal to them the next winning numbers of the National Lottery, and watching Roger use his white flag to smear the lustsweat from his face just about sums it up for me.

Anyway, that's Roger's problem (and mine, from the sounds of it) – now what about Sarah?

She's right up the creek without the necessary equipment. She's got this sex demon of a man coming round to her flat in a few hours' time with a verbal mandate to do with her what he will. That was the easy bit. Now that she somewhat belatedly comes to think about it, how's she going to get rid of him once Anita's got enough evidence on her home movie camera to save James, save the company, and no doubt the whole world, from extinction?

Somehow Sarah reckoned that the old pulling your tits out of their bra cup to embarrass him stunt wasn't going to be quite as smart a move when done in the privacy of her own flat. Do Liberty's sell stun guns, she wondered? Would a timely call from Suzanne at seven-fifteen be enough to put him off? Or would he just invite her round to join them for a threesome?

For a moment, Sarah's heart sank, you know, like women's hearts are supposed to do. When we just can't cope – plosh! What had she let herself in for? She must be mad; Anita would be no use in protecting her. What if Anita didn't turn up anyway? What if Anita and Roger were in this together and had just set Sarah up so Roger could get his revenge?

Just as these thoughts were tobogganing through Sarah's head, James happened to walk by her office. His handsome, bulldog-like features appeared the other side of the large glass window, his beautiful bloodshot eyes gazed into hers, his sensuous, slimy lips mouthed hello and smiled.

He was walking past with clients, so this tender scene lasted but a few seconds. But those few seconds were enough to remind Sarah of her mission, some would say her destiny. No matter how great the risk or the danger, she would have to go through with it: professionally and emotionally, her boss needed her right now, and she was going to be there for him.

What I want to know is, why doesn't Sarah just go for Roger and make them both happy and save us a lot of grief? He's suitably revolting, isn't he? I guess his problem is that he's too explicitly keen, he makes no bones about fancying her. She can sense that, however bumptious and crass his approach, Roger actually quite likes her.

Whereas James is more devious, more ambivalent in his affections, and that's the challenge she wants. She wants things as tough as possible, otherwise she doesn't feel she's fulfilling her personal pain targets for that month. No pain, no gain is Sarah's motto.

So what's she going to do for a denouement once she's got Roger slobbering over her in her flat? As Sarah's in advertising, strategy is obviously not her forte, but she's going to have to rustle up something strategic if she's going to save herself from complete rape that evening.

Just as Sarah was about to put mental pen to paper, however, the phone rang and it was the MD from her cereals clients, Mr Muesli himself, telling her she had to get over to their offices for a brainstorm on the packaging. One fears that it's not really her brain he'd like to storm, but that he's accepted her brain was going to have to do for the time being.

When the man who pays the mortgage calls, you

gotta go. So Sarah went, and decided to worry about what to do with Roger later in the day.

Tempus fugit, that's what I say.

Seventeen

Never put off till the evening what you should do early afternoon. God, I tell you, this is more than a book, this is a bloody manual of life. We'll have to give it a red cover and make it the little red book for the nineties, a doctrine for success and happiness. Read this and you'll never have another unhappy relationship.

Never put off till the evening what you should do early afternoon. You've been warned.

Down in Slough, Mr Muesli didn't want Sarah to go. He kept thinking of new ways of configuring the packaging which ideally were going to keep them there until dinner time when he would, all impromptu-like, suggest they went for a meal together. Sarah had to invent dramatic excuses, not to say lies, about having to take one of her cats to the vet's before his gammy paw fell off. Mr Muesli (I keep calling him this stupid name because for some reason I just can't remember what his real name was, and it hardly matters) offered to send his secretary to take the cat for her, so Sarah had to embellish on the gammy paw with descriptions of infection and pus so realistic that they kind of dampened the poor chap's ardour.

At 5.45, Sarah escaped and raced her Range Rover (I wasn't going to mention this in case it put you off her, but yes, her Range Rover) (so handy for all those rocky terrains in Notting Hill Gate) back to London. She's Aquarius, is Sarah, and the great traffic stars in the sky were obviously in her favour that day as it only took her just under an hour to get back that evening, but even so, when she arrived, Anita was already on her doorstep. That's Anita as in not very happy Anita.

'Where the bloody hell have you been?' Anita enquired affectionately. 'This is no time to start fannying about. He's going to be here any minute, he already took half the afternoon off to go to the hairdresser's and buy a new tie. Come on, don't stand there gawping, hurry up and open the door so I can get sorted.'

It was only then that the full horror of Sarah's predicament struck her. She'd been so concentrated on manoeuvring her Sherman tank through other cars at eighty miles per hour in built-up areas to get home on time that she'd kind of forgotten why she had to hurry home in the first place. I guess the mind plays strange tricks on you in the face of adversity, and women's minds are pretty strange at the best of times, let's face it, eh lads?

In half an hour, Casanova on speed would be sailing in through her door, helping hands and God knows what other body parts a-flailing. She could put the moment of truth off no longer. 'Anita,' confessed Sarah in a state of angst, 'I'm terrified, I don't know what to do, I've tried to think of a plan, of a clever way of doing this, but . . .'

'You don't know what to do? What are you talking about? We went over all of this earlier. You just act surprised when he turns up, then . . .'

'No, no, I know what to do about that, I mean I don't know what to do, you know, when he starts, when he expects to . . .'

'To actually shove it up you, is that what you mean? Don't worry about that, that's the least of your worries, I've got the solution for that one.' Anita produced a large baseball bat from her aerobics bag. 'I'll give him a good whack on the head with this, it'll take more than a few Nurofen to sort his head out after that.'

'But you'll kill him!'

'Don't talk rot. Just a gentle tap to cool his ardour for a few minutes, then I'll drive him up to the Notting Hill Gate tube station and dump him there. Or would you rather go through the full business with him, eh, Sarah?'

'No, no,' said Sarah, beyond desperation. It was ten to seven. 'The baseball bat sounds fine. Just fine.'

They hurriedly positioned Anita behind the door to Sarah's study. Sarah decided not to change but just stay in her work clothes, to give her appearance the I've-just-got-home-from-work look. This would make her performance all the more credible on the video when she had to feign surprise and confusion at Roger's arrival.

Other than that, it's hard to know how to get yourself ready for a man who you find physically repulsive, who you want to semi-seduce you before you assault him with a baseball bat. A recharge of deodorant would have been nice, but did seem rather inapposite in the circumstances.

Now imagine this is a film, like Anita's trying to. The scene suddenly cuts to Roger, sitting back at the agency at his raw-hide desk, all fine and dandy with his new hairdo and dapper new tie. He's also changed his socks and Y-fronts for the clean spares he always keeps in his bottom drawer at the office for just this ilk of occasion and, unlike Sarah, has applied liberal, perhaps too liberal, in fact positively gagging amounts of Gieves and Hawkes cologne to his face, armpits and genital areas (that's ninety per cent of Roger's body surface).

At 6.30 p.m. he rings through to his secretary to tell her to ring his wife to say he will, once again, be on the late side due to an unexpected and unavoidable meeting. As he plans to leave at 6.32 for Notting Hill Gate, this will leave minimal time for telephonic recriminations.

Just as he's smoothing down the lapels of his cashmere coat to leave, Melanie, his personal secretary, the woman with the constant faint golden glow just behind the back of her head, comes through, chokes politely on the exhaust fume effect of the cologne and tells Roger he'd better ring home.

'Now for fuck's sake, Melanie, I've asked you to carry out a simple task and I'd be grateful if you would just do it. I really do have to go, now, right now, do you see?'

Melanie, talking with a strange voice as she tries to speak and hold her nasal passages closed at the same time, simply says: 'Roger, I've made the call. If I were you, I'd just phone home.' Yeah, Roger, just phone home: it's good to talk.

There was something about Melanie's expression, not to mention her squeaky voice, that alerted even Roger to the fact that all was not well. He took off his coat, went back to his altar to a dozen calves of a desk and dialled his number. His wife, Trudy, was not at home, but the answerphone was on.

'Hello, Roger and Trudy are not at home right now. Roger will be back later, right now he's no doubt just screwing another little something he's picked up along the way today. I will never be back, I've decided to leave Roger for the very nice man with whom I have been enjoying a very nice relationship for three years now. My friends will be hearing from me, with my new number. Roger will also be hearing from me, via my solicitor. Cheerio.'

Roger's head started to throb with anger and fear. For Roger to feel anything anywhere above his gut-line is a novelty, so I guess every cloud does, as they say, have a silver lining.

The old cow, his cash-cow, had just walked out on him. His financial support system, his old-age pension, his middle-aged pension, his account at Gieves, his country club, his town club, his everyfuckingthing, had done a bunk. Of course, he earned a fair old whack at the agency, but a racehorse like Roger costs one hell of a lot to stable.

How could the slut do this to him? Relationship for three years? The filthy slut, the filthy slut. While he's hard at work, she's putting it about behind his back. And Melanie had heard the message. What was he going to do? Abandoned by his wife, homeless, penniless, what was he going to do?

He decided to go home to switch off the answering machine before anyone else could hear it. But as he leveraged his generous backside into the Jag, he realised that he just couldn't face it right away. He couldn't go back to that empty house on his own. Suddenly, Sarah's sweet and loving voice on the phone echoed in his ears. He'd go to her, she'd console him, she'd give him strength . . .

He bolted down to Notting Hill Gate and rang her bell. Sarah opened the door. She was about to begin the performance of a lifetime.

'Sarah. Hello.'

'Roger, oh! oh! Goodness me, what are you doing here?'

'Please don't tease me, Sarah. Can I come in?'

'Well, of course, Roger, I mean, you're my Finance Director, if you'd like to talk business . . . I mean it's rather odd doing it at my house, but please, come in,' staccatoed Sarah in true RADA scholarship style.

Roger more or less fell into the house and onto Sarah's sofa. Cecil B. de Anita Mille practically had to run to keep up with him.

'Er, can I offer you a drink, some coffee perhaps?'

'Yes, a drink, a whisky, big as you can make it.'

'Er, a whisky?' said Sarah loudly in the direction of the microphone. 'A large one? Er, well, all right, if that's what you really want.'

Sarah poured the drink, gave it to Roger and sat down next to him, pulling her skirt well down over her knees, waiting to be ravished. Roger said nothing, he did nothing. This kind of action is not going to pack 'em in at the Acton Odeon. This just won't do. Roger was slumped over his drink, completely immobile. Sarah could see Anita hovering in the shadows of the kitchen door and sensed her irritation.

'Well, Roger, could you let me know what it is you wanted to see me about. That new contract perhaps? Couldn't it have waited until tomorrow? I mean, I'm anxious to know why you're here. Is anything wrong at the agency?'

Roger was still doing his impersonation of a rock. The camcorder whirred away. For the first time since he'd arrived, Sarah looked across at him. Was this really Roger? Perhaps she'd let a complete stranger into her home. He certainly looked like Roger, smelled like Roger (smelled very strongly of eau de Roger in fact). But the jaunty Mr Come Over Here And I'll Spank You had been replaced by a dead duck.

'Roger, is anything wrong with you?'

Roger burst into tears.

Oh dear, cut, cut, this is going all wrong. This was going to be the scene that made *Rocky IV* look like an episode of *Bill and Ben*. Now Roger was making Little Weed look like Rambo.

Roger got out his hanky (aaargh!) and blew loudly and wetly into it. 'I'm sorry, I'm sorry, Sarah,' he howled. 'Only, my wife's left me.'

'Oh, Roger, I am sorry,' said Sarah with genuine concern until she remembered why he was there in the first place, and that if there was no wife to threaten him with, there was no point in him being there in the first place in the first place.

'Can I spend the evening with you, Sarah? I feel so lonely, so confused, I don't know what to do.'

'Well, Roger, I'm so sorry for you, but I really don't think that there's much that I can . . .'

'Women, they always let you down,' he snivelled dejectedly, the famous hair losing its balance in his distress and lolloping about all over the shop. 'They always deceive and abuse you. The only woman who never deceived me was my wonderful mother. My mother was quite the most magnificent woman, you know.' Roger was wandering off into some kind of verbal coma.

'That's lovely, but . . .'

'You know, my mother, my mother was quite a terrific lady in every sense. I enjoyed a perfectly splendid relationship with her. And do you know what was so wonderful about my mother? She was a real woman, a lady, who knew her role, who enjoyed being a woman who was there for her man. My mother was the most humble, the most accommodating creature anyone could wish to meet. She raised me and my brothers with total devotion, one couldn't have wished for a more dedicated mother. She put up with my father's problems with great grace and dignity. I don't think I ever heard her complain once in all those years, and when she felt it was all getting too much, she'd just go into her bedroom, shut the door, cry quietly and with dignity, and then reappear when it was all over.

'Of course, we knew she was upset, we knew she had been crying. But she did not wallow in it and neither did we. She had dealt with it and life went on. No buggering off with relationships of three years for her.'

'Roger, I understand you must be upset. Would you like me to call you a cab?'

'And the way she dealt with her illness, that was equally magnificent. She told no one that she was ill, preferring not to make a fuss. She knew how important she was to all of us, even though my brothers and I had left home by then, she knew it was important that we could pop in at any time to have a meal, simply to be at home and relax. When the cancer really started to get to her, she just turned up at the doctor's one day, said, "I've got cancer, I haven't got long to go now, I don't want any treatment, put me in a nursing home till I've gone, will you?'' Simple as that. And that's just what she did and two weeks later she was dead. And you hear these stories of these ruddy women with their breast cancers, clawing and grasping at life, festooning themselves with wigs and wotnot to cover up the bald patches and the scars and I think, Christ, learn to die with a bit of dignity, can't you, without pulling all the rest of us down with you. Women have no sense of dignity, no loyalty any more. And now I'm all alone. Oh Sarah, come here, come and sit next to me and cuddle me. I feel so alone, so helpless, so hopeless. Come and give me a hug.'

This emphasis on the hugs and cuddles of consolation led the wily Sarah to ask herself whether Roger had not in fact concocted the whole scene and made up the whole story just to get a grope of sympathy in the final Act.

'Are you sure she's left you?' she asked.

'Yes, yes, dial my home number, you'll see,' sobbed Roger, wiping back the hanks of errant hair from his face.

'What, to speak to your wife!' cried Sarah.

'No, no, she's left me, I tell you. Look, look, give me your phone, listen to this.' He dialled his own number and shoved the receiver against Sarah's ear.

'Oh my God,' said Sarah after a few moments. 'It's true!'

Just then they heard the front door bang shut. It was Anita ending her directorial debut in a very bad mood. If the old bag had left him already, there could be no video, no blackmail. Anita was going to have to go to Plan B, as soon as she had decided what Plan B was.

Roger went white through the red blotches of tears on his fat face. 'Do you live with someone?'

'Er, yes, that's my boyfriend. My boyfriend, John. Just back from rugby training, I should imagine. Just gone through to have a shower, I would think. These scrum halves do build up rather a sweat!'

Roger leapt up unsteadily. 'I have to go Sarah, do you understand? I'm sorry, I'll make it up to you.'

'Of course you will,' smiled Sarah as she bundled him into his coat. 'You can start by telling James not to fire me.'

'Tell James not to fire you?'

'Come on, Roger, let's stop playing games, you and I.'

'I swear, Sarah, I swear I don't know what you're talking about.'

Sarah looked into his watery eyes. She could see that he didn't. The lying bitch.

'All right, all right, ignore that. You'd better go now, Roger, and I'd better get John's steak on the grill. He gets anxious if his rump steak isn't waiting for him when he gets out of the shower.'

Roger gulped and dashed out of the door. Sarah flung her back against it and gasped with relief.

All we need now is for Brian Rix to come in through another door in his underpants. Except that none of this is really very funny, it's actually very sad.

Our heroine, Sarah, has just got herself into a very dangerous situation – for James. Now she's going to get herself in an even worse one – with James. It shows how stupid she can be when she wants to, how her bright and brave brain can turn into a swamp when she lets it.

It looks like it's all downhill from here. I don't know why. I'm beginning to lose sympathy for her. I don't know why she behaves like a moron when she is far from moronic. She's run a risk now for James, but she didn't get hurt. How much further is she prepared to go for him? Does she want to get hurt? Does she actually want to get hurt? Would that prove to him how much she cares about him? Or would it prove to her how little she cares about herself?

All I know is, there's no point in criticising men all the time when women allow themselves to be victims. There's no point in saying, why do men do it? The question should be: why do women let them do it? Why don't they open their mouths and make it stop?

All you have to do is say stop, stop now, and mean it. Just say no.

In the meantime, it looks like it's all downhill from here. Sorry.

Eighteen

Next thing you know, it was Friday afternoon. Sarah left work at lunchtime claiming a mysterious doctor's appointment, as you do. Fortunately Anita was not in the office that day, so there were no raised eyebrows. Once home, she spent two hours checking that all her weekend clothes had just the right essential accessories, like earrings and scarves and tights, which really bring out the real you in an outfit, and which men really notice. The Gospel according to *Elle*.

Before you could say '40 denier in barely black' the little hand was on its way to four o'clock and James was on his way to collect Sarah from her flat.

In out of work togs, he looked much younger. His height complemented his width and it has to be said that he was quite attractive in an overwhelming sort of a way. For all his forty-six years, James could look the part when he set his mind to it. And, however principled you are, a Saab convertible with the roof down revealing a tanned chest against a yellow cashmere sweater definitely reaches the parts on a bird that a Ford Fiesta can't.

Just as Sarah was putting the finishing touches to herself so she looked like the kind of woman she thought James would like her to look like, the phone rang. On no. Is this James calling to blow her out? Don't worry, Sarah. James is on his way. It's your Mum.

'Sarah?'

'Hello, Mum.'

'Can you come over?'

'Not today, Mum, I'm going away for the weekend.'

'Oh.'

'Are you OK?'

'No.'

Sarah frowned. 'Not again, Mum. Please tell me not again.'

'Yes. Don't be angry with me. I couldn't help it.'

'But why?'

'Your father rang last night. He wants a divorce.'

'So? You've been separated ten years now. You should be thrilled. You should be the one asking for the divorce. I don't know why you haven't. We've been through all of this a million times. Why's that upset you so much? How much have you drunk?'

'A lot.'

'But why?'

'Sarah, I love him.'

'No you don't. He made your life hell. The police got so fed up with coming round to stop your fights that they gave up. You got so smashed up by him that I had to miss half my lessons at school taking time off to look after Caroline while you were in hospital. Don't you remember any of that, for God's sake? It seems like yesterday to me.'

'He wants a divorce because he's got a new girlfriend. He wants to marry this one.' Sarah held her breath. Her mother didn't add 'because he's already got two kids by her and now she's expecting a third she's putting her foot down' so she obviously still didn't know about that bit. 'Did you know he's got a girlfriend, Sarah? Why didn't you tell me?' Sarah could hear her mother drinking, slurping back the vodka. It was usually vodka, because she thought no one would be able to smell it on her breath as she fell over in Tesco's and stepped into oncoming traffic in the street.

'Mum, please, listen to me, you're well rid of that

man, he caused you so much harm, real harm, he beat you up for years, he robbed you of every inch of your self-confidence, he would have ruined you completely if you hadn't got out when you did. Give him this divorce with your blessing and consider yourself a free woman.'

'I still love him. I love him.'

'Look Mum, I'll be back on Monday and I'll come and see you, sometime next week, early next week. I would come now but I just can't. Don't be sad, and stop drinking.'

'All right,' whined her mother, 'if you don't want to talk to me, I'll give Caroline a call.'

'Caroline! No, uh, no, that's not a good idea. She's away this weekend I seem to remember, er yes, now I come to think of it she told me she and Edward are definitely away this weekend. So just wait for me, and I'll be round as soon as I can next week.'

Her mother did her usual trick of putting the phone down without saying goodbye, leaving Sarah feeling lost, frightened and just cut off. How could her mother still love that man, after all he'd put her through? He'd taken her to hell and back, without the back. Now that Caroline had buggered off to New York, Sarah had been left to cope on her own with the alcoholic mother, the neurotic father, his depressed fiancée and an ever increasing number of half brothers and sisters.

Then she remembered Caroline, who still hadn't rung to say when she was coming. Sarah would have to give her a call when she got back as well.

Sarah was exhausted by it all. In the midst of all the chaos, she understood just one thing: she had her own life to lead, and she wasn't going to make the same mistakes. No man was going to smash her to a pulp and put her down and humiliate her. It was her life and she was in charge.

Hallelujah and I wish.

The door bell rang. Through the glass in the front

door she could see the outline of Prince Charming standing on the doorstep. Her own life and she was in charge.

James: Hi!

Sarah: Hi!

Boy meets girl. The language of love. Sarah grabbed her things, and followed James to the car. She snuggled into the leather seat and hoped the neighbours were watching. This was it and this was how it was meant to be. Young, unattached, independent, bright, advertising, Saab, leather seats, a high flyer driving you off to somewhere lovely, leaving work early on a Friday like a kid who's playing hookey.

More dialogue:

James: Tina Turner OK for you?

Sarah: Great.

Don't change channel – it does get better. It's just that she's a bit nervous and he's a bit boring. You might have guessed the taste in music – the typical 'I might be middle aged but I'm still hip'. All the pre-wrinklies like Tina because she's still so damn sexy even though her chicken is now more autumn than spring. It gives them all hope. At the back of his leather cassette pouch Sarah thought she saw an Abba CD, but she said nothing.

Not a lot was said until they got to the Chiswick roundabout. Then James announced that they were going to spend that night, Friday night, at the home of one of his best mates, Gerald, who's managing director of some publishing company or other.

'Their house is in a little village just outside Hungerford. It's pretty much en route and it'll save us having to pay for dinner somewhere.'

Sarah laughed at what she was sure was a joke. They had been invited for dinner. They. He was already telling his friends about her. He wanted his best friend to check her out before it started getting too serious between them. That was lovely. She relaxed, felt the glow of the seat heater up her bottom, and all seemed right with the world.

They sped along the M4, vroom, vroom. James drove at a steady 100 miles an hour and hooted wildly at any car that dared to try doing anything approaching the speed limit on the fast lane in front of him. He didn't seem particularly chatty and, as the roof was down, even though it was actually rather bloody freezing and had started to drizzle, it was hard to hear much anyway. But let's face it, if you're taking a bit of skirt away for the weekend in a convertible, you keep the roof down even if it's snowing.

James has that kind of concrete hair which never seems to move. Sarah's not so lucky. Even though she'd spent three quarters of an hour that afternoon lovingly moussing and blow drying them, her flowing locks were flapping all over the place. It's difficult to look like the cover of *Tatler* when you've great gobs of hair slapping you across the chops. All she could think of was whether she had any gas left in her Braun hair styler for a rapid resuscitation job when they got to Gerald's.

Is this romance?

James, sensitively, noticed her distress. While his sensitivity didn't quite run to offering to put the roof up, he did suggest that she might want to use the silk scarf in the glove compartment 'which often came in handy'. Jolly good. Nice to know that many hundreds of eager female bums have been on this very car seat before you.

Relax, relax, she thought to herself. He's single, attractive – what do you expect, that he spends every evening in developing his wrist muscles? What do you want out of this relationship anyway? Marriage and babies? Somewhere very far away, a little voice squeaked a nervous 'yes please', as it always did when she embarked on any new affair, but Sarah pretended she hadn't heard.

No, this was the life, no ties, no commitment, just fun in the fast lane. So she put the scarf on, ignoring the very long blond hair that fell out of it onto her lap, then put her head back on the head rest and tried very hard to look like an ad.

Just over an hour later they were there. Chez Gerald. The house was everything that the country home of a leading publisher should be. We're talking a bohemian, cosmopolitan look of chaos that costs thousands to achieve. We're talking a decor so stylised that even the kids match the wallpaper.

By the time they arrived, Sarah knew every word of 'You're Simply The Best' off by heart, having heard it about seventeen times as James flipped rewind on the CD whenever the track was over, just to 'hear it one more time'. It was a relief to get out of the wind tunnel and take a break from Tina.

As they drew up the long crunchy drive, one of the colour-coordinated accessories ran out. He was about three or four, with ringlets all over his face like a permed sheepdog, freckles and spotty dungarees. 'Cunt! Cunt! Cunt!' this little kid was crying at the top of his voice.

A lanky, well-manicured man was running after him. 'Quentin! Come here at bloody once!'

But Quentin was too fast for him and was waddling off towards the horizon when the man noticed the car and stopped running.

'James!'

'Gerald!'

'You look fucking marvellous, old man.'

'That's because I know the secret to eternal youth, whereas you, you poor miserable old bugger, you've blown it.'

By now James was out of the car and the two men were giving each other affected bear hugs. 'You mean the wife and kids. You know, you may be right, you old sod. They're all driving me bonkers. But I guess you're still young, free and single, sowing your oats in all and sundry? Of course you are. God, it's good to see you.'

More hugs.

'Come in and have a drink, old man. Good trip down? Remembered to bring your tennis kit?'

James and Gerald disappeared into the house.

Sarah was left standing by the car. She watched Quentin running hyperactively up and down the garden, like a bee that had gone berserk. He was still screaming 'cunt' like his life depended on it while a terrier yapped excitedly at his little fat heels. After a while, Sarah followed the men into the house.

'Sarah, come on, stop lolling around outside. Meet my old chum Gerald,' said James with exuberance.

The men were sitting on the kitchen bar stools with large tumblers of whisky. Gerald nodded a grunt of recognition in Sarah's direction.

'Gerald, where's your lovely lady?' said James, through a slurp of whisky.

'She's here,' said a sultry voice which had just walked in at the other end of the kitchen. 'James, you big swinging dick, get over here and give me a big snog.'

A very slim woman who'd smoked more fags and had more bottles of wine than her complexion could take went up to James and gave him a very full kiss on the lips. James gave her a good squelch of her breasts.

'Antonia. Still looking marvellous, absolutely bloody marvellous. Gerald, when are you going to lend her to me so I can give her another good porking?'

'Come on, Jamie,' said Antonia, delighted. 'That's all history books now.' Seeing Sarah wilting by the entrance of the kitchen, Antonia barked, 'Who's the bird this weekend, James?'

'This is Sarah, a colleague from work.'

'Oh, right,' said Antonia, as if he'd just announced that Sarah was a pot plant and therefore required no further personal attention. 'Come on boys, dinner is all ready next door. I thought we'd have an early supper to give us more time to catch the evening light for fun and games afterwards. Gerald, did you give Quentin a good walloping?'

'No,' said Gerald wearily, 'the little bugger's too fast for me.'

'So where is he now?' asked Antonia rhetorically as she poured herself a large drink.

'Somewhere in the garden with the dog. He'll be all right.' Whether 'he' was the dog or the child was not clear. The welfare of either did not seem a subject worthy of further pursuit. They traipsed through to the banqueting hall of a dining room, with its massive vaulted roof and great iron chandeliers.

Supper consisted of bread, a hunk of ageing cheddar, some not-quite-baked baked potatoes and a salad. Antonia explained that she was simply too shagged to do anything more complicated and that anyway it was bloody Gerald's fault as he hadn't done the bloody shopping he was supposed to do when he went into the bloody village that morning. Gerald explained that if Antonia didn't sleep all fucking day she would be able to go and do the bloody shopping herself.

None of them seemed particularly interested in food anyway. While Sarah nibbled on a piece of very hard cheddar cheese which smelt like you would imagine athlete's foot to smell if it had a smell, the other three ploughed through as many bottles of red wine. The talk was books, affairs, indiscretions, media. Wonderful things.

After a while the phone rang. 'Yes, yes, we're on our way over,' trilled Antonia. 'No, no, it'll be no problem. Jamie's brought someone who'll look after the kids.'

She put the phone down. 'That's Hugh – he's ready for us. James darling, you did bring your tennis stuff, didn't you – or do you want me to lend you some of G's? Susan,' she said, addressing Sarah directly for the first time, 'you won't mind looking after the kids while we have a quick game of doubles over at Hugh's? There's a telly next door. They won't be any trouble.'

'Be a sport,' said James, coming over and giving Sarah a big kiss on the cheek. 'We won't be long.'

'But there's only one child, isn't there?' asked Sarah, completely lost.

'What?' said Antonia, as if Sarah was mad.

'You said look after the kids.'

'Oh yes,' said Antonia, impatiently. 'There's the baby upstairs. Lorenzo. He's asleep, he's fine. Anastasia and Tamsin are having supper with friends. Quentin's in the garden – don't worry about him, he doesn't like strangers anyway.' With this last remark Antonia threw Sarah a look which seemed to say, and if they're strangers like you, who can blame the little chap.

'Thanks,' said James affectionately as they all lurched out into the car. 'We'll be back before you know it.'

Sarah wondered how any of them would be capable of holding the right end of their racquets, much less play a game of tennis after all that wine. After a few moments of depressed thought, she went through to the kitchen to make herself a cup of coffee. She was too thrown by everything to know whether she felt angry or upset or bemused. Perhaps what they'd done was perfectly reasonable. Perhaps it was incredibly rude. She couldn't quite make it out.

She looked out of the window. Although Quentin and the dog were about a hundred yards away, they seemed to be all right. Quentin was playing a fun game he'd invented which involved grabbing the dog's tail and pulling it as hard as his small chubby hands could manage, but the dog didn't seem to mind.

She opened the fridge to look for milk for her coffee. A blanket of stench hit her, the stench of food which had enjoyed its sell-by date many moons before. A brown cauliflower snuggled up against a plate of mildewy cake. Something pink was dripping from an overturned yogurt carton on the top shelf onto a joint of what looked like leg of werewolf below. In the door compartment, there were four bottles of white wine and one milk bottle with an inch of caked orange milk at the bottom of it. Sarah decided to take her coffee black.

Just then, she heard a desperate scream, closely following by an even more harrowing whelping. She ran out to the lawn – in the distance she could see Quentin beating the dog with a croquet stick. Although she ran as fast as she could, by the time she got there the little dog was motionless and whelping no more. 'Bad!' exclaimed Quentin with glee.

'Oh my God!' cried Sarah, holding her face in her hands. 'What have you done?'

'Bad!' cried the mini-murderer. 'Bad dog!' Quentin held out his hand to show Sarah some little red teeth marks where the dog, finally pissed off with having his tail pulled out, must have bitten him.

'Quentin, that's very naughty. Very naughty.'

Quentin squinted at her with his single visible eye through the curtain of curls. 'Cunt,' he said to her emphatically, then turned to waddle at full speed back to the house.

She wanted to stay and see how bad the dog really was, but she was more scared to leave Quentin in the house on his own. She ran after him.

By the time she got back to the house, loud baby screams were coming from somewhere upstairs. Quentin was sitting happily on a huge antique sofa covered in dog hairs and biscuit crumbs, intently watching the evening news on the television.

Sarah, ran panting upstairs and eventually located a tiny red-faced baby, his nappy drenched, who had been screaming so much it looked as if he were going to burst. She grabbed him and went to look for a new nappy. The nursery had a stale, dank odour of ageing turds from a pile of unremoved ex-nappies on the floor.

It was a very beautiful room with a large, joyous print on the walls, with curtains, borders, swags and furniture that some sod-the-cost Fulham Road designer had obviously been summoned to put together. Finally she found a pile of clean nappies at the bottom of an immense mahogany chest of drawers.

Sarah had never changed a nappy before. She was a career girl and babies had never been necessary on a CV. She peeled off the clammy folds of cotton wool. The baby's bottom was soaked in urine and a very pale avocado purée which had slipped all up his back and down his legs. It took almost half an hour for Sarah to clean him up, including regular breaks for going outside the room and taking a good gasp of uncontaminated, non shit-smelling air next door. The purée clung to her fingernails and seemed to seep down into the crack between skin and nail in a way that no amount of soap scrubbing could remove.

By the time she took the baby downstairs, she was exhausted. Quentin was still in front of the telly, gleefully watching a debate on hospital funding as if it were the latest Walt Disney, his mouth overflowing with digestive biscuits and snot.

It was clear that this child's parents had not made strenuous efforts in the brother bonding department. When Lorenzo appeared in Sarah's arms, Quentin's eyes lit up like he would like to mete out the same treatment to his baby brother that he had given the dog. 'Cunt,' said Quentin to the baby.

'Quentin,' said Sarah, talking to him as all non-parents do to little kids, with a slow and sincere enunciation as if they're talking to a martian, 'you really must stop using that horrid word. It's not a nice word.'

'Daddy say Mummy cunt,' burbled Quentin through the biscuit. 'Daddy say Mummy cunt, cunt.' Then, suddenly bored with the television, the baby and Sarah, he buried his face in the furry pillow, yawned a massive yawn and fell instantly asleep. The baby, worn out by crying and hunger, so relieved not to have his lower half swimming in a sea of sewage any more, had also fallen asleep. Like some goddess of fertility, Sarah sat on the sofa for another hour with sleeping children either side of her, wondering how James could do this to her, until the Wimbledon set finally got home.

The tennis match had not been a success. Gerald had accused James of pawing Antonia and she had told Gerald that he was a jealous, impotent fart who couldn't get a hard-on even if he were to put quick-drying cement on it. Gerald replied that with a frigid bitch like her for a wife, it was hardly surprising.

Sarah knew all of this because these were the exchanges that bounced through the house as the front door opened. Sarah's pulse began to thud. The baby started screaming and Quentin started crying. This was not the ideal environment to inform these loving parents that their mutilated dog was out enjoying a spot of rigor mortis on the lawn and their eldest son probably needed to be sped off for a tetanus injection.

Feebly, nervously, Sarah went out to the kitchen and waited for one of the three of them to remember she might be there. When this did not happen, and neither her presence nor the children's wailing were acknowledged in the midst of the on-going circus of verbal abuse, Sarah decided to take action.

'Excuse me,' Sarah shouted above the din. They all stopped ranting and stared at her, like Mrs Rochester had finally revealed herself. 'Excuse me,' said Sarah again, a tad less confidently than the mark one excuse me, 'but Antonia, Gerald, there's something you must know. I'm afraid I have to tell you – I think your dog is dead.'

'The dog is dead?' demanded Gerald.

'Yes. I'm so sorry. He's out there, on the lawn.'

'For Christ's sake,' cried Antonia, grabbing the baby. 'What's all this bullshit about the dog, you ridiculous woman. Why didn't you let Lorenzo sleep? He'll be up all bloody night now. [You have to be a parent to understand the logic of that one.] And his nappy's so tight he can hardly breathe. Don't you barren bloody business types know anything about children?'

'Antonia! Please! Will you just shut up and listen to me!' wailed Sarah. 'There's been an accident. In the garden.'

'An accident?' demanded Antonia, in the tones of 'a handbag?' 'What do you mean an accident?'

'The dog,' pleaded Sarah, 'the little dog. He's dead. Quentin clubbed him to death on the lawn with the croquet stick.'

'Churchill? What's wrong with him? He's fine.' Antonia bent down to caress the dog, who was sitting perkily at her feet, as right as rain.

'Oh, thank God, thank God,' cried Sarah.

'Are you complete mad? Have you been drinking?' said Gerald, waving his glass of whisky in her face. 'To think we left the kids with you all afternoon! Is she on drugs, old man?' he asked, turning to James with sudden interest, as if he might know whether Sarah had brought any with her that she might fancy sharing out with them.

James was irritable after the argument and could hardly be bothered whether the dog was dead or alive anyway. 'We're all tired,' he said. 'I need a shower. Let's all have a wash, a bit of a rest and a few drinks, and forget about all of this. Sarah, come on, let's go upstairs and get sorted out.'

Sarah picked up her bag and followed the captain of her ship with a look of love and gratitude. He was a natural leader, she reflected in her swelling bosom. He was the one, in any situation, who took control, the one that people listened to and obeyed. Mmm, doesn't that kind of fella just make your skin tingle, girls? Ooh Sarah, hang on in there, sweetie. If you're very lucky, he might give you a shirt to iron and tell you what colour lipstick to wear that evening. Would you be able to take that? Or would you simply swoon from the sheer pulsating, dominant virility of it all?

As Sarah trotted dutifully upstairs after him, the excitement mounted. With each step that she took on the magnificent staircase, her heart missed a beat, so it was a wonder she was alive at all by the time they reached the top of it. Will she or won't she be sharing a room with James? This would be the clincher! Had James told his good friends that she was just a work colleague, or was she officially The Girlfriend?

Are they an item or not, is frankly what Sarah needed to know, and the answer is about to be revealed to her. Separate rooms would mean amity, camaraderie, bonhomie and sundry other French euphemisms for you ain't getting it tonight. A double room would mean togetherness, it would mean a Peter Jones wedding list, Volvos and names down at St Paul's: in a word, it would mean love.

Sarah had, of course, already been upstairs, but had also been in such a state of frenzy to grab the screeching baby that she hadn't thought to check out the sleeping arrangements. As she panted along eagerly behind James, her eyes sparkling, coat shiny and tail wagging, past one, two, three, four bedrooms in the corridor, she reflected that, whatever the answer was, he was very sure of himself: there had been no discussion as to whether she might be happier on her own for the night, no tender suggestion that he might be happier if they were together . . . James was certainly a man who knew what he wanted and acted on it. Gosh, what a guy.

Finally, they got to the end of the long, cold corridor (you know the type of big, old country houses that are cold even in mid-summer, with no nice London exhaust fumes to warm them up). He flung open the door and, tra la!, all was revealed. All, everything, everyone, altogether in the altogether. The original open-plan bedroom. 'My God!' said Sarah, using the expression that seems to be becoming her catchphrase since she's known James, 'What's this?'

'This is the bedroom, Sarah,' explained James patiently.

'But there are about eight beds in here!'

'Yes,' said James, relieved, given what he was paying her at the agency, that she was so strong in the counting skills department. 'So what?'

'Well, I mean, is this to be our room?'

'Well, yes,' replied James. 'This is sort of everyone's room really. This is where the adults sleep. The kids each have their own rooms, all along the corridor, but Gerald and Antonia decided that they would open this side of the house up and make just one massive room for themselves and their guests. It's rather splendid, isn't it, don't you think? So much light; such wonderful views.'

Heavens, all that power, all that steely determination, and now the man's an artist too. Some people really do have it all. I'm getting jealous of Sarah already, aren't you?

'So,' continued Sarah, not liking these Woodstockesque sleeping arrangements one little bit, light or no light, views or no views, 'do we just choose a bed?'

'Yes, whatever, throw your stuff wherever you like, said James. 'It's academic. We'll be moving around, so it hardly matters. Actually, I must have a piss,' he concluded gravely, in the way that bladder-rich men do, and disappeared into the equally vast, equally communal, en-suite bathroom.

Oh-oh. Oh-oh. Moving around. Moving around? No, I'm sorry. Sarah does not do moving around. Maybe in your cosmopolitan, world-weary and other-worldly kind of advertising meets publishing kinds of lives you do moving around, but Sarah most emphatically does not do moving around. No, she doesn't. Sarah's idea of getting kinky is doing it with the lights on, and that's about as far as she gets, so you can keep your funny stuff to yourself, thanks all the same.

James reappeared from the lavvo (his word for it, not mine), scrummaging affectionately with his flies in that unpleasant way that men do. 'James,' said Sarah, assertive when she wants to be, 'James, what exactly do you mean by moving around?'

James chuckled. Actually it was more of a snort than a chuckle, but of course, when you're in love, sounds, like vision, often distort. 'Come here, you silly old thing.' He grabbed Sarah by the arm and then cupped her face in his hands. 'You're always worrying about something, aren't you? Just stop worrying and start enjoying yourself. Why don't we got out for a walk, just the two of us, and catch the last of the evening light before the sun sets?'

Well, you know by now how Sarah's going to react to this kind of talk. You know that James only has to turn on the tender tap for a moment for Sarah to think she's swimming in a warm bath of bliss.

'All right, James,' she said. 'I'll try and relax.' And before you tell me that try and relax form a contradiction of terms, remember I'm just telling you what happened, it's not me who needs the lecture. So, as violins serenaded in the background, our heroes walked off into the setting sun together, pausing only to invite Gerald and Antonia to join them at the pub later on.

Now I'd like you to cast your mind back many years: do you remember, can you remember, that heady sensation of the zingling and twingling in your lower stomach, when you know you are on the brink of a new affair? What a sensational feeling. Everything to play for, your adrenalin is on overdrive and your sense of the sensible gets locked in the cupboard . . .

Let's give Sarah just a few moments of that cloud cuckoo kind of happiness, shall we? Hand in hand with James, giggling as she skips to avoid the horse manure along the way in her apricot kid leather

Russell & Bromley bootees, while they crunch down the country lanes.

The air is warm and lazy, after a long Friday's sunshine. It is the end of a lovely day, the beginning of a drowsy and completely wonderful English summer weekend. The hedgerows are full of birds and butterflies, the fields full of rape and cowshit. There they are, just two city people, enjoying the new experience of putting one foot in front of the other for a distance longer than from the office to the company car-park, swanning past lovely little country cottages full of overpaid London executives who have just arrived, ready for a weekend of the family rows they had no time for during the week, past the old farmhouses full of ex-City has-beens selling organic turnips to each other.

'James,' murmured the lower-stomach-twingling Sarah as they sauntered along in romantic silence, 'tell me more about yourself, I feel I don't really know you.'

'Well,' said James – and you can guess that there's nothing that James likes talking about more than James, so I'd settle back for a good session if I were you – 'what exactly would you like to know?'

'Oh, I don't know,' said Little Red Riding Hood, 'tell me about advertising, about the agency, about how it feels to have that kind of responsibility, for all those accounts, for all those people's jobs?'

Come back Shirley Temple, all is forgiven.

'Well, what can I tell you, Sarah,' said the wolf. 'I'm an adman. I've been in advertising all my life. Sometimes I feel like I invented the game. But today, today advertising is no longer the business that it was. There's little pleasure left in advertising now. I know I've seen the best of it and that, in many ways, I was the best of it.'

Somehow James's reply was not the fairy-tale reply that Sarah would have liked. 'My goodness!' she squealed. 'No pleasure left in advertising! That's rather cynical, isn't it?'

'Not cynicism, Sarah. Reality. Advertising nowadays is tired, washed-out, the fanny that's been shagged just that once too often.'

'Oh,' exclaimed Sarah. It's true she'd never thought of her profession in that way. How much she still had to learn.

'The customers keep getting older and wiser,' James continued, 'while the admen grow younger and greener with each campaign. It used to be the other way round: you had the admen calling the tune and the customers dancing to it. This way, nowadays, it doesn't work, it's inverse, perverse, unworkable.

'You see, the whole trick of advertising is making people believe what you say. What disillusioned post-recessionary sod out there is going to believe anything any more? And what do the tots running advertising nowadays think they're trying to make them believe? I've got people working for me, kids straight from their first fucks at university, they stride in and tell me "what consumers want". What consumers want! And I look at them, and I tell them – learn one thing and you've learnt it all – consumers don't know what they want, you have to tell them, that's your job, that's what advertising is, you miserable, half-cocked pricks. And they look at me like I've blasphemed, because they've just spent three months in Daddy's holiday home in Florida, genning up on geodemographics and psychographics, reading how you need to profile and segment and target a customer before you can go anywhere near one and I'm saying sod that! Sod that, OK! Get your product, get your ideas, and do your job! You're an adman, not a lab assistant. Sod the science, chuck the sex at them, make the dream flicker in their weary minds and you'll get grandmothers buying Tampax if you get it right.

'These boys, armed with their degrees in economics

and their sodding MBAs, they think they've dipped their dicks in vats of twenty-four-carat gold. I've got these prats on my payroll telling me I can't do what I want to do because market research shows us that it is incompatible with the product profile, or analysis of the database tells us that it would be better to reach a different socio-economic target group, and I say, who gives a fuck, OK? I mean, who gives a fuck, right? Don't tell me who you want to sell to. Tell me what you've got to sell and I'll sell it.'

'Oh,' said Sarah again. She was sure James was right, just not sure how he was right.

The sun had gone in, she was starting to feel quite chilly. James's hand was sweating not pleasantly in her own, and she really didn't follow, or like, much of what he had said to her.

'Well, I guess as one of the MBAs who thinks I've dipped my dick in gold, I have to say I think I probably disagree with you, James. I think advertising is more exciting today than it's ever been. I think the opportunities available through sophisticated consumer analysis are fantastic, and given the fragmentation of the marketplace and the consequent diversification of consumer types, good market research, and market analysis in general, are essential prerequisites to a successful campaign.'

How lovely – it seems they deserve each other after all.

'What people fail to realise,' James went on, ignoring her comments completely, for, like most men, his orals are far better developed than his aurals, 'is that advertising is all about brands. Brands are the twentieth-century icons that have replaced statues of the Madonna, national flags and old school ties. A good brand is your parent, your ally, your mentor. And what the fuck is a brand? No more than a good ad. Now tell me who has more influence over people's lives: a president, a doctor, a teacher, or the man who brings the brands into your home? They eat my brands, they wash with them, they go into the red for them and spend most of their lives aspiring for them. Now tell me don't get heady about advertising. I gave you advertising and you left home at seven-thirty this morning to work to get more of what I'm selling you, so don't tell me who's on top. Right?'

'Well, yes, in a way,' Sarah mumbled as James paused for breath, 'but in a way also – '

'All these fucking schoolboys running the show, all these twenty-something twats who think that advertising is about recall rates and balance sheets. No, it's not. No, it's not, I tell them. Advertising's about fun. If you have fun, the shoppers have fun. Be a bit cheeky, have a bit of a laugh, that's what my ads say. Because humour sells. Humour sells. That's what I tell these po-faced anal adolescents I have milling round the agency nowadays. And they talk to me about their strategies and their analyses and I say – look, fuck all of that, fuck it. If we're not having fun, it isn't working. And they look back at me and I think to myself, Christ, this lot couldn't have fun if they had a circus up their backsides. I despair, I really do.'

'Despair – gosh, that's a dramatic word to – '

'I've built my agency up from nothing to everything, and it's my name that people are buying when they work with us, it's the James brand and everything it stands for that the clients want. I know it, everyone else knows it. People listen to me because I've got success tattooed on my arse. I've won more accounts than they've popped zits. They can throw theory at me, I can throw billings, awards, revenue. Don't give me tosh, give me results, I tell them, OK? They grow up eventually. If they don't, I let them go. I'm quite happy for the competition to pay a monthly cheque to dorks I don't want. I'll give you an example: Ralph. He does his best, but he's run his course. I've tried to give the guy my help and my input but I can see it's only a question of time before I get someone to leave a black plastic bin-bag on his desk one Monday morning.'

'Really?' said Sarah, because she was still there, as I hope you are after such a sea of monologue.

'Yes,' said James, suddenly bringing the verbal stream of consciousness to a halt. 'Why? You sound surprised.'

'Well, yes, I am,' said Sarah, thirty-two going on twelve, 'because he's more or less told me he's going to accept another offer for a partnership from that new agency that Mark and Paul set up when they left a few months ago.'

So the rumours are right about him as well, thought James. Fuck. I'll have to hurry and give the bastard his notice on Monday morning, before he gets in there first. 'Yes, well, you know, when people know they've failed that's the kind of story they invent. He's run his mile. I've seen it all before – a young bloke, all burnt out, not enough talent to finish the course, I've seen it a hundred times.'

You'll be glad to know that this doleful reflection was James's finale. Now all he had to do was make sure that Sarah didn't let on to Ralph that she had told him what she'd told him when she'd told him.

'By the way, Sarah, I know I can trust you to respect absolute confidentiality in all our discussions.'

'Of course, James!' cried Sarah, thrilled. 'Everything you've ever told me, including all that stuff in the restaurant the other evening, I understand how absolutely confidential it all is.'

'What stuff in the restaurant?'

'You know, about the Birksomes account.'

'About the Birksomes account?'

'Yes,' said Sarah, looking conspiratorially around the deserted country lane in case an errant rabbit might be taping their conversation. 'About how you're going to pay Frank to hang on to the account.'

James felt the contents of his bowels turn to taramasalata. 'I told you that?' he whispered, so the bunny couldn't hear.

'Yes,' said Sarah, with pride, 'don't you remember?' Well of course James didn't remember – his brain had been busy running a brewery at the time. He couldn't believe that he'd got so rat-arsed he'd told her about that. What an idiot! He'd have to make sure he kept an eye on himself with the booze while he was with her, if that was the kind of effect she had on him, the witch. He'd have to make sure, too, that this woman was so devoted to him that she would never spill the beans to anyone.

'Sarah,' he said, suddenly stopping and swerving his bulk round towards her.

'Yes, James.' Sick bags at the ready, folks.

'Sarah, I want you to know you're a very beautiful and intelligent woman.'

'I'm glad you think so, James.' In fact, make mine a bucket.

James moved his body very close to her. Very, very gently, he pressed his perspiring lips against hers. She breathed in the fumes of alcohol, tobacco and, well, let's be frank, signs that he'd ignored the 'your visit to the dentist is now due' reminder card just that once too often. Lower down, she feels what I believe is at this stage called his manhood pulsating against her valley of dreams.

'Sarah,' he said, moving away after the kiss, if this lip-wiping exercise can in fact be deemed to have reached kiss status, 'Sarah, I want us to be very good friends.'

'Yes, James. I think we're going to be very special friends,' croaked Sarah. Heads down between your legs, everyone. The hands re-entwined as they tenderly pushed open the gate to the garden of the Rat and Carrot.

In fact, James needn't have exerted himself thus. Sarah was already hooked. Although she didn't actually agree with or like or comprehend most of what he'd said to her, she knew that this was because of her own inadequacy and ignorance.

This was the first time that she had had a relationship with an older man, someone whose first instinct was not to jump into bed with her, someone who really wanted to develop a rapport with her. He'd talked to her, he'd confided in her. He was honest, open, genuine. She felt a pang when he spoke with so much pride about his agency, about his achievements. He had such a weight to carry on his shoulders. She knew things were not going particularly well for the agency right now, but it was only a blip, she was sure. James had so much conviction, so much determination, and confidence, and experience. He had integrity, that was the word.

She felt inspired by him, exhilarated through him. He was taking her up to a new dimension, into a new world. He was enriching her with his own knowledge and ideas and strength of character. She was about to start a wonderful relationship with a wonderful man. And life was wonderful.

Sarah, we're all thrilled for you.

Nineteen

Gerald and Antonia arrived very soon afterwards. They brought with them their eldest, Anastasia, who had had a row over at Pansy's and had decided she didn't want to spend the evening at her house after all. Apparently Pansy's mother had a funny smell which made Anastasia feel sick, so she'd got a cab and come home.

Anastasia was eleven, in the middle-aged way that so many eleven-year-old women are. Anastasia had not wanted to be left at home with 'the children' so she'd come too. Right now she was in speciality sulk mode because Gerald had got her beef and onion crisps instead of the cheese and onion she had specifically ordered.

'Gerald, you know I don't eat beef and onion.'

'Well, Annie, that's all they had. Leave them if you don't want them.'

'Don't tell her to leave them,' barked Antonia. 'You should be pleased she wants to eat anything at all.'

'Aren't you a big eater?' said Sarah pleasantly. 'I was just the same at your age. My mother had to shout at me to get me to eat my dinner.'

'Please don't patronise me,' said Anastasia. 'Gerald, what about sandwiches, don't they have any sandwiches?'

Her dad obediently shuffled off and brought back a plate of sandwiches. 'They had cheese and tomato, ham salad and prawn mayonnaise. I didn't know which one you wanted so I got you one of each.'

'Prawn mayonnaise! Dead molluscs swimming round in raw eggs. Gross! I'd rather die than eat that!' But the good news is that the other two sandwiches were acceptable. Well, that is, parts of them were acceptable. Anastasia took a half slice of the processed cheese out of one, carefully scraped off all the tomatoes and butter, peeled away one piece of lettuce from the ham salad sandwich and wrapped it round the cheese. This she nibbled at the rate of one nanobite an hour, but appeared happy enough.

The rest of them all stared at their drinks. It seemed that no one had anything they particularly wanted to say to each other.

'Where's Quentin and Lorenzo?' Sarah asked brightly.

No one spoke. Gerald nudged Antonia. 'Oh, the boys? Oh, Mrs B next door is going to pop round every so often to check them,' replied Antonia with great effort. She was clearly not in a good mood and didn't care who knew it. Eventually Gerald suggested that he and James got another round, and they both leapt up at the idea and dashed off.

The three women were left in uncomfortable silence, Anastasia sitting in the middle, still munching loudly through her slither of food, like she had to cream every minute morsel into a pulp in her mouth before she would concede to let it slip down to her stomach.

Suddenly, Antonia faced Sarah head on. She seemed to have decided that it was time for war.

'I suppose you know what you're doing with him?' Her overmascaraed, massacred, cynical little eyes locked into Sarah's.

'I'm sorry?' said our mild-mannered girlie. 'What I'm doing with him?'

'Yes. Please don't play *la innocente* with me, my

dear. With James. I suppose he's told you everything about himself?'

'Antonia, are you planning on doing a Mrs Danvers on me? Because I have no interest in James's past. That's his business. James and I are friends, that's all.'

Antonia thought this to be marvellously funny, for she threw her head back and laughed, ha ha ha. 'My God, he's had some daft ones, but it looks like you're going straight to the top of the hit parade. You know nothing about him, nothing about the women in his life, nothing about Belinda?'

Sarah's bottom squirmed on the greasy pub sofa and she took another sip of her drink. 'Antonia, look, I'm not interested. Can we change the subject? I'm just not interested in any of this.'

'I bet you're not. If I were you I'd shut my eyes to it all as well. Oh well, don't say I didn't warn you. Maybe you're into that kind of thing, God knows I'm not, God knows that poor cow of a wife of his was glad enough to get out when she eventually did. The stories she had to invent at the hospital to explain the cuts, the bruises, the bits and pieces they used to find up her, in her, the toys, the tools, the – '

'Antonia!' interrupted Sarah, pointing to the lettuce mulching Anastasia. 'For God's sake! Please!'

'Oh yes,' said Antonia. 'Oh, well,' she concluded, wiping her mouth of the spittle which had foamed there. 'It's not my problem any more. I've done my turn with him, I've paid my dues. Good luck to you.'

The men came back. Sarah reminded herself never to heed the deranged rantings of bitter ex-girlfriends, and Anastasia, an eighth of the way through her meal, ran off to the loo.

'Are you all right?' said James to Sarah. 'You're very pale.'

'Yes, yes, I'm OK,' said Sarah with a look of contempt in Antonia's direction.

'Is she all right?' said Gerald, staring at the fleeing skeleton of his daughter. 'Shouldn't you go with her?'

'Yes, yes, she's OK,' said Antonia impatiently through the bubbles of her G&T.

Ten minutes later, when Anastasia was still not back, someone near their table said there was a commotion with a little girl found on the floor in the ladies toilets. Anastasia had fainted: she wasn't used to having so much food in her stomach all at once and had blacked out chucking it up. An ambulance was called. 'Look,' said James, 'I'd better go with them. Take a cab back and look after the boys. I'll be back when I can.'

Once again, in times of stress and choppy seas, her Captain was immediately at the helm. 'Of course, James,' said Sarah. 'Take care.'

'I will,' said James. 'I'll be back as soon as I can.'

'Of course, darling. Don't worry, I'll be fine.'

'Right. I'll see you later.'

'OK, James. And, James.'

'Yes?'

'I love you.'

'Fine. See you later.'

And so it was that, while Captain James went off to do whatever it is a Captain has to do, Sarah went back to the house, checked the boys, then picked a bed in the adults' dorm, fell fast asleep, and didn't have to move around once all night.

The reason why Sarah was denied her musical beds that night was that James, Gerald and Antonia did not return until nine the next morning. Anastasia had regained consciousness, but the doctors wanted to know why an eleven-year-old only weighed three and a half stone, so they had decided to keep her in for observation. It was not clear where the three of them had been all night, although fretting by the bedside of the little one seemed an unlikely explanation.

As soon as they turned up, James appeared keen to

201

leave. Antonia went straight up to bed 'too shattered to do anything but sleep' and it was true, she did look shagged out. So, after a terse and unaffectionate farewell to Gerald, Sarah and James got back into the Saabmobile and left.

Back in the car, the mood was not good. James was clearly tetchy and tired. Even Tina was thrown ungraciously onto the back seat and ignored. Sarah tried to express concern about Anastasia but her interest was met with a flurry of gruff monosyllables.

Sarah was anxious to recreate the tender atmosphere that had existed between them when James left the pub the night before. As ever, her idea of creating intimacy was to start a bit of Cosmospeak, a bit of the old relationshipanalysis. It's so sad that a woman's idea of intimacy is a man's idea of hell. No wonder they never get on.

'I gather you and Antonia go back a long way,' she initiated earnestly.

'Look, if you're trying to ask me if I've fucked her, yes I've fucked her,' he yapped back at her. Wow! Mr Brusque! But at least he's got beyond the monosyllables, which is a start. Trying is definitely two syllables, and fucked, well, when you read it, it looks as if it could be two, although I guess when you actually say it, it is really only one.

'James, you're being very defensive! I only mention it, not because I'm prying, but because she seemed keen to talk about it. She seemed keen to talk about you and all your relationships with women, especially Belinda.'

The car swerved. They both had to pretend it hadn't.

'Fine,' said James. 'You want to talk about Belinda, let's talk about Belinda. Belinda was my wife.'

'Was, or is?' said Sarah, stupidly.

'Please don't be clever with me, Sarah. Be what you like, but don't be clever. I've had enough of women thinking they're clever to last me a lifetime. If I say was, I mean was, not is.'

'OK, I'm sorry. When did it end?'

'Years, years ago. When I began to feel trapped by the marriage, by Belinda trying to reduce me to the infinite smallness of her own tiny conception of what I should and shouldn't be, that's when I got out. When my physical energy rose up against me, against her. When I felt myself gagging and choking on her small-mindedness.'

Sarah was amazed by this sudden and intimate confession.

'What you need to understand, Sarah, is that I am a very physical, a very sexual man. I take my sexuality very seriously, very intensely. Work is important to me, but so is sex, you know, sex and work, it's the yin and yang thing. And I think one of the reasons I'm so creative at work is that I don't coop up my sexual needs in some worn-out relationship. Most men today have lost all contact with their own sensuality. They spend their whole lives rubbing themselves up against the same tired body of a woman, then they wonder why they don't enjoy it any more. They end up locking themselves away in dirty hotel rooms to shaft some tart who smells of chips and semen. Then they're surprised that in their work they are dull, uninspired, unoriginal. I don't find it surprising at all.'

Sarah was appalled. But there was more to come.

'When I see a beautiful, young, fresh woman, my immediate desire is to have her. And, unlike most other men, I usually do. I enjoy sex. I enjoy my own sexuality. I must toss off three or four times a day. It does me good; I know it does my work good, it makes me think more creatively in everything I do.'

'OK,' gulped Sarah. 'OK. How does this fit in with Belinda?' What she really wanted to know was how this absurd *weltanschauung* fitted in with her, but from what she'd heard already, she wasn't sure she could really cope with the answer to that.

James sighed. 'Look, Belinda was a wonderful woman. We married when I was only thirty. After six years together, we both realised that our relationship was just not allowing me to develop into the man we both knew I had to become. She would be the first to tell you, I was honest with her, right from the start. Right from the start, she knew what kind of a man I am, a very physically active man. I'm a very active, creative individual and you can see this in my work, in my private life. My energy has taken me to where I am today, it's going to take me a lot further and I need to give this energy, this drive, an outlet, do you see? My sex drive is exceptionally strong and vibrant and anyone who's around me needs to be able to take this on board.'

Sarah had gone very pale.

'I like to have sex and it's not that important for me who I do it with. If I like the look of someone, if I want to shag them, I ask them out, we have a good fuck and that's it. I'm very open and honest in my sexual behaviour. I have a very strong, almost violent, need for sex: for me the sexual aspect of my life is, well, it's essential. Men who pretend otherwise, men who make out that fucking isn't the number one priority on their daily agenda, well, I've got nothing but contempt for men like that. They're welcome to their miserable, monogamous relationships. The truth is that man must fuck, and one woman is not only never enough, this is not the point. It is only by enjoying a wide variety of women that a man can fulfil himself, otherwise it's like trying to play a sonata with only one key of the piano. If a man does not fuck, he does not breathe, he does not think, he does not grow.

'This is how I am, this is who I am. I'm open with people, up-front, and they have to be able to deal with it. They have to deal with it, not me. It's not my problem, right? When I agreed to marry Belinda, we both thought she'd be able to deal with that, we both tried to work with her, to help her understand it, and it was a great disappointment for both of us when we realised she couldn't and that the marriage had to go. Belinda was a wonderfully intelligent woman in that she could come to terms with this, and in fact she was actually the one who finally said, James, I'm holding you up, I know it, I've got to let you go. And I will always admire her because of that.

'And I must add, in all fairness, that she is a super mother. My kids couldn't have a better mother, and I think that she too, finds bringing them up a very fulfilling experience, and I am so glad that I have been able to give her this.'

'You've already got kids!'

'Already? Why, who else am I going to have them with? Yes, I've got three kids. But I don't see much of them nowadays. I think that seeing me is disruptive to the routine she has built up for them, and, to be honest, I'm just too busy to get down to Esher that often.'

James settled back into his seat, clearly not in the mood to discuss the subject any further. Frankly, I think we've all heard enough. Men intellectualising their need to treat women like dirt never was my favourite topic. But what about Sarah, as she crosses her hands nervously in her lap and reflects on the thoughts of Chairman James. Guess what Sarah's thinking. Quiz – is she thinking:

[1] Where's the nearest Little Chef on this road so I can say I'm nipping out for an Aero bar, slip round the back and thumb a lift with anyone to anywhere knowing it will be safer than staying with this jerk?

Or is she thinking:

[2] This is amazing, amazing; it's true that older men are so much more in touch with their bodies, their

feelings. How refreshing, how stimulating to be with someone like him. Someone so sure, so bold, so mature. James is about to open new doors of experience for me [that's true enough] and I can't believe my luck.

It's your call, Sarah. My own very personal advice would be to get that Aero bar and sod the calories.

You can't be that besotted with this character, can you? Can you? Why do you want to get hurt, because you can see it coming now, can't you? He's getting nasty now, he's doing you a favour, he's showing you how nasty he might get. You've already had enough warning signs, Sarah. The allure of the big man is one thing; the actions of a self-confessed screwball are another.

I'd get your act together now. Like the ads say, all you've got to do is just say no. Open your mouth, while you still can, Sarah, and just say, 'No, I don't want this.'

But Sarah picks up her pencil and ticks answer [2]. Although she's a bright lass, quizzes never were her forte, alas.

Twenty

When they arrived at the hotel, Sarah was suitably
impressed. It was gorgeous. Big, old, plush and very
expensive. The fellow who came to collect the bags
from the car called James by name and winked at him.
'They get better every time, sir,' he commented
appreciatively.

They were shown up to a room which was the size of
her entire flat in Notting Hill Gate. There was a massive
double bed.

'Oh James', she exclaimed. 'It's lovely!'

'That's the power of an expense account for you,' he
replied. What an old romantic.

She looked around the room and at the sumptuous
view from the many windows of their suite. She
caressed the four poster bed and admired the ornate
dressing table. No smorgasbord of beds here, just the
one big four poster for the two of them, reflected Sarah,
suddenly more desperate for a bonk than she had ever
been. Sarah was hoping he might suddenly fling her
onto the bedsprings and yin-yang her with a bit of his
strong and vibrant sexuality.

In the very same time-frame, James was wondering
whether he shouldn't just take her there and then as
she metaphorically fondled the bedposts. But for the
past half-hour he had been dying for a crap, not having
had a really satisfactory one since before dinner on
Wednesday when all that drink had thrown his bowels

out of kilter for a bit, and James always worked on a bowel-override principle.

'Right, well, I think I'll just get changed and head on down for the pool. I guess you want to sort your stuff out and you can join me down there.'

The passion in the minds of both was duly dispelled. Sarah suddenly felt all her dreams going down the waste disposal unit. What had all that talk been in the car about his sexual energy? Did he not really fancy her? Was she not beautiful, young and fresh enough? Was she past it at thirty-two? When he said young, was he trying to tell her something?

All the inhibitions, all the doubts came gurgling back. She was never going to get this sex thing right. Half the time she never wanted it, the other half she wanted it but hated it when she got it. This man had made her feel excited, really excited about him, about herself. He was supposed to be her teacher, he was going to open doors for her. She felt confused, alone.

'OK,' she said, head bowed, as James toddled off to mark the territory as his own.

After fifteen minutes he reappeared, visibly relieved, wearing nothing but a pair of skimpy swimming trunks which would have looked great on a man half his age and with half his stomach. Still, all those beers and business lunches had to end up somewhere. 'Swimming time!' he announced. 'I'll meet you down there when you're ready?'

Sarah nodded. He went. She padded forlornly into the now rather smelly luxurious marble bathroom to get changed. What was the deal here? Was this the start of a love affair or a business trip? If he wasn't going to jump on top of her, why were they sharing the same room?

She felt miserable and tired. This was not what she had expected. She considered calling a cab and going home. Then she remembered that she had a mortgage to pay and a job she had to go back to on Monday.

James was not a man to upset lightly. She decided that she would change downstairs and leave the bathroom to get its breath back. She took off her shoes, grabbed her swimsuit and that week's copy of *Campaign* (yes, I'm afraid so) and made her way down to the pool.

By the time she got there, James was already surrounded by a small crowd of people at the bar in the leisure club. He was telling an animated story to an audience who looked as though they would feel more comfortable sitting cross-legged on the floor, or indeed in any position that would give better access to fawning at the feet of the master.

'Ah Sarah, here you are' he said, taking her arm. 'This is Sarah, everyone, one of my assistants, here to help me out with a little project.' Cue the titillation of giggles. 'Sarah, this is Bob, Tricia, Tim, Richard, Beverley, Chris, Linda and Natalie.'

A sea of faces nodded indifferently at her. They all looked like grown-up versions of the kids who would nick the chocolate biscuit from your packed lunch at primary school. People with hard and cynical features. Men who knew what was expected of them – aggression, attitude, ambition. Women who judged their own self-worth from the depth of their cleavage. Sarah's arrival created but a slight pause of mutual appraisal. The men reckoned she looked a bit snooty but OK, nice tits. The women dismissed her immediately as no threat. Anyone who comes down to the pool with no make-up on, like they seriously intend to swim and mess up their hair, doesn't stand a chance.

James went on. He was recounting a long story about his trip to the annual TV advertisers' shindig in Barcelona the year before which he had attended with a young woman called Vicky. Anyway, it appeared that everyone standing round the bar knew who Vicky was, because they too had attended the Barcelona conference, which in advertising land is the equivalent of the oil barons' ball in *Dallas* – i.e. an excuse to shag a lot of people on expenses. By the time Sarah came down, he had got to the bit where he was giving Vicky one behind the screen in the conference hall. This must have been a very funny story. Everyone laughed to within an inch of wetting themselves.

James got another round of drinks and remembered another story, a secret story which he only wanted Tricia to hear, because he started sniggering and whispering it very closely into her ear, with his arm round her waist.

Sarah took her drink and went for a walk round the leisure centre. The air was scented, its balmy heat contrasting lusciously with the austere tingle of the marble floors under her feet. Piles of thick white fluffy towels and robes were piled on every corner so you could pick one up, mop a brow and drop it, where some minion would immediately scurry out like a ballboy to snatch it up again and remove it lest the sheer soiled sight of it might offend you. Tall and gilded mirrors reflected gracious greenery and huge ferns billowing out of glass ceilings, leafy bowers erupting from still corners where the latest glossy mags were tossed on wicker tables. In the gym, glistening iron soldiers of equipment saluted you in rows while nervous little bodies pumped away at them to classical music. Lighting was moody, soft and then suddenly bold on a creamy statue of Venus with her arms chopped off, or a tasteful reproduction of a famous painting with colours that matched the wallpaper.

Meanwhile, the staff floated about like heavenly air hostesses, all in white, no one over the age of twenty-five, scooping up empty glasses, providing full ones, saying 'Hello' – big white teeth – 'Mr Layton', or 'Hello' – big white teeth – 'Deborah'(men are always second names, woman always first) whenever they met a guest. They all spoke in whispers and had smiles of beatific bliss sprayed permanently on their faces as if to say, dreamily, 'Isn't this simply the most lovely place you've ever been to?' – big white teeth.

In spite of all the opulence, it seemed to Sarah that it was not. With the exception of a few tourists, most of the people there were affluent ageing singles trying nonchalantly not to look as if they were hoping that you were watching them and desperately hoping that you were. Well-padded hips sashayed past well-padded guts. Sagging bosoms greeted drooping buttocks.

These people had spent too much time making money at their desks all throughout their twenties and thirties to remember that they were supposed to have lives as well. As middle-age started to creep up and seep into their bodies, as second and third chins began sprouting ominously from behind the first, as hairlines staring wilting and receding, they were trying every unsubtle means to flaunt their bodily wares to whoever may still be interested.

The atmosphere was self-conscious, over-controlled. All the women wore coordinated leotards in pastel colours to show that they weren't aggressive feminists but just normal women who had also wanted a career but now, before it was completely too late, could they please find a man who was going to take them away from all this and give them a couple of babies before their biological alarm clock went off. And the men wore T-shirts with the name of their management consultancy or blue chip company indiscreetly emblazoned all over them, to show that they may be losing head- and gaining nose-hair but they were solvent, heterosexual and had careers that you'd be proud to tell your mother about. They swam purposeful lengths up and down the pool, stepped sincerely on the step machines and rowed intensely on the rowing equipment, all with a look of vague irritation. A look that said: hey, I'm really very busy, you know, and I really should be somewhere else because I've got a whole address book of friends who are probably leaving me a message right now on my answering machine, so I'll just finish this exercise before I carry on with my busy, popular and definitely not! lonely life.

The whole place made Sarah feel edgy. James's voice and loud, excited laugh echoing off the marble walls made her feel uneasy. She decided to get changed into her costume, have a swim and generally calm down. She got a locker key from one of the celestial steward-esses and found the women's changing rooms right at the end of a long corridor (men design leisure clubs).

Opening the door to these changing rooms was like suddenly turning on the radio to find that someone has left it on maximum volume on clashing airwaves. A wall of women hit her – women's bodies, women's chatter, women's various women smells, from the fra-granced to the foul. Everywhere, the sight of hundreds of naked breasts jigging about, big breasts, little breasts, tanned ones, white ones, pink ones, black ones, great boisterous exuberant ones, funny pokey little mean ones, flat ones, ones which were all nipple and no flesh, ones which were sucked down by the force of gravity, ones which were held up by the force of sili-con. Tits, tits everywhere. Expensive frilly panties, chirpy little G-strings, rather nasty looking grey knick-ers. Tight, firm little bums, great sloppy buttocks like African elephants' ears. Long sleek legs, squat stubby tree trunks. Long straight wet hair, tight frizzy dry curls. Perfumes, scents, BO, deodorants. Hairsprays, footsprays. Creams, lotions, potions being slapped on, smeared over. Hairdryers whirring. Talcum powder fluffing. Yak, yak, yak. Noise and skin and towels.

Sarah found her locker and realised that she was going to suffer from her usual post-adolescent problem of not being able to change in front of people. She knew they'd all stare at her. There was nothing at all unusual about her body, but they'd all stare at her when she changed, she knew it. She slowly took off her shirt and jeans. So slowly that by the time she was down to her smalls, the changing room had emptied and there were only a couple of women left. Feeling more confident in this emptiness, Sarah finally yanked off her underwear.

Just then, Natalie came in. 'Hello. I thought I'd find you in here,' she said with a conspiratorial laugh. As Sarah had never met this women before, apart from James's brief introduction twenty minutes earlier at the bar, this familiarity threw her a bit. She giggled back politely. Natalie disappeared up to the other end of the changing room.

Once her swimsuit was safely donned, Sarah walked up there to look for the loos. Just as she turned the corner she was confronted by the sight of Natalie, naked, in one of them, having a pee with the door wide open.

'Hello!' she said again as if they were meeting over the garden fence.

Sarah stopped in her tracks, and desperately thought of something she could pretend she could have come down that end for, anything other than joining Natalie for a group wee round the camp fire. She swung herself round and started assiduously washing her perfectly clean hands. 'Hello,' replied Sarah, all Janet and John style friendliness.

Natalie flushed (the toilet, that is, not her cheeks – there is no sight left in this galaxy that would make Natalie flush) and came over to the handbasins. 'As soon as James introduced you, I felt very attracted to you,' she said.

She was standing right next to Sarah who was now applying soap with a passion like her hands hadn't been washed for several months.

'Do you have a problem with that?' Natalie said.

Come on, Sarah, thought Sarah. Don't be such an old fart. This woman's being perfectly straight with you, stop feeling like you're living through an episode of *Star Trek*. Sarah rinsed her hands and grabbed one of the super-fluffy towels. She forced herself to look into Natalie's face to give her a firm no.

This Natalie, I should tell you now, has one of the loveliest faces you've never seen. She's got large brown eyes, dark blonde hair, very white teeth. Most of all, she's got an expression: a warm, intelligent, self-assured expression that you'd like to wrap yourself up in like a thick blanket round you when the wind is howling in the night.

Nothing came out of Sarah's larynx. The firm no ended up as a strange, strangled gurgle in her throat. Natalie looked like her best friend at school, like Zelda the ice maiden in *Bunty*, like her Brown Owl. Natalie was very beautiful. She was standing so close to Sarah that Sarah could smell how beautiful she was, see how soft her skin would feel, see in the intelligence of her eyes how clear her mind must be.

'Are you attracted to me, Sarah?'

'I'm sorry,' was all that Sarah could say.

Natalie's heartwarming face broke into a wide smile. 'You're sorry? Is that a yes or a no?' she asked.

'I'm sorry,' Sarah said again, and ran out of the changing rooms back into the land of the semi-living.

James, his laugh and its audience were still at the bar. Sarah took a couple of the magazines and went to sit down on one of the recliners near the edge of the pool. They obviously put some kind of aromatic herb in the air conditioning, so that every so often a scent of pine and lavender caught your breath. She lay back on the heavily padded chair. She sipped the drink that one of the big white teeth had brought her and closed her eyes. She thought of the shape of Natalie's eyes and the smell of her hair. She thought of James.

James. Sarah asked herself whether she really liked this man. She was excited by him, challenged by him, she wanted him to want her, but now she thought about it, she really didn't like him that much. He was playing games with her. He actually was not a very nice person.

He asked her nothing about herself, knew nothing about her and seemed not to want to know anything about her. But still she wanted him, and feared his rejection. Although she knew she did not like him, she ached for him to want her.

But now it seemed that this had always been planned as a group jolly, that it was never going to be just James and her having a romantic weekend *à deux*. The thought of any romance with James now seemed ridiculous. Ridiculous and impossible. Almost impossible, her hopes added squeakily.

She took another sip of her drink and closed her eyes. The lovely smells filled her head. She shut her eyes, stretched her toes and started to dream and drowse. The pool made lovely lappy noises at her feet. The air was warm and close.

Just then she felt a cold, wet hand on her thigh. 'I can see where all the little hairs are starting to grow again round your fanny.'

It was James, on his knees by her chair, peering very closely into her crotch. He had been swimming and looked very different with his hair stuck to his head and water dripping from his nose and eyebrows. He was inspecting her upper thigh and stretching the skin apart between his fingers, like a marine biologist who's just found a rather unusual specimen of sea shell that he wants to prise open.

'Get off, James' said Sarah, pushing his hands away.

'But it's true, isn't it?' he continued. 'I'd say you've got about three or four days' growth there. So you must have gone to have your bikini line waxed last week. Or don't tell me you shave it?' He grinned and continued to drip all over her, his wet face and whisky breath right in her face.

'You seem very knowledgeable about this subject,' said Sarah, hoping that a mix of flattery and confidence would shut him up.

'Oh, but I am, sweetie. I am. When you've banged as

many women as I have, you get to know a lot about them. Women are my hobby. I know what you girlies do to yourselves to make yourselves look nice for us. You get yourselves plucked like chickens from head to toe. Not to mention calves and thighs and kneecaps and armpits and especially the little moustache which you get on your upper lip. All bald and shaved and plucked so it's nicer for men to run their hands all over you. But then it all starts to grow back, gets all spikey, all little pussy in-growing hairs, all little stubbly nasty patches. So then you've got to do it all over again. And that's what's happening, right now, to your fanny, isn't it? It's a plucked chicken coming back to life, back from the dead to haunt us.'

He belched a large cloud of whisky burp and flung himself onto the end of her recliner. Sarah felt revolted and ashamed. He was right. She had been to have her legs done exactly four days before. It was true that the hairs were starting to grow back.

James was grinning at her now. 'Come on, lighten up. Don't look so terrified, we're only having a bit of fun. I'll go and get you another drink. Perhaps that's what you need to cheer you up a bit. And then we can go and get some lunch.' He burped again, giggled and walked away.

When he came back with the drinks, he was all fun and friendly, lolling on the lounger, reading the papers, slurping at his whisky, happy as Larry. Sarah pretended to read but could not take her eyes off him.

If you've ever wondered why they call them swimming trunks, you would not wonder once you had seen James in his. His appendage was definitely a trunk. It bulged and strained through the flimsy material of the hip huggers. You could almost see the outline of the veins as they longed to tank up on blood and get into gear with a major erection. Given half the chance, a nod's as good as a wink, and they'd be off. For now, they were snarling around in their sateen cage, prowling and snarling and just aching to be let off the lead.

Sarah was mesmerised. She had never seen a penis quite that big. It was so big it was almost offensive. Yet it was hypnotic. Perhaps it was Natalie's warm skin in the changing rooms. Perhaps it was all that prodding about that James had put her through a few minutes earlier. She couldn't tell whether it was the pool water that had dripped off his hands or something else that was making her feel so damp. His dick was leering at her now. 'Can't take your eyes off me, can you, sweetheart?' it sneered.

She realised with a start that James was also staring at her. 'Big, isn't he?' he said. Go for it, said the little character on the left of her head, the one with the horns holding the fork, grab him and say I thought you'd never offer. But no! cried the character on the right, the one with wings and a halo, that's not the way to have a love affair!

'I think I'll go for a dip now,' said Sarah, and dived into the pool water to wash away her quandary.

She spliced through the water. It felt wonderful. She began to relax. Perhaps she should just let herself go and start enjoying it all a bit more. This was one of the best hotels she had ever been to and there was no point in letting him spoil it for her. She was over-reacting; she had always been accused by previous boyfriends of being over-sensitive and now she was doing it again.

If only she could understand what James wanted from her. He had made no real advances towards her. Maybe this was a bona fide work do after all. Maybe she had been stupid to ever think it was ever going to be anything else. She would try talking to him about work and get everything back on an even keel. She had let her imagination run overtime. This was how work was done at the top of the tree. They would probably be up all night discussing strategy on the account. That's why the shared room. She began to feel much better, although a little part of her remained quite sad, the little part that wanted a loving man, please.

She had seen a sign for a sauna tucked away round the corner at the other end of the pool and decided to go and unwind in there for a while. She looked round to see what James was up to. He appeared to have dozed off in the chair.

As the sauna was empty, Sarah gave her inhibitions a brief holiday and rolled down her swimsuit. There's always that moment in a sauna when the heat really hits your skin and the pores start to release their sweat. Suddenly you feel this glorious greasiness running all over you and all the toxins in your bloodstream come spilling out. The warmth rolls over you and dribbles down you. The heat slobbers all over you like someone is smearing warm clotted cream over your flesh.

It was exhilarating and liberating. Sarah felt the juicy sweat streaming down from her neck to her bare stomach. Hot, hot, hot. Blissful. She ran her hands down her arms and felt her skin melting. All her gritty tensions, all her anxieties and knots all evaporated into hot air.

She thought again of Natalie. She realised that she was kind of hoping that Natalie might join her in the sauna, as she lay there with her swimsuit rolled down, her eyes closed. Natalie would come in and start pressing her hot, perfumed skin against her, she would say over and over 'I'm attracted to you.' Sarah would just be the object of her desire, she wouldn't know what was happening to her, she would not be responsible for what she was doing, she would just feel a beautiful person loving her in a warm and loving way. But no one came in. Sarah started feeling like her head was exploding with illicit thoughts, which were wildly careering down tracks she rarely let herself even acknowledge.

After a while all the fantasies and the heat of the sauna became too much. She looked at the timer – she had already been in there fifteen minutes. She rolled up her swimming costume and tried to stand up. She really had been in there too long. When she got up, everything started to swim lopsidedly in a mist round her eyes. She fell back hard onto the wooden seat.

She stood up again, much more slowly this time, gripping a handrail. She put out her hand to push open the door.

The door didn't open. Although it was definitely a push not a pull door. Through dry ice that now seemed to be swirling round her head she saw big letters. P–U–S–H. Her head was so hot, maybe that meant pull. Does push mean push or pull? She tried pulling. The door still didn't open.

She couldn't think at all, her head was boiling and spinning, she could feel the blood in it bubbling like a cauldron. She couldn't breathe, couldn't breathe. Still the door wouldn't open. Perhaps pull did mean push.

Black waves began whooping over her mind like a toreador's cape. The ground went flimsy beneath her. She focused all her concentration to bang on the door and scream. As she moved her fist slowly forwards a face appeared at the little glass window in the sauna door. A big grinning face. A face with wet hair stuck down all round it. The face raised its eyebrows and mouthed the word 'hot' and smiled again.

The blood throbbed in Sarah's head. Bang, bang, bang went the blood. Bang, bang went Sarah's weak fist on the door. She felt the heat climbing up her stomach and rushing at her head. The toreador's cape was coming at her again, bigger than ever before. Whoosh, it went over her head. Suddenly the face let go of the door and Sarah's body slumped out on to the marble floor.

Twenty-one

From the blackness, Sarah came round. She was in the big bed in the room, with James smoking and drinking at the end of the bed, reading a car magazine.

'Sarah, you are a twit,' said James. 'Fancy going into the sauna on your own and then staying in there for such a long time. You could have killed yourself. I didn't realise you needed a bloody nursemaid for the weekend. If I hadn't come looking for you, you'd probably have copped it by now. We'd all be having roasted Sarah for supper.'

Sarah remembered fragments of a nightmare she'd had where she'd fought to get the sauna door open while James kept it shut from the outside, laughing at her. She said nothing. Her head ached where she'd fallen. Perhaps he'd think she'd gone bonkers.

'Sorry, James' she said weakly, 'I just didn't realise I'd been in for so long.'

'Oh well, let's just forget about it. Don't want to let something like this ruin our weekend, do we?' He smiled at her. Unlike the smile in her dream, this was a friendly, almost affectionate smile. 'You've missed lunch now but I've arranged for us to have tea with that crowd you met earlier. Why don't you get yourself together, and I'll meet you down in the library.' He left.

It was only then that Sarah realised she was on the bed with just a sheet covering her and nothing on. The sheet was creased and puckered, as if there had been a dog fight on it. She saw her swimsuit in a little wet heap by the side of the bed. She could remember nothing about getting back up to the room or taking it off.

She looked at the clock – it was already five, which meant she had been out of it for several hours. She rang down to the leisure club and asked for the manager. He was very pleased to hear that she was feeling better, very pleased because nothing like that had ever happened at the club before and he had to remind her that her personal safety in the leisure club wasn't the hotel's responsibility, as was clearly shown on various notices posted throughout the club.

'But how did I get back to the room after I'd passed out?'

'Your friend took you up, Madam. He carried you in his arms and wouldn't let anyone else help. He said you were quite all right and that he'd call us if there were any problems. I have to remind you, Madam, that guests of the hotel enter the sauna at their own risk.'

Exhausted, Sarah put down the phone. She had been on her own in the room with James for over four hours. He had taken off her costume and put her in the bed. She looked down at her body. Her skin was all red and blotchy – it looked as if someone had been pummelling at it. That must be from the heat in the sauna. Her breast and legs were starting to bruise, they felt as if someone had been slapping her around. That must be from where she fell down and from flinging herself repeatedly at the sauna door.

Her body looked back at her, raw and sore. It could tell her nothing.

Twenty-two

Tea-time. Sarah spent a long time in the bathroom trying to calm herself down and use creams and colours to soothe her microwaved skin and take the pale look of terror from her face. She wedged a pile of magazines in front of the bathroom door to keep it open, as she couldn't bear the thought of the door shutting and leaving her closed in a small space again.

Our Sarah is a good-looking woman by anyone's standards, but it's hard to look cool when you've just done a sharp impersonation of a corn-fed chicken on a spit. She smeared foundation into her face to balance out the red patches and she attempted a bit of assertiveness training in the mirror: Sarah, you are thirty-two years old; Sarah, you are a bright, clever woman; Sarah, don't let this man treat you like shit. Then she glanced over nervously to check that the pile of magazines were still standing guard at the bathroom door.

She put on black trousers and a beige jumper. She's one of these annoying women who doesn't look like a sandcastle in beige. She just looks kind of lovely really.

She took her very long hair and flipped it up into a casual but creative pile on her head. She hooked in earrings in the shape of starfish and put some rinky-dinky aromatherapy perfume on her wrists and neck. She's the sort of women you see in Bond Street and think, never mind, at least I've got a nice personality. At least I'm kind to animals. She's the kind of woman that men see and think – it's Annapurna! As soon as they meet her, they feel this compelling instinct to get their climbing gear together, get on top of her and stick their flag into her. She's too tall and independent and beautiful to leave unmolested. Conquest of her is imperative.

So why is this kind of a woman going to let someone like James treat her so badly? And why is a banana skin yellow?

She went downstairs, wading through the lavish carpet pile and beating a path through the sumptuous antique furniture of this amazing hotel which only Americans or business accounts can truly afford. They were all there in the library, surrounded by trays of scones, clotted cream and silver teapots which had been pushed aside to make room for the G&Ts. James was, surprise surprise, in the centre, waving his arms round wildly as he recounted yet another tale which left the others either open mouthed with obsequious awe or contorting themselves with hilarity.

He's an amusing old bugger is James. He can tell a story all right. If you met him at a party, for the first five minutes you'd be thinking what a great bloke. Then you'd be thinking, what a wanker. But this lot couldn't get enough of him.

Sarah arrived at the bottom of the grand staircase. Now there are two kind of difficult entrances you can make. The one where you go into a room and everyone stops talking and stares at you like you're something that just fell through the roof from the lavatory of a passing plane. Or the one where they all ignore you. Press button B for this scenario, friends. Sarah sat down at one of the empty armchairs, ripped all her clothes off and sang the first two verses of 'Blue Suede Shoes' juggling oranges on her tits and no one even vaguely acknowledged her presence.

Some remote-controlled waiter eventually came to help her out and asked her if she would like tea, coffee or something from the bar. At this point, as if the waiter's words had been the abracadabra that threw back a magic curtain, James suddenly noticed her and got very excited.

'Sarah, Sarah, where have you been! We've all been missing you madly, haven't we, Tricia?' He pulped Tricia's thigh. Tricia went another shade pinker under her blusher and burped with delight.

'Come here, come here, gorgeousness,' he continued, beckoning to Sarah. 'Come and sit on Daddy's knee and tell him where you've been.' James took another stiff swig of his drink and motioned animatedly for her to come over to him.

'James, really, I'm fine where I am,' Sarah said.

'James! Really! I'm fine where I am!' he trilled back in a high-pitched squeal. 'No, you're not. No, you are not. How can you be fine until Daddy gives you a big cuddle. Now get over here.' No one seemed shocked that James should treat one of his work colleagues like this. It was all just a bit of fun, after all.

Sarah looked at this man, red in the face, pissed and hyperactive. He was her boss. He employed almost two hundred people. He worked on very important accounts – accounts that sold millions of products, sales that made profits that made employment for thousands of people in their factories and their offices up and down the country. He had interviewed her. He paid her salary each month. He decided on her promotions and her pay review. Now he was Daddy and if she didn't go and sit on Daddy's lap this minute, Daddy would give her a good spanking.

Sarah walked over to him. 'That's better,' said the Chief Executive of one of the best-known advertising agencies, the man whose face regularly leers out at you from *Campaign*, the man whose throwaway lines in the pub on a Friday evening used to be every advertising executive's mantra in the office on the Monday morning. 'You see, you can be a good girl.' He grabbed her hand and pulled her down onto his podgy lap. He started jigging her up and down. 'Get this woman a drink,' he hollered. 'She's tight as a nun's fanny.'

'Just the way you like them,' someone bellowed.

James began to burrow his face into Sarah's neck. 'Kissy wissy, kissy wissy, Sarah.' He was mouthing kisses like a goldfish, sucking his cheeks in and rocking his head from side to side. Everyone thought this was hilarious.

'Go on, give the poor sod a kiss,' one of them shouted. 'Can't you see the old bugger's desperate?'

Sarah leant over and gave James a peck on the cheek with a look that was meant to say: make sure this shuts you up, mate, because it's all you're going to get.

'What's that?' says James, all irate. 'What's that? Call that a kiss? That's not a bloody kiss, girl. We want to see a real kiss, don't we, boys and girls?'

'Yes, yes,' shouted the kids watching Dame James on his stage.

'We want to see a really big kiss, don't we?'

'Yes! Yes! Yes!' the children cried.

'This is the kiss that we want to see.' He pushed Sarah's head down onto Tricia's thighs and kept it down while he swooped his great hoary face into hers.

Now his mouth has grown larger, wider, wilder. The goldfish has turned into a big whale. A big sweaty old whale that has cruised through many oceans and gobbled up many smaller fish before. A big red greasy tongue of a whale that has swum through seas of G&Ts to get to her.

And now she was going to end up like Jonah, inside this great whale. It bashed at the narrow crack of her clenched mouth, fighting to get in. It was an angry whale. It smashed and thrashed its tail. It pushed and banged and finally forced her mouth open. The immense encrusted whale swam in and filled her mouth with its huge size and forced itself down to the back of her throat. She was suffocating, drowning.

This slimy whale cruised round and round her mouth. She could feel the crusty old scabby skin of this whale's body rummaging against the skin inside her cheeks as he swished about and explored the spaces round her teeth, under her tongue, in her throat. And as the whale was exploring, one hand kept her head yanked back on Tricia's spongy legs, and the other pawed at her bosom.

After a while, James pulled away, wiping all the spittle from his mouth with the back of his hand. And how the children laughed and sang to see such a wonderful sight!

The waiter brought in a new tray of drinks and everyone, now bored with that game, started talking about who they thought was going to win the radio awards that week.

Sarah extracted herself from Tricia's legs and stood up. She was very angry, she realised with a bit of a shock. James had made her very angry.

'James, why don't you go fuck yourself,' she said and turned to go back upstairs to the room.

They all started a slow mocking handclap of applause. A voice shouted out 'What a performance! Give this woman an Oscar!' As she walked away, she could hear that someone had started to follow her. She walked on slowly, but she knew it was him. He was walking right behind her. She kept on walking, up the stairs, back down the corridor. He stood behind her as she opened the door to the room. Her armpits broke into splinters of nervous sweat. When she got into the room she turned abruptly round to face him. What now? The spanking she'd been threatened with earlier?

James shut the door behind him. His face was puffy and purple. He took her by the wrist and led her to sit next to him on the bed. 'Sarah, Sarah. I'm so sorry. So sorry. I really am. I've had a bit too much to drink today and I've behaved like a complete prat. That lot always have a bad influence on me. Look, I'm really sorry. I was out of order. Please can we just forget it happened? I'm sorry. I've been a moron, I was showing off, I can't seem to stop myself. Forgive me?'

She looked at him. This tired and drunk middle-aged man, wearily wiping the sweat off his brow, was the head of her advertising agency. He was her hero. He had won awards, he spawned fashions. She had heard stories of clients, way back when, in tears of veneration at some of his legendary presentations. She had admired him from afar for years, never dreaming that he might one day take an interest in her. Now she was with him, with her dream, with her fantasy. Her anger burrowed back into its retreat.

'OK, let's forget it,' she said to her boss.

He took her hand and squeezed it. 'Friends?' he asked, pathetically.

'Is that what we are?' Sarah asked back.

'What?' he said.

'Friends. Is that what we are?'

'Well of course we're friends, you silly sausage. Of course we are.'

'James, I'm not a silly sausage. It may be true that you are a fair bit older than me, but why this means you have to address me in this, I don't know, this avuncular form, as if I were a prattling child, is not clear. I'm one of your senior account directors. You pay me quite a lot of money each month to be that. You've invited me away for a weekend and I want to know what's what.'

Poor James looked genuinely confused. Mind you, I think I am a bit too at this stage. He also bristled somewhat at the mention of his age, of the difference in age between them. Who the hell was she to throw his age in his face? This woman was starting to get on his tits.

'Look, Sarah, I'm sorry, I don't follow you. What's your problem? I've brought you to one of the most expensive hotels in the country, you've got a whole crowd of some of the brightest bonces in advertising sitting downstairs to get to know. Aren't you having fun?' He looked red-eyed and bored by this little scene which Sarah wanted to make happen and he wasn't having any of. He badly wanted another drink. 'Do you want us to go?'

While there wasn't menace in his voice, this was a top-gun loaded question. Was she really going to make such a fuss that he was going to have to drive her all the way back down the M4 and ruin the whole weekend, just because he'd had a bit too much to drink, because he'd let a bad joke go too far? It would be all over W1 by lunchtime on Monday – Sarah the virgin maiden who is so politically correct she thinks joke is a four-letter word.

'OK, OK, James. I'm not going to make an issue here. I'll just ask you one more thing – why the double bed?'

James stood up and winked at her. If there's one thing I cannot stand it's men who wink at women. 'Play your cards right and you'll find out,' he chuckled. He obviously thought this was very funny and laughed a lot. Sarah got so fed up with her own unease that she laughed too. It seemed the best thing to do.

Big wrong, Sarah, big wrong.

The best thing to do, my dear, would be to get angry, stay angry, pack your bag there and then, and get the hell out.

Twenty-three

They walked back down to the library together, but all
the rest of their merry gang had already gone through
for dinner. 'Yoo hoo, Jim,' trilled Tricia. 'We've saved
you a place.'

You'll note, as Sarah did, the single form of the noun
in that sentence. They obviously hoped that Sarah
would have left or died or done whatever was necessary in the interim not to have to impose her humour-
less presence on them over dinner. James sat down
and Sarah hovered in a state of embarrassment while
another chair was brought across by a waiter from one
of the adjoining tables.

There's something about media people. They're
usually very pleasant one-on-one. But get them
together and it's like the damp washing you forgot in
the machine during your three-week holiday in
Minorca: not nice. They feel that so much is expected
of them and, although they do have a lot to offer, it is
not so much. Their product, unfortunately for them,
is intangible, amorphous. Something a bit creative, a
bit commercial, a bit psychological, a bit odd. Which
makes them defensive, loud, embarrassing.

Here we go again. Martin was holding forth on what
happened after the latest trip to Monte Carlo for the
newspaper awards when the awards chairman failed to
turn up. He was eventually found in bed with a fifteen-
year-old girl by the Monte Carlonian police who broke

down the door to his hotel room after his secretary, who read a lot of books, suggested that he might have been kidnapped.

Righty ho. You'll be glad to know this meant that this evening's topic was sex. It could have been work or sex. It was sex. Martin had got the proverbial ball rolling. Now it was up to the others to make sure that whatever else they came up with was more shocking, more disgusting, then his offering. If it had been work, they would have had to produce more prestigious clients, more exasperating accounts, more lucrative business wins. As it was sex, it was a question of bigger willies, younger girls, dafter situations, closer shaves.

Debbie told Martin he was a fine one to talk after he was found shagging one of the organisers under the reception desk at the same event. This story, which they'd all heard before, all told before, was recounted again with yet another veneer of hyperbole, everyone slathering on another coat of innuendo and fantasy.

Meanwhile, po-faced French waiters served up exquisite courses which were scoffed down and munched through as they all vied to get their words in edgeways. You could see sauces and terrines which some poor underpaid sous-sous-sous chef in the kitchen had taken hours to prepare being swilled round chattering open mouths like so many pairs of underpants going round in a washing machine. It was all fodder to them. This lot had such a constantly rich diet that a fishfinger sandwich would have seemed like a luxury.

And, of course, there was booze. Booze and booze. Alcohol dribbled from every orifice, into every orifice. Fine wines were glugged down like lemonade; full glasses of claret were discarded for Chardonnays which were pushed aside for champagne.

By the time it got to their main course, the posse of super-trained French *maîtres d'*, sommeliers and whatever else they call the people who serve you your dinner in a posh restaurant, were getting complaints from fellow diners. I do not pay to come to place like this to hear how some girl got her breasts rubbed down with olive oil. That kind of thing. Some people walked out.

The manager was called. He tried to unruffle a few feathers but basically he let James and co get on with it. This lot had a block booking for fifteen people. They were a regular crowd. They spent more per head when they stayed than any other guests. The alcohol started with the *oeufs benedict* and the caviar at breakfast. All the women had one beauty treatment after another in the health club. The men ate non-stop, drank non-stop, bought expensive presents in the hotel shop for their guilty consciences, to take home after their 'business weekends'. They made expensive transatlantic phone-calls, they sent long faxes, arranged bikes to take unnecessary things to their office in London, to get something unnecessary delivered from their office in London.

In short, where they could add to the hotel's margins, they did so. They also had a habit of bunging the waiters fat tips at the end of each Bacchanalian event. This meant that, while they might well be *agacés par le comportement des sots*, the waiters all turned a blind *oeil*. Le twenty quid note is le twenty quid in any language, *mon vieux*. These were not the kind of guests that you took to one side and said, would you mind very much keeping the noise down as your story about Hammy the hamster who was found suffocated up a creative director's bottom is putting the other diners off their *sablée aux fraises*. If their antics meant that a few other guests were lost by the wayside, so be it.

And so the party continued unabashed. But what of our heroes, the lovely Sarah and the somewhat less lovely James? Well, Sarah, in a surge of determination to enjoy, had forced down at least a bottle and a half of wine. This was a piss in the ocean compared to the others, but for her the greatest excess since she fell off her chair at her sister Caroline's wedding. That was almost five years before. No matter that her sister, who was four years younger than her, had got married before her. It mattered so little that, on the wedding day, Sarah had drunk herself into a state of total oblivion.

This evening, she knew that the only way to deal with everything was to take the same course of action. Alcohol always made her melancholic, but at least she was pissed, visibly pissed. If she was going to be the odd one out, at least they couldn't hold sobriety against her. All tanked as she was, the crappy fun and games going on around her seemed pretty harmless. She kept a fixed smile on her face, said little or nothing, and systematically forced back more wine.

Young James on the other hand. Now he was another story. James was in his element. He was a man with a mission. He was Attila the Hun dressed for battle. He was Yogi Bear at a picnic, a kookaburra up a gum tree. There was nothing he enjoyed more than finding himself in the midst of plenty of grub, plenty of plonk and, most of all, plenty of fanny. There were two of the latter in particular that he was considering giving a good stuffing. Linda and Beverley. He'd have Beverley from behind and Linda on his face.

Don't ask James why that way round, i.e. why not Linda from behind and Beverley on his face. For some reason that image, that configuration, had loomed into his mind as soon as he'd sat down at table and he just hadn't been able to shake it off, hard as he hadn't tried.

It wasn't helped when Beverley, who was sitting right next to him, reached out for his hand and put it between her knickerless legs in the middle of his steak tartare. Beverley was telling a story about how she'd been pursued by an eighteen-year-old copywriter in her previous job. She was waving her fork in the air, conducting her tale, and with the other hand she was positioning James's paw where she wanted it.

James was also happy to put his ambidextrous skills to good effect. He could still shovel fresh raw meat into his mouth with his left hand and shovel even fresher raw meat with his right. His steak was delicious – wet and juicy and runny with the egg. Just like Beverley. She was so wet it was like putting your hand under a tap. But she was also very loose. This woman must have had a whole *Generation Game*'s worth of cuddly toys and toasters up her in her time.

Now she was on to the bit about how the guy was waiting for her when she got into work, lying in just his socks and boxer shorts on her desk. In her rush to tell this story, she was feeding her cleavage as much food as her mouth as she talked, as lumps and crumbs spattered down from her chomping chops full of exquisite *brioches aux champignons*.

Meanwhile, James was beavering diligently away. He had tried stuffing three fingers up her but there was still plenty of room to spare. Beverley carried on energetically with her story – now she was on to the bit where the copywriter asked her round to tea at his mum's. James's efforts didn't seem to be making any difference to her life, in spite of all his shoving and rubbing and pushing. In the end, contorting his arm with not inconsiderable discomfort, he was ramming his whole fist up her to try and get her going, yet she hardly seemed to bat an eyelid as she raucously munched her way through the finale where this boy hands in his notice and puts his passion for her as his reason for leaving in his resignation letter.

Eventually, James realised that he was getting nowhere. Sweat was pouring off his face with the concentration of his task, and his arm was starting to hurt. He could be there all night.

He retrieved his soggy hand and wiped it down on his napkin. After that, a strong odour, not dissimilar to that of a supermarket fish counter, belched at him every time he took a forkful of meat to his face. He left the rest of his steak.

Occasionally, he remembered to look across at Sarah, and felt himself tense up. Bringing her here had been a stupid idea. This bloody woman had no sense of humour and wanted melodramatics at every corner. He didn't even really fancy her that much any more. She looked like she'd had too much to drink and it gave her features an unattractive blotchy flush. Compared to the other buxom girls around the table, her body looked a bit stringy. Far, far better to have Beverley from behind and Linda on his face. He'd just have to hope that Beverley's rear wasn't as well worn as her front, he reflected wistfully.

But what was he going to do with bloody Sarah, bloody holier-than-bloody-thou Sarah, who wouldn't know a good time if it whacked her round the face? He'd only gone and got them a double bloody room, idiot that he was.

While he was desperately dreaming up schemes to remedy this plight, Sarah herself suddenly provided the solution. She stood up, staggered a bit, and announced politely that she was going to bed.

Everyone stopped their gabble and a hush fell as they all waited to see whether James was going to offer to go with her. He knew it. She knew it. There was a silence.

'Sleep well, then,' said James, toasting her with his glass. There were giggles as Sarah walked out.

'Hardly the honeymoon couple, are you?' smirked Martin.

'I've got other fish to fry,' said James, sniffing his hand thoughtfully.

How to define these thoughtful thoughts of James? Something along the lines of: yabba dabba bloody doo. Ms Frump has bogged off, he was thinking. Now I can have some real bloody fun. James was suddenly elated, released, reborn. Pudding was served. Everything in the world was beautiful and James felt his *joie de vivre* spring back into action.

'How about it then?' he cried triumphantly to Linda, as the splendid *mousse aux trois chocolats* was presented to him.

'How about what, James?' she replied, in her own endearingly stupid way.

'How about eating this chocolate mousse off my dick!' he roared.

There was a shock of silence. Even Martin *et al* thought this was a bit much. James had stood up and was undoing his trousers.

Two more couples got up to leave. 'You are absolutely a disgrace, sir,' said one man on his way out.

James retorted by shaking his now fully exposed willy at him. 'My good man, if you join the queue like a good fellow, I'm sure I can fit you in somewhere.'

At this, Martin let out a whoop of laughter and suddenly it was all going to be all right. Sod it. Why not? It was a bit of fun. It was a laugh. It was quite a spectacle for the dining room of a five star hotel restaurant. It would make quite a story on Monday.

The few remaining guests and assembled staff stayed transfixed, half aghast and three-quarters captivated by the scene they hoped was about to ensue. 'Well, Linda, how about it?' James went on, thrilled by his audience. He took his now massively erect penis and held it right in front of Linda's nose.

Now, I know I just intimated that Linda was stupid. She is, but she's not that stupid. She's a junior account wannabe, and what James was dangling under her nose was her ticket to ride, it was the shining pink key that would open the door to a better future. Everyone knew that if you had someone like James, old duffer that he was, or, more to the point, if someone like James had you, he could help you really go places.

By now, the others were stamping their feet, ringing their knives against their glasses, banging their fists on the table. Opportunity knocks. So Linda took the exquisite mousse in both hands and smeared it all over James's fleshy spoon. Then she stuck her full fat lips over it and chomped and sucked and slurped and gagged a little too if the truth be told, until James added his own ingredient to the mixture.

When it was all over, Linda swallowed up while James wiped himself down. Everyone applauded, James ordered another dessert and they all debated their liqueurs. It had just been a bit of fun, after all.

Twenty-four

Up in their room, Sarah started packing her things. It was too late to leave now and she felt too drunk anyway. She'd rung down to reception to ask if there was another room free but apparently the hotel was completely full that night. She would get a cab to the station first thing in the morning, James would no doubt be spending the night in someone else's room anyway. He had behaved like an idiot all evening. She found him ridiculous. She no longer cared what he did. Well, she did care but she didn't think he cared about her any more. Well, she hoped he might still care but she wouldn't be surprised if he didn't. He didn't seem to care. If he did turn up, she'd be fast asleep with the lights off.

She contemplated locking the door. She didn't. If she had, then it would have been impossible for James to turn up, take her in his arms and tell her he loved her. Which he might still do, although she was sure he wasn't going to do anyway, but you never know, he might.

She lay in the bath and ran the water slowly. It crept up the sides of the bath until her kneecaps and breasts were little islands of tranquillity. After a while her knee islands drowned. Then her breast isles were washed over. She had left the light off in the bathroom. From the pale hall light her body was a long dark corpse in the water. She felt as if it belonged to someone else.

She wished it did. Her skin was still sore from the sauna, she could only bear the coolest of water on it.

Somewhere down in the silent, dark, tepid water her female was having a little sob. No one wanted it, no one loved it, no one wanted to be friends with it. It sobbed quietly in the dark and cried lonely tears into the water. Sarah felt she had let it down. Why couldn't she find someone nice for it? Why didn't James want it?

She ran her hands down her chest. Why wasn't she Tricia or Linda or Beverley? Why didn't she just let herself go? Have a giggle, have a laugh, have a fuck. Why didn't she want to? Because she didn't want to. She didn't care if she never had another man inside her. That wasn't what she wanted.

She thought of a man, what a man is like, what he looks like. Like a woman, but with a pair of saggy, hairy sacks dangling down. Scrawny scrotal sacks, like leather balloons with the air gone, drooping sulkily like Deputy Dawg's cheeks. And a shapeless, sapless aubergine, a purple stump slumped aimlessly, meaninglessly, between the sacks, under a ripe shelf of gut. Then, when the stump filled with blood, big red veins start bulging on the surface and that stump wants to prod you, pork you, shove and push its way into you, contaminate you, make a mess inside of you. Great. I can hardly wait.

Oh dear, oh dear. Sarah felt so miserable. She didn't want sex with women. She just didn't want that kind of sex with men. Where was the pleasure in that kind of act? She did not want anyone inside of her. It was her space. The very thought made her suffocate. If she had a space, it's because she wanted a space. She didn't want that space filled up, made airless, closed, compressed.

A couple of times, men had even tried to shove themselves up her bum. Why not stuff something up her nostrils too, while you're at it? A pair of socks, one up each nostril, and why not a packet of peanuts in each earhole? And the mouth, the mouth, you could stick a pound of sausages in there. The belly button, good idea, rip out the umbilical cord, stick something in there, oh I don't know, you could roll up the Sunday papers and stuff them in. Take an eye out and stuff up the socket with a hanky.

Stuff it all, stuff her up, close up those holes, those airways, stuff, stuff, stuff until it's all airtight, sealed, shut down, shut up.

The thought revolted her. Nauseated her. What did that have to do with desire? I love you. So I'm going to shove myself inside you. She imagined what it must be like, to be a man, to have that limp then livid skin between your legs. She tried to think how it must feel to be a man, to see a woman, to want that woman, to have the thing go stiff and to force it up the woman. That's how men love women. She felt sick.

Did she want James to do that to her? No. Not really. But she wanted him to want her, to notice her. And the only way James wanted women was by hurting them, humiliating them. She could see that now. Is that what she wanted? Anything from him, anything, as long as it was from him to her? Maybe. Did she always want men to hurt her somehow? They usually did. Why was she only attracted to men that hurt her? Did she enjoy being hurt? Probably. Maybe. Not really, actually, now that she thought about it.

Downstairs, James was also thinking about pretty much the same kind of thing: pain and sex and how much he wanted it. Beverley was definitely willing for a shilling. She was gazing at him like a kid who's just seen the lid taken off the sweetie jar. The sight of James's mammoth dick usually had this effect on them. That's why he liked to give it as much of an airing as possible.

However, since his last couple of glasses of whisky, that Tricia had also taken on a decidedly appealing appearance. This was strange, because normally he didn't go for redheads. A mate of his had told him once that they had a funny smell, but this one looked like she might be a bit of a goer, nevertheless.

How was he going to fit them all in? And how was he going to fit himself into all of them?

Beverley, noticing his roving eye, pre-empted. She announced that it was her bedtime and would James go with her to the room as she was afraid of the dark. James winked at Tricia with a look that said 'see you later, darling' and then, to the accompaniment of such benevolent felicitations as 'way to go, Jimmy boy' and 'give her one for me', the happy couple made their way up the fully-lit staircase and down the fully-lit corridor, past the room where Sarah was going through her bathtime soul-searching, to Beverley's boudoir.

Even as Beverley turned the key seductively in the door (you're going to ask me now how you turn a key seductively – you know what I mean), James realised that his chocolate mousse *tour de force* had been a big mistake. Even the sight of Beverley's voluminous rear guiding him up the stairs had not put him in pole position. He had a quick footle with his undercarriage now. *Rien de rien*. His codger had definitely put up the 'do not disturb' sign.

This is very unusual, thought James, trying to ignore the knot of panic forming somewhere in his groin.

When they got into the room, she poured him a drink from the minibar and turned on the porn video on the TV. 'Just to get us in the mood,' she said, thoughtfully. Then, picking up a pile of clothes, she added: 'I'll just go and change into something that'll even more put us in the mood.' Poor Beverley. Syntax never was her strong point.

Luckily for her, her syntax was not currently a priority for James who had other things on his mind. Her absence gave him a good window for some self-arousal techniques that he'd learnt on the forty-six-year specialist training course he'd been on. As he rubbed and cosseted himself, he watched the TV screen. The camera was so close to something going in and out that he wasn't sure what was going in and out of what. The camera panned back. It looked as if two blondes were attacking some chap underneath them, but he must have been enjoying it as he asked for more, more every time he was allowed to come up for air.

James yanked and tugged at himself in ways which normally produced results within seconds. This time, however, it was definitely a case of dead meat. Blankety-blank. This time his pride and glory lay inert in his clammy hands. Sweat crept insidiously out of pores James didn't even knew he had. What the fuck wasn't he going to do now?

Suddenly: tra-la. Beverley the wonderdog reappears from the bathroom, clad in a red rubber bra, all laced up like Julie Andrews' bodice in *The Sound of Music*, and lace split crotch panties in black shiny pvc. Yummy. A little outfit she'd packed in her weekend bag in case this kind of situation should present itself. Beverley hadn't been a Girl Guide all those years for nothing.

She tottered over to the bed on black stilettos and lay down, legs apart, split crotch and all its contents open to the seven winds. 'Come and get it then,' she said simply (for Beverley's verbal skills excelled at simplicity).

James took another swig of his drink and mopped his brow. His star of stage and restaurant was obstinately refusing to do a second performance that evening. James was pleading, cajoling, negotiating and wanking like hell, but his precious possession lay like a moribund worm shrivelled up in the palm of his hand.

This was a nightmare. This was the drink. It had to be the drink. He knew that booze could do this to you. It had just never done it to him before. James felt a rush of terror. What if it wasn't the alcohol? What if it was – gulp – his age? As in – gulp, gulp – old age? He was

241

forty-seven next birthday. Was that it then? One half century of fun and then you're rumbled ?

'Come on, James,' said Beverley running her delight-fully manicured claws up and down her inner sanctum. 'Come and fill me up, bring your big tusk to Beverley, you big randy old rhinoceros.' (Oops! I'd avoid using that 'o' word right now, Beverley love!)

Perhaps it would help if I got undressed, thought James. Then he thought, perhaps it would help if he had another drink. Having done both, he kneeled his way clumsily over the huge bed towards Beverley's gaping chasm.

She spread her legs as far apart as she could get them and pouted her freshly lipsticked chops provocatively. 'Oooh, who's a lucky boy then,' she giggled.

Not our James, that's for sure. Here was prime pussy, staring him in the face, begging for it, gasping for it. But it wasn't having any of it. It hung limply down like a very used washing up cloth that had dried one too many dishes.

Just then a new guy appears on the telly: he's got a dick that's about the size of a police truncheon and then some. The camera homes in on it so it takes up practically the entire screen before one of the girls descends on it.

James choked with frustration. Beverley, who had been caressing herself avidly for five minutes and was by this time about to explode, noticed James's non-reciprocation and realised that all was not well. He was just kneeling there, peering down at himself. Time to get into full action, girl, she decided.

'Fuck me, fuck me,' she started groaning, rubbing her hand up and down her steaming vulva, tossing her head from side to side on the pillows.

'Take me, take me,' came the echo from the TV. James howled and hurled his limp bits against her like a battering ram without the batter. The more he lunged and thudded, the more his by now bruised and terrified dick retreated into itself.

'Yes, yes, yes, I'm coming, I'm coming,' squealed the voice from the TV.

'Is anything wrong?' said Beverley on the bed.

James collapsed in a sweating, seething pile by her side. His willy was throbbing with pain from all the rubbing and banging.

'Yes, yes, you're so big, so big, yes!' gurgled the TV in ecstasy.

'Turn that fucking thing off,' commanded James.

Beverley, who was basically a kind and considerate girl, did her best to sort out the situation. She clicked off the television on the remote and took the shrivelled skin between her well practised fingers, pulling and stroking with words of encouragement such as 'Come on, big boy, give Beverley a smile.'

But big boy, so to speak, refused even to look her way, much less smile. Beverley gave it one final yank of exasperation. James yelled out in pain and instinctively swiped out at her with a hefty wallop using the back of his hand.

'Why don't you piss off and leave me alone,' he shouted.

'Why don't you piss off yourself, you dirty old man. It's not my fault you can't get your smelly old dick to work,' wailed Beverley (Bev to her friends) from somewhere on the floor where the back of his hand had landed her.

'Shut up, you stupid tart,' said James, as he flung his clothes back on, demented with frustration and humiliation. Old man, old man, he thought hysterically.

He gave Beverley a kick in the side for good measure on the way out. She started howling.

'You can keep your tart's mouth shut about this if you know what's good for you,' he called out by way of farewell before slamming the door behind him.

Well, lucky Beverley. At least she's allowed to shut her own mouth.

Twenty-five

James went downstairs to find something to drink. All the others had gone to bed. The whole place was deserted, apart from a tired-looking middle-aged woman who was doing the night shift at reception. 'Where the fuck is everyone?' barked James, appearing suddenly from nowhere.

The woman let out a small howl of shock and then, holding on to the edge of the reception desk to steady herself, said, 'Who, sir?'

'Everyone, anyone, you stupid cow.'

'Everyone's gone to bed. It's two in the morning. And I'd be grateful if you didn't use that kind of language, sir, thank you.'

'Bloody hell,' roared James. 'What is this place? Sunnyside fucking retirement home? Everyone already in bed and only an old crone like you still hanging around?' The woman went pink. 'Get me another room,' he said, banging his fist on the desk. 'I demand another room.'

One thing James knew he couldn't face was going back up to spend the night with Little Miss Muffet. He couldn't bear to see her sad beleaguered little expression of questioning unhappiness which had followed him everywhere since they had arrived at the hotel.

'I beg your pardon, sir?'

'Are you deaf as well as senile?' enquired James. 'I said I need another room.'

'Haven't you already got a room, sir?' said the woman courageously.

'Of course I've got a bloody room, you ugly trout,' blasts James, 'I just want another one.'

She had dealt with drunks before. They were all the same, their bark was worse than their bite. You just had to be firm with them.

She took the telephone receiver and held it defiantly in front of her. 'I'm sorry,' she said. 'I've told you. The hotel is completely full. If you don't go immediately to your room I will call the manager in his cottage. Which is just a few yards away,' she lied. James didn't move. 'Or I will call the police' she said, her voice breaking with terror.

'All right. All right. Keep your knickers on. I'm going. This isn't bloody *Hawaii Five-O* for God's sake,' he muttered as he ambled off towards the stairs.

No doubt the silly bitch has locked me out anyway, he thought hopefully. But the door to their room slid open easily and silently. He wandered past the sitting room area into the bedroom. Sarah was nowhere. Fabulous. She must have cleared off. He got undressed. Then a withering thought came to him. What if she hadn't left? What if she was in one of the other bedrooms with someone else, the filthy tart? He stomped into the bathroom and had his hand poised to switch on the light when he saw her there, asleep in the half light in the half-empty bath.

She looked so pure and pretty. Compared to the vision of womanhood he had just wrestled with three doors along, compared to the bouncing dolls on the TV screen, she was another gender. Her damp hair lay all over her shoulders. One arm was crossed protectively across her chest, the other across her stomach, as if to ward off the evil spirit of the night.

Me, I suppose, thought James. God, she thought she

was so bloody marvellous, didn't she? So innocent, so special. She lay there, asleep, and she was laughing at him, laughing at his old age, his droopy dick, his aching balls, his fears about the agency. She was laughing her head off, her sides were splitting. She was killing herself laughing at him.

He wanted her so much and as she slept she was saying, don't even think about having me, you miserable wreck of a man. With her closed eyes, she could see right through him, she saw him for the tawdry old shit he was, she saw the man who had bonked and buggered his way through so many women that he couldn't begin to remember one from the other, they were just so many peas lined up in a pod, nameless, faceless, just a line of holes queuing up to be full-filled by him.

The alcohol whirred and buzzed round his skull. Except. Except. Except, fuck it, he couldn't even do that any more. He couldn't even get his fucking cock to fuck. And this silly bitch, lying there, asleep in the bloody bath, who did she think she bloody was? Too good for him? Too good for anyone, that's what she thought. With her pert tits, untouched by human bloody hand, her cutesy little never-been-kissed fanny with every hair just so. Who the fuck did she think she was? He'd had a thousand women. A thousand women better than her, who was she? She was scum. Scum. And he wasn't having it. He'd show her what he thought of her.

He moved close to the bath. Holding his penis with both hands, he began pissing a hot, steamy soup up and down the length of Sarah's body.

Sarah woke to see the jolly green giant, looking none too jolly, urinating over her stomach. The strong stench of his pee shocked her more than anything. At first, it occurred to her that he'd been aiming for the loo, which was right next to the bath. She could see how very drunk he was. But the look of intense concentration, as he stood with his tongue between his lips, like a schoolboy trying to work out his algebra, revealed that his target was indeed her crotch, her chest and, of course, a finale in her face and hair.

Now he'd finished. She thought then that he looked a little mad. His face was bloated and reddened like a sumo's. Sarah realised that she was suddenly quite scared of this man. She smelt the acid odour of his piss in her hair, on her skin. She lay completely still in the bath. He watched her, and mumbled to himself.

Now she was frightened. Now she understood that this man very much wanted to hurt her, that he needed very much to hurt her.

'I've saved you a bit,' he said.

She said nothing. Say something, Sarah.

'I said, Sarah, I've saved you a bit.'

The use of her name made her stomach flip with fear. It personalised her in him. It was the anonymous phone-caller who knew who you were.

'Open wide like a good girl.'

Sarah didn't speak and she didn't move. Say something Sarah. She looked at the emergency cord at the other end of the bath. She thought of lunging towards it. Then she thought of James lunging towards her. She kept still.

'Open wide, Sarah.' Tell him to stop, Sarah.

He grabbed her pee-sodden hair, shoved her mouth over his groin and finished off. The hot and bitter syrup blasted into her, corroding every corner of her mouth. James removed himself, clamped her jaw shut and kept it clamped.

'Now swallow.'

She swallowed. The warm filth went down her throat into her chest. The pungent poisons that James's kidneys had so efficiently expelled entered her system and started coursing through her. He was cleansed, she was fouled.

Sarah: say go away; say stop; say no. Sarah says nothing.

Now it got nasty, as if this wasn't nasty enough. (For Sarah, evidently not.) Now she was being dragged, her legs clanking and banging and bruising on the sides of the bath, on the bathroom door frame. Naked and still dripping with wee and bath water, she was being pulled into the bedroom and pushed into one of the armchairs.

James had saliva on his lips and he's started muttering again. Muttering under his breath like the wicked witch in the gingerbread house. Sarah was so scared.

She wasn't going to move. She knew this man had to purge himself through her. He had urinated on her. He had knocked her up a bit. That wasn't enough. They both knew that. He was going to have to do her real harm to get the anger, the anger for which she was responsible, which she owned, out of his system. She had to receive his anger because he simply couldn't carry it. He wasn't big enough for it. Whereas she had all those soft bits and all those holes all over the place, all those secret little cosy spots where he could bury all his anger, all his fears. He could dig deep and put his bone in a safe place far inside her where no one else would find it. And anyway, it was her fault he had all this anger. It was only fair that she should be hurt for it.

Sarah said nothing.

He sat on the edge of the bed and stared at her. She wished he'd just get on with it. The waiting for pain was worse than the pain. He was staring at her with such a look of hate. He wanted her to have all of that hate. But he didn't know how to give it to her. He could beat her up. He could try and fuck her – except he still wasn't sure if he could do that any more.

Oh God. He looked so wretched. Sarah was thinking perhaps she could help him, perhaps she could show him what would hurt her most. Poor, wretched, miserable man.

She said nothing. Say something, Sarah. Say stop.

They stared at each other, and he was still babbling away under his breath. A long time passed. It was getting almost embarrassing. She was getting cold.

Suddenly: uh-oh. He was taking action. The mumbling stopped.

'You know you make me want to puke,' her boss said.

'Yes,' she replied, trying hard not to sound patronising.

'You know that just looking at you makes me sick.'

'Yes.' Say no.

'You think you're so immaculate. Don't you? Don't you!'

'Yes.' Say go.

'Missy Sarah. So fine. With all her airs and bloody graces. I can tell you that I'd rather fuck someone like Beverley any day of the week.'

There was a pause.

She looked across at his large, white, sweaty body twitching on the bed. He looked rather revolting. Something about him disgusted her.

'So why don't you?' said Sarah, getting brave at just the wrong moment, with just the wrong thing to say. James did not like this. You and I know why.

'Come here, you slut,' he yowled, leaping off the bed and grabbing her. He pulled her down on to him on the dainty little chair in front of the three-way mirror on the ornate dressing table. The triple image of their two heads loomed around them and stared back at them like some crazy six-headed monster.

'Sarah, Sarah,' he said, stroking her smelling hair. 'Queen of the agency. Every man's desire. We think we're so bloody wonderful, so very amazing. Just too perfect for words, aren't we?'

Sarah hung down her head. He yanked it up again to make her confront her image and his.

Sarah, open your mouth and tell him to go.

She could see he had to hurt her. She could see now that's how he operated, how he communicated. He hurt people. He passed on the pain of all his inadequacies and insecurities. Did she really want him to do this to her?

'I suppose you're going to hurt me now, like you used to hurt Belinda,' Sarah said.

James laughed. 'Belinda, yes. You're very interested in Belinda, aren't you? Do you really want to know about Belinda? I'll tell you about her. She thought she was perfect as well, stuck-up little cow. But she was the first one to show me how cheap women really are, how low they crawl, how much they like a man who does them harm. Yes, does them harm. That's what women like, men who hurt them. She made me hurt her. She nagged me with her stupidity, she suffocated me, she wanted me to get angry. She loved it when I hit her. She would wail and bleed and whimper, she would leave home for days, for weeks, but she always eventually came wheedling back for more.'

He was talking to her like hairdressers do, their reflection talking to your reflection in the mirror, like two ghosts. Sarah shivered.

Will you just tell him to go, Sarah, before it's too late?

'I don't always hurt my women, you know. You're going to have to consider yourself lucky. I only hurt the ones I really like, ones like you, Queen Sarah Bee. When I fuck some common or garden tart, I fuck her and that's it. But the clever women, the clever ones like you, Sarah, they inspire me, do you see?'

Keep him talking, keep him talking more, thought Sarah. Get him to talk himself to sleep or to tears or to pity, just keep him talking.

'James, tell me more about Belinda, about how it was with her.'

'You want me to hurt you, don't you?'

'I was asking about Belinda . . .'

'Why do you want me to hurt you?'

251

'Why do I want you to hurt me?'

'Do you go looking for men to hurt you? Is that what you want?'

'No, of course not.'

'You knew what I was like. I told you what I was like. You did know, didn't you?'

'No.' You're lying, Sarah. Tell him to go.

'Why do women always want to be hurt by men? Why do you want to be hurt by me?'

Sarah did not answer. She'd been asked this question a thousand times. She'd asked herself this question a thousand times. Suddenly it seemed like a good question.

She stared across at the mirror image of his bloated, rabid face. The hate look was back in his face. She could see his fingers were twitching, nervously pushing the pots and tubes from her make-up bag on the dressing table this way and that, shifting, fiddling.

He looked grotesque. Her James. Her mighty man. He looked pathetic. From the sublime to this. She had been captivated. How could she now be so revolted?

'James,' she pronounced, stoically, and I think almost ironically, 'if you want to have sex with me, if you really want to hurt me, why don't you just get on with it?'

James seemed not to hear this kind offer of her services. His eyes were fixed on something on the dressing table that he had tipped out of her bag.

'Otherwise,' Sarah went on, 'I'm going to go now.'

He turned his face slowly towards hers. He'd heard that bit all right. 'Yes, you'd like that wouldn't you? I suppose you wouldn't mind nipping along to Martin's room to get yourself a bit of a shafting from him. Or Andy. Nice young chaps. They'd show you a good time, wouldn't they?'

He gave himself a rapid grope. Still no sign of life. Rage stalked him.

'Well, I'll tell you what, Sarah. I just don't want that.

I don't want Martin running himself up you. I can't have you. And if I can't have you, no one's having you. No one.'

Sarah, say it again, say it like you mean it. Stand up and say stop, say no. Say you're leaving and mean it.

'You'd like to ask them to fuck you, wouldn't you? I don't want you telling anyone to fuck you if I can't. You keep your filthy mouth shut. I don't want you blabbing. I don't want you talking to people, telling them what you know. You know too much, I've told you too much. I don't want you telling other men to fuck you.'

He was poking around with the little sewing kit he'd found in her make-up bag, pulling at the threads, jabbing the table top with the thimble.

Sarah, just say bloody no.

Sarah was asking herself why she had packed that sewing kit. James was playing with the needles. He was winding the thread tight round his little finger until it went white.

'You know too much, you ask to much, you need to shut up, big mouth. I'm going to make sure you shut up.'

Now he was carrying her to the bed, with the sewing kit in his hand. The little sewing kit. Her sister had given her that sewing kit. He was pushing her down on the bed. 'Do you want me to stop, Sarah?' Sarah stared at him.

Sarah, say stop. Open your mouth, open it while you still can, and say yes, I want you to stop.

He was kneeling on the bed. She had carried that sewing kit with her everywhere. He was sitting on top of her, pinning down her arms with his knees. Her sister had said she should take it with her everywhere she went.

Now he was trying to get the thread through the needle. Now he was crying. Now he was sobbing his heart out, slobbering and blubbering: 'No one, no one, if I'm not going to have you, no one will.' His eyes were blurred, his hands were shaking.

Sarah, stay stop.

Sarah was silent. He got the thread through the needle. He was sitting on her chest, clamping down her arms with all his weight. 'I'm going to shut your mouth up, shut up your fucking mouth, so I can't hear you say those things to me any more. I don't want you to say those things to me any more.'

Sarah lay there. She has been mesmerised, magnetised. She has needed him, she has loved him, she has longed for him. She has been grateful for his undivided attention, however barbaric, anything which has shown that he cared about her, that he was aware of her, any recognition from him at all. But now, but now, he's really going to hurt her; sticks and stones are going to break her bones where words haven't done enough.

He started pulling at her upper lip. He's going to sew her mouth up, I tell you. Sew it up, clamp it shut, so he doesn't hear her voices in his head. The sweat from his forehead was dripping into her face.

Oh, I tell you what. Sarah, if you can't say no, if you can't even say stop, even now, why don't you just let him get on with it? You've seen it coming, you've had it coming, if this is really what you want men to do to you, have it, have it all.

'James.'

Hang on. Someone's said something.

'James, I don't want this. Stop it now.'

Someone's definitely said something. I think, well, I think it might have been Sarah, but I wouldn't like to . . .

'James, will you stop it and get off me. You weigh a ton. Just get off me, will you, you fat git.'

'If I can't have you, no one will have you, no one will.' James was still slobbering and puffing away on top of her with the threaded needle poised.

'Oh do shut up, for God's sake. And I said get off me!'

Sarah yanked his blubber to one side and got up. Dithering and jerking and wittering to himself, he rolled over on to his back on the bed, his right hand still clutching the needle. In dawn's merciless light, his ample white torso had the appearance of something eskimos spend the winter dining off. Sarah looked down with revulsion at the quivering mess of a man. She was angry. So really angry.

'And I tell you what, you fat shit, you ever come anywhere near me again to try and hurt me, you'll be wearing your balls as earrings. You got that?'

James started crying again. Sarah rolled her eyes to the heavens. 'Shut up, James,' she snarled at him. He sobbed even more loudly. 'I said, shut the fuck up,' she yelled, eloquently, with her face right in his. God his breath was bad. He shut up.

She pulled on leggings and a sweatshirt – the casual clothes she was going to wear on the lovely country walk they were going to take after breakfast on Sunday morning, with the warm summer sun in her hair and James's warm hand in hers, etc, etc. She chucked all the rest of her stuff into her weekend bag and made for the door. But then she stopped and went back to the blubber on the bed.

'You know, you came close, you came very close, but the answer is no, no I don't want your shit, I don't want your pain, I don't want any of it any more.'

James was on his back, his head lolled to one side, wordlessly mouthing some nonsense or other, his hairy blancmange of a stomach beached forlornly upwards, his penis wet and wilting like a clubbed baby seal.

Now she realised she'd had enough – from him and from all of them. Her eyes filled with tears. She put her fingers to her lips and thought of what he might have done, what he had done, what they had all done to her, all her men. How far would she let them go? This far. And this far, she decided then, this far was far enough.

James rolled over and belched.

Time to go. Sarah left the room and headed back downstairs.

By now it was gone 5 a.m. How time flies when you're having fun. It was too early to leave, too late to stay. Dumping her bag at reception, she slipped out through a little open door in the library and found herself in the hotel gardens.

I don't wake up early enough to know what mornings are really like, but with a little imagination I'd say that at that time the sun was just starting to wince through the ether. Pink feather boas of cloud laced a baby blue sky and the air felt like pure oxygen. Perky, twinky, friendly.

Sarah walked along the hand-selected bits of gravel on the paths through the flower beds, and went to sit on a small wooden bench next to an ancient brick wall. Although there were no birds, no animals, definitely no people about, somehow she wasn't on her own. The gardens were so pretty. The place was so tranquil. She was exhausted but she was happy. Something had clicked in her head and pierced her consciousness.

That's it, she thought. I've done it. I've stopped the rot, I've made a move, that's it. No more pain, no more degradation. No more working for work's sake. No more chasing after the ones who want to do me down, no more rejecting the ones who don't want to, just because they don't.

She thought of her grandmother. Same film, different cinema. No, she wasn't going to repeat anyone's life. She was going to build her own. By herself. Be herself. For herself.

All the blossoms and leaves and the big trees sat and watched her. They were looking at her, not she at them. And they were saying, about time. She could hear them. About time, they said. The fat, orange petals of a big chunk of rose smiled up in her face. The paws of a juicy green ivy patted her on the cheek. A great chorus of purple clematis sung up into her face. Way to go, Sarah, way to go, it sang.

Just like the girl in the Nescafé ad on TV who sees in the dawn with her cup of coffee, Sarah watched the day slowly come together in that garden. She sat there until seven o'clock, when she went back into the hotel and got a cab to the station. Sometimes it seems that ads aren't imitating life, it's we who are all living out ads. Sarah had almost been one of James's. But now, she had got up and turned the telly off.

It can be done, you know.

Twenty-six

Monday. Back in the office. It had been a long day, Caroline had rung to say that Edward had come home and she was going to stay with him. Suzanne had rung to say she was seeing Stuart again. Her mother had rung to say she was taking the train to see Sarah's father to convince him to take her back.

After the last call, Sarah had just sat and looked at the phone. That was me, that was me, she thought with frustration and relief. She rang Virgin to get tickets out to New York to see Caroline the following weekend. She arranged dinner with Suzanne. She asked her mother to come and stay. She was going to talk to these women. She was going to talk them into action, talk them into happiness. She knew how to do it now.

On her way out late that evening, Sarah stopped to photocopy some notes for a meeting with her cereal clients early the next morning. Someone had left the photocopier jammed: the office equivalent of leaving the lavatory with no paper. She looked to see if there were any secretaries around who could help. They had all left early to go to the pub for Ralph's leaving do. She remembered then. Someone had told her he was starting the next week as senior planner in another agency. Today, Monday, had been his last day. She realised that he hadn't asked her to go along for a drink. He hadn't even said goodbye to her.

Cursing and kicking the machine, Sarah opened up

its innards and started pulling levers, turning dials. The internal rollers spewed up a clog of paper. Some berk had got a whole pile of stuff jammed and just left it all. She ripped out the chewed-up paper and dumped it all in the recycle box.

As her notes whirred cheerfully through the copier, she sat down on the pile of boxes of new paper and reflected. Tomorrow, at the meeting, she was going to tell her clients that she had handed in her notice and that she planned to be out of the agency by the end of the week.

She knew that the MD there had been thinking of offering her some sort of directorship in the marketing department. But Sarah had already rung the head of the third world charity they were doing the joint promotion with to see if there was a job going with them, and she had said she'd be glad to consider taking Sarah on.

It would mean less pay, it would mean working in a clapped-out office in Putney. It would mean going a little bit backwards to start going forwards for once.

Tired and impatient for the photocopying to finish its work, Sarah gazed blankly round the little room. Suddenly she realised she was looking at an image she knew. It was James's ridiculously grand signature. His signature on one of the sheets of photocopied paper she had dug out of the bowels of the photocopier and chucked on the recycle pile.

She fished out the page. It was his personal letter paper. It was marked 'Strictly private and confidential'. It was letter to Frank, the marketing director at Birksomes, at Frank's home address. It was just three lines of text, handwritten by James.

It read: 'I'm glad for your confirmation today that the account is safe. As agreed, each job will be over-invoiced by 15% and we will split the difference. To start with immediate effect.'

Sarah finished her photocopying. She took James's

letter round to the fax outside her office, the one that Anita had set up with a code which automatically sent the same document through to the fax machines of every marketing correspondent on every national paper and trade magazine in the country. She put the letter on the fax and pressed the code button.

Then she left, to go and buy Ralph a pint in the pub.